The Genesis Files

The Genesis Files

Bob Biderman

Walker and Company
New York

First published in the United States of America in 1991
by Walker Publishing Company, Inc.,
720 Fifth Avenue, New York, NY 10019.

Originally published in Great Britain

Library of Congress Cataloging-in-Publication Data

Biderman, Bob, 1940-
The Genesis files / Bob Biderman.
p. cm.
ISBN 0-8027-5797-9
I. Title.
PS3552.I335G4   1991
813'.54--dc20   91-25483
CIP

Printed in the United States of America
2 4 6 8 10 9 7 5 3 1

To A. E. Biderman:
Poet, Humanist, Man of science

There is a striking similarity between nuclear science and genetic engineering. Both major scientific accomplishments confer a power on humans for which they are psychologically and morally unprepared. The physicists have already learned this, to their dismay: the biologists, not yet.

Liebe F. Cavalieri
Bulletin of the Atomic Scientists
December 1982

Chapter 1

Something caused him to look up. It was the same uncomfortable sensation that ran down his back when someone was watching him from behind. This time it was his front.

Outside his study window was a tiny park with a great banana tree which the Nicaraguan gardener had planted a few weeks ago, hoping, by some miracle, it would bear fruit. An elderly woman was rummaging through the trash bin underneath the tree. She was staring at him. Or, at least, he thought she was.

He had seen her before. Maybe not her, but someone like her. Someone who could have been her sister or her cousin, he supposed. They all dressed the same in their loose-fitting slacks and dark cotton blouses and their embroidered pill-box hats. They all had the same coal-black eyes and they all had those grotesque wooden plugs fitted in their earlobes like a tribal lip.

The woman sifted through the discards with a practiced movement, taking the waste remains and putting them into a cloth sack before moving on. It was all done with a certain methodical poise, a certain dignity that one rarely found among the urban poor. But these people were different. Back in their native land, he suspected, they had been hunters and gatherers. Here, in San Francisco, rubbish bins, not fruit, were underneath the trees.

The ring of the telephone sitting on his cluttered desk just inches away from his ear was so startling that it made him break the point of his pencil on page thirty-two of his *magnum opus*. He picked up the receiver and let his raw nerves explode: "Hello!" he shouted. "Who the hell is it?"

"Is that you, Radkin?"

Joseph let out a sigh at the unwelcome voice from the past. "Yeah, it's me, Lamont. Who do you expect to answer when you dial my number? Frank Sinatra?"

"Sinatra, no. A drunken ex-reporter with the scruples of an agent from the Comintern, perhaps."

"What do you want, Lamont?" Joseph asked, gritting his teeth. The day had started out bad, it was bound to get worse.

"You want an assignment?"

"An assignment?" Joseph almost laughed. "I thought you fired me . . ."

"I did. Now I'm asking you whether you want an assignment. You've got the choice of saying 'yes' or saying 'no'. And the way I figure it, if by some strange quirk of nature you happened to find another job you'll say 'no'—after all, there was that paraplegic who got hooked up to mechanical water-wings and managed to swim the English Channel, so anything is possible. Otherwise you'll jump at the chance to work for me again."

"What makes you so loveable, Lamont?"

"Maybe it's my good looks and charm, Radkin. You got ten seconds to make up your mind."

Joseph groaned. For some reason his stomach began to hurt. Maybe it was the fatty chicken soup his mother had brought down last night to fill up Polly's bottomless pit. More likely it was the thought of working for Lamont again.

"What kind of assignment did you have in mind, Lamont? Counting the number of glory holes in Frenchy's porno shop?"

"Nothing as grand as that, Radkin. I save the really good stuff for our aces. This is more your speed. A simple, uncomplicated accidental death."

"Then why don't you get Johnson to write an obituary for you and save yourself the two bits for the phone call?"

"Because you knew the guy, Radkin. And maybe there's more to it than what's coming out."

"Who are we talking about, Lamont? Do I get a hint before I have to decide?"

"Malcolm Greene, the director of the People's Medical Clinic—or should I say ex-director. You did a story on him once."

"Greene's dead? You're kidding!" Joseph remembered him well. He had done the story last year on the struggle to save this last and final refuge of community medicine. Malcolm Greene was the only administrator Joseph had admired—and that was probably because Greene had never seen himself as one. He had hated bureaucrats as much as Joseph did.

"I don't joke about labs blowing up, Radkin. Especially when they're part of hospitals."

"So that's what happened . . ." Joseph muttered. He could usually sleep through anything. But last night Polly had shaken him awake and had forced him out of bed to shut the windows even though it had been uncomfortably hot.

"Shut them yourself!" he had snapped. "You're always getting up to piss anyway!"

"Is that what you're going to say when the baby is born? 'Feed it yourself! You're always getting up to go to work anyway'!"

To avoid the unwanted drama of a midnight quarrel, he had stumbled out of bed and that's when he had heard the infernal sounds of the fire-engines racing through the streets.

"It must be a five alarmer," he had said, climbing back into bed after pulling the windows shut. "When did you start hearing them?"

"If it wasn't for the fact that you join the land of the living dead every goddamn night, you'd have known it's been going on for hours," she had said somewhat resentfully. Pregnancy for her hadn't been all bliss.

"For God's sake, stop mumbling Radkin! It's bad enough trying to make sense of your New York twang!" Lamont shouted through the phone.

Joseph cringed at the pain in his ear. "What the hell was Greene doing in a hospital lab in the middle of the night?" he asked after twisting his index finger into his ear-hole a couple of times. "The clinic is a separate building."

"The question is what he was doing there with Professor Krohl."

There was a note of exasperation in Joseph's voice. "Come on, Lamont. Every story doesn't have to have a sex angle . . ."

"In my paper it does, Radkin!" Lamont cut in.

"That's just one of the reasons I don't write for you anymore, Lamont. Besides, people don't have affairs with genetic engi-

11

neers. Guys like Krohl are too busy splicing buzzers to bees and waiting for their Nobel to be delivered. Anyway, Greene wasn't like that."

"This is San Francisco, Radkin, lest you forget. People screw sheep on the subway here. You'd be amazed at all the things that people choose to have affairs with. But am I gonna write the story or are you?"

"Let me call you back, Lamont . . ."

"Forget calling me back, Radkin. I want an answer now. Yes or no?"

"OK." It was like reaching out and grabbing a moldy piece of cake just because you're hungry. He knew he'd regret it later."

"OK what?"

"OK, sir?"

"I can't believe it!" Polly said that evening when she had come home from work and had let her puffed-up body drop like a lead weight into the easy chair below. "You swore up and down that you'd never work for that . . . that . . ." she searched for the appropriate word, and finding none that would truly fit she resorted to generalities, "that creature again!"

"You used better epithets before," he said, bringing in her ration of white wine.

She took the glass and drank and then let out a deep sigh—a response which Joseph thought was either gratitude for the wine or pining for the time when she had been articulate.

"I seem to be walking around in a cloud of pink fluff these days," she admitted.

"At least it's pink," he said. "My cloud seems to be more muddy brown."

Which brought her back to the subject at hand. "But why Joseph? For heaven's sake, I thought we decided you'd work on your book for a while. After Spinach comes you're not going to have much chance, you know."

Joseph shrugged and took a drink from the glass of Scotch

he had poured himself when he fetched her wine. "We could always use the money."

"Money?" She stared at him and then burst out laughing. "How much money has Lamont ever paid for one of his 'assignments'?"

Joseph cringed. "That's not the point . . ."

Polly raised her eyebrows. "Oh, no? I thought it was."

He stared at her. Sometimes, these days, she was absolutely radiant: all blushing with baby and smelling of health and vitality. Then she was the spirit of optimism itself. But other times, especially after work or in the middle of the night when she had gotten up for her hourly pees, she was like a human blimp that had mugged itself in the dark. Then nothing he could do was right.

"I'm interested in the story for other reasons," he said. "It's not every day that the administrator of the only decent health clinic in town decides to get blown up in a research lab with a genetic engineer."

"This isn't the best of times to start playing detective, Joseph," she said patting her magnificent protrusion.

"Who's talking about playing detective?" he asked with more than a trace of annoyance in his voice.

"What are you talking about then?"

"I'm talking about ironies. Don't you see? Here's a man who spent his life trying to fight for the right of basic medical care blown to smithereens with another man whose idea of public health was giving every frog an extra head."

"I think you might be climbing out on another precarious limb, Joseph. Genetics made it possible to check Spinach for Down's Syndrome," she said pointing to her stomach.

"And what would we have done if Spinach hadn't been cleared of that particular crime?" he asked narrowing his eyes.

"Aborted," she said quite simply.

"You're awfully smug for someone who sweated like hell," he shot back. "When it actually got down to it . . ."

"Yes?" she said, as his voice trailed away. "When it actually got down to it?"

13

"What if they mislabeled the amnionic fluid? Things happen, you know."

"That's why they run the test twice, Joseph."

He glared at her. "Mistakes can happen twice, too."

She took a deep breath. "We've discussed this before . . ."

"Many times," he agreed.

She struggled to her feet looking tired and vulnerable. She gazed at him with her soft green eyes and said, "Why are we arguing, Joseph?"

He shook his head. "I don't know." He walked over and took her in his arms. He stroked her hair. "You're so warm," he said.

"My oven is on. I'm always warm when my oven is on," she replied.

He put his hand down low. "Can I feel it kick?"

She smiled. "I'll tell you when." She waited a moment. "Now!" she said. "Did you feel it?"

He nodded. "Yeah. It's alive."

"You're telling me! It's eating me out of house and home!"

"You look pretty well fed to me," he said, stepping back a pace and admiring the view.

"OK, male sexist pig. You try having one and seeing what it does to your figure!"

"I like what I see," he answered. "I always thought you looked good fat!"

She swatted at him with the flat of her hand. "Joseph, sometimes you are a perfect ass!"

"We all strive for perfection, my dear," he said with an endearing smile.

Polly closed her eyes. "All right, that's enough. It's getting out of hand again."

"I know," he agreed. "This was supposed to be the best of times."

"I feel so raw around the edges, Joseph." Tears started to trickle down her cheeks. She smiled. "I don't even know why I'm crying."

He looked at her guiltily. "I'm sorry, Polly. I'll call Lamont tomorrow and tell him to go to hell."

"No," she shook her head. "I don't know why I jumped down your throat like that. It could be an important story."

"Really, Polly. It's no big thing. In fact I ought to have my head examined for even thinking of working for that baboon again."

Her eyes brightened. She looked at him kindly. "Sleep on it, Joseph. You might feel differently about it in the morning."

"I doubt it," he said.

"Whatever you decide, make sure it's your decision. I don't want to stand in your way."

He nodded. "Sure . . ."

"Anyway, what's for dinner? I'm starved!"

"Ummm . . ." He looked down at the floor. "Spaghetti."

"Not again!"

"I'm sorry, Polly. I just didn't have time . . ."

She glared at him and then turned on her heels and stomped toward the door.

"Where are you going?" he called out.

"Upstairs to your mother!" she shouted. "At least she knows how to cook a decent meal!"

They were lying in bed with the lights out. The shades were pulled down and the room was as dark as the moonless night.

"So she dosed you full of chicken soup? And what else?" he asked suspiciously.

Polly giggled. "Women's lib. Imagine! Your mother filling me with women's lib!"

Joseph grunted.

"Then she went out with some guy . . ."

"Who?"

"I don't know."

"What did he look like?"

"Nice . . ."

"Fat? Skinny? Large? Small? Two heads? Horns? Nice is no description at all, Polly. I've told you that before."

15

"Mature, gentlemanly, unsarcastic—in short, everything that you're not."

"So after lecturing you on the perils of the male gender she goes out with a guy. Can you beat that?"

"She's got a right to her own life, Joseph."

"Polly, did I say she doesn't have a right to her own life? Who in this room heard me say that my mother doesn't have a right to her own life?"

"Are you expecting someone to answer?"

"I'm expecting you to tell me if you heard me say that."

"Joseph, they went to a meeting together . . ."

"What kind of a meeting? Is he going to get her arrested again? What's our kid going to think about having a grand-mother who's an ex-con? Did you ever ask yourself that?"

"Spinach will be very proud when it's old enough to under-stand the reason. Besides, you're just saying that because she's your mother. Everyone else who got arrested at Livermore Radiation Labs gets the hero of the year award in your book."

"That's just it, Polly. Who wants a mother who's a martyr? Why can't she just grow old gracefully like everyone else?"

"Who the hell grows old gracefully in this country, Joseph? Half the aged in the communities I work in live off dog food and sour milk. Your mom's got the right idea. A wrinkled finger can still poke you in the eye."

"Don't I know!"

"Look, Joseph, your mother's finally coming out of a long period of mourning. She's decided that her life didn't end when her husband died. She idolised your dad, you know. And now she's overcompensating a bit . . ."

"You can say that again!"

"Why can't you understand? She's changing course at seventy years old! You have to applaud her for that."

"I do?"

"Oh, Joseph!"

"You're always taking her side, Polly. You know that, don't you?"

16

"I'm just trying to tell you that you're not being totally objective."

"Polly, you tell me one person who's objective about their parents."

"Spinach."

"Besides Spinach."

"Oedipus?"

"Besides Spinach and Oedipus."

"You made your point, Joseph. Don't run it into the ground."

"What's the use of making a point if you can't run it into the ground, Polly?"

Polly let out a quiet sigh. "I don't want to argue with you tonight, Joseph."

"What do you want to do then?"

"You know . . ." she said in a soft, seductive voice.

"That?"

"Yeah." He felt a warm hand work its way down his thigh.

"But Polly, you know how hard it is for me now. Whenever we do it these days I keep feeling like I'm going to bump into its head!"

"You're not going to bump into its head, silly! It's in a waterproof sack all tied up tight. Spinach will never know what's going on."

"How do you know, Polly? I mean, how do you know for sure? Maybe it's got a peep-hole. Maybe it senses things we know nothing about."

"Come on, Joseph . . ." she said determinedly. "I promise you. Spinach will be none the wiser. It's fast asleep, in a dark, watery bag, deep in a primeval sea, safe from all worldly harm." She drew closer, pressing her gigantic belly next to his.

"But Polly, it's so obscene!"

"Yeah, but obscene things can be fun, too."

As usual, she had her way. He didn't complain.

"Feel better?" he asked. Her head was tucked into the crevice between his arm and his chest. He fancied he could see her eyes glowing in the dark.

"Yeah, I do," she said.

The room was quiet. All that was heard was the rustle of sheets and the occasional car passing outside their house, alone in the depths of the night.

After a while Polly said, "I need you to be a little gentler now. Do you think you could try?"

"Yes," he said. "I'll try."

"It's so strange having a baby inside me. Someone's there, a person, an honest-to-goodness person, who you've never met. It's so strange."

"From two to three. I'm glad it takes nine months. It gives you a chance to get used to the idea."

"From nothing to something," mused Polly. "From zero to one. From seed to flower. Sometimes I get so frightened . . ." She grabbed his hand and squeezed.

"Frightened? Why frightened?"

"What if . . ."

"What if what?"

"What if it's got twelve toes?"

"It probably could keep its balance better than us. Twelve toes wouldn't be so bad."

"What if it doesn't have arms? I mean I know it has feet. The poor thing kicks like a demon!"

"If it doesn't have arms we'll teach it to use its feet as hands. I saw a documentary once about this guy who didn't have arms and he became an extraordinary painter. He used his toes like fingers."

She sighed. "Sometimes it talks to me, you know . . ."

"No, I didn't know. What does it say?"

"It asks me to sing it a lullaby. It says, 'Mommy, I'm frightened. It's dark down here and I'm afraid.'"

"So you sing it a lullaby?"

"Yes. I sing it a quiet lullaby. I rub my belly very softly and sing: 'Hush little baby don't you cry. Mama's gonna sing you a lullaby . . .'"

He leaned over and whispered in her ear. "I love you, Polly"

"I love you, too, Joseph. Let's be friends, OK?"

18

"OK."

Again they were silent. Time passed. Time stood still.

"Are you asleep?" asked Joseph after a while.

"No," she replied.

"You used to go to the People's Medical Clinic, didn't you?"

"Yeah. Not only for myself. I used to bring some of the homeless people I worked with too. It was the only place in the city they'd be treated with any respect."

"Did you ever speak with Greene?"

"Once or twice. I liked him a lot. He was one of the most dedicated people I think I ever met."

"A rare breed," Joseph said. "You don't find too many doctors like that."

"I never heard you say a good word about doctors before."

"He was different, Polly. He wasn't out to control the real estate markets. Personal wealth didn't mean much to him."

"There was a good feeling in that clinic," said Polly. "You could tell it right away. There was a sense of trust. No one felt like they were going to be disposed of by a petty bureaucrat who couldn't have cared whether they lived or died. There's a rocking chair in the waiting room that has a little plaque on it—'In the memory of Sarah Brown' it says. Once I asked someone who she was. You know who she was, Joseph?"

"No."

"She was an old lady from the community who used to come to the clinic because she had no one to talk with at home. She used to come there and just sit in the rocking chair and talk with the patients when they came in. When she died, they put a plaque on the chair so they'd remember her."

"A little corny," said Joseph, "but that's the kind of a place it was."

"You think it will close now that he died?"

"I hope not, Polly. But sometimes things like that depend on one man."

"Or woman . . ."

"Yeah. Anyway, I'm sorry he died."

"It's a real tragedy, Joseph. Besides, he was so young."

19

"Young or old, it's the way he died. He didn't die of a heart attack or falling off a cliff. He got blown up in a lab with a genetic engineer."

"I guess you ought to do the story, Joseph."

"Maybe . . ."

Chapter 2

Joseph riffled through the cards in his address file till he found
the right one. Then he dialled the number for the clinic and
waited. There wasn't any answer.

He hung up and studied the source notes he had made last
year. Gerry Saunders had been Malcolm's administrative assist-
ant. He decided to try her. He got her number from directory
information and then placed the call.

"Yeah. Who is this?" The voice that came on the line
sounded exhausted, as if it had been drawn through the wringer
of an old-fashioned washing machine.

"This is Joseph Radkin. I did a story on the People's Medical
Clinic last year."

"Oh . . . you're calling to do an obituary."

"I'm . . . I'm sorry . . ."

"Jezus! A reporter who apologises! What paper did you say
you work for again?"

"The *Defender*, but . . ."

"Yeah, I remember you! About a year ago. You brought
those bagels. That was sweet."

"Well, actually, my mother had bought a ton of them and
they were going stale."

"Whatever. You wrote a decent story. Malcolm had cut it
out. We made some copies and put it in our propaganda pack."

"I hope it helped . . ."

"Helped? Say, don't you know?"

"Know what?"

"The clinic's dead. I thought you were calling to do an
obituary?"

"That's right. I'd like to come over and talk."

There was a silent moment. Then Gerry said, "I guess so.
Let me give you directions. It's a little hard to find . . ."

*

The cottage he was looking for was on Hill Street in the Noe Valley district. It was tucked behind the fancified edifice of a redone Victorian. The Victorian had the style, but the cottage had the view. It overlooked the city, perched above the morning haze like a mountain look-out post, keeping watch on all the nonsense far below.

He knocked on the door a couple of times before she opened up. She was a tiny woman, slim and pretty in a waif-like sort of way. She had short black hair that hung down the sides of her face like a wilted mop. Her eyes were red. She had obviously been crying.

"You're Radkin from the *Defender*?" she asked.

"Yeah—I guess . . ."

"Come in," she said half-heartedly, holding the door open for him.

Inside it was as green as spring. The place was covered with so many ferns, it could have passed for a summer camp in Brazil. There was a thick rug, lots of throw cushions and not much furniture.

"You want some coffee?" she asked brushing by him as she walked through an opening in the wall that led to a tiny kitchen.

"Yeah, thanks."

There was a wooden desk covered with potted plants against one of the walls. Propped up against a cactus was a photograph in a simple chrome frame. Joseph walked over and picked it up. It was a staff portrait taken at the People's Medical Clinic. They all had their arms around one another, with great big smiles on their faces. It was obviously taken in happier days.

Gerry came back in carrying a tray. She placed it on an occasional table and then, staring at him sullenly, said: "I better warn you, Radkin, I'm not in much of a mood to talk. I've been up since four this morning . . ." She was obviously fighting hard to hold back the tears. She stuck out her hand. "You got a smoke on you?"

"Yeah." He reached in his pocket and pulled out a pack of Camels and handed it to her.

"Light?" she asked.

He took out his lighter and held it out for her. She lit up and took a puff and then started to cough. "Shit, I haven't smoked one of these things in years!"

"You have any idea at all what happened?" he asked.

She shook her head abruptly and then took another quick puff on her cigarette.

Joseph poured a cup of coffee. "You take milk and sugar?" he asked.

"Just black thanks," she said. Then realising she had invited him over to her house she said, "Let me do that."

"It's OK," he said. "I'll get it."

"You want a Danish or something?" she asked.

"Not for me . . ."

She sat down on one of the pillows. "Hey, go ahead, sit down if you want."

He looked around for a comfortable cushion and then sat on it. "I won't stay long."

She started to speak. Maybe to him, maybe not. "I can't believe he's dead. Not Malcolm. He was one of those people who you think are gonna live for ever . . ." She was holding her coffee in one hand and the cigarette in the other. The ash from the cigarette was growing long. It was clear that she didn't know what to do with it.

"You have an ashtray?" he asked.

She shook her head. "No. I don't like people to smoke in here." She let out a short, ironic laugh.

"How about a saucer?"

"Yeah. I'll get it."

"Stay put," he said. He got up and went into the little kitchen.

"First cabinet, lower shelf," she called out.

"Right," he said, taking one from a stack and bringing it in to her.

"Thanks," she said, letting the ash fall into the white china dish.

"How long had you known him?" he asked.

She shrugged. "I never really knew him, I guess . . ."

It sounded to him like an unhappy admission. "I mean when did you meet?"

"About fifteen years ago." She closed her eyes. "I know, I don't look that old . . ."

"I wasn't going to say that," he replied.

"What were you going to say?"

"Nothing. I just wanted to know if you were there from the beginning."

"Yeah," she said taking another puff, growing used to the rhythm and the narcotic effect, "from the first idealistic throw to the final shot of dung!"

"I don't understand," he said, trying to make sense of her words.

"You think I do?" she replied stubbing out her cigarette in the newborn ashtray and then downing the rest of her coffee. "Can I have another?" she asked.

"Cigarette?" He took out the pack again and handed it to her. "If you're going to be a chain-smoker you might as well just keep them."

"Thanks," she said. "Your mother buy a ton of these too?"

"My mother doesn't smoke. At least not yet. She's seventy and still determined to try everything once."

"Good for her," said Gerry lighting up and then starting another fit of coughing.

"You've got to watch it for the first couple of weeks," Joseph warned her. "It takes a bit of time to break in your lungs."

"Thanks for the warning, doc," she said.

He nodded. "So what happened, Gerry. You want to tell me?"

She looked over at one of the hanging spider plants. "It wasn't that we were starry-eyed kids, but if you could have heard us talk back then you would have thought we'd just invented the moon."

"When was that?" he asked.

"In the early seventies. Back in the days when money was growing from trees and ideas were free for the asking." She took another puff, coughed, and then smiled. It was a far-away smile.

"And then came the crunch," said Joseph.

"Yeah. The Crunch. The Drought. The Guillotine. The taps were opened, the taps were shut." Her face suddenly got tense. "Nobody gives a fuck about the poor anymore!"

"But you survived . . . till now. What went wrong?"

"What went wrong?" She looked at him curiously. "Nothing. The goddamn irony is that we were extremely successful. Listen, it's not easy to gain the confidence of the people in the communities we were trying to serve. There were constant conflicts to battle through. It took years, Radkin. I mean years. And then, when we finally got to the point where we had actually made it work . . ." She shook her head. "Pour me another coffee, will ya?"

He went over to the tray and felt the pot. "It's cold," he said.

She held out her cup. "Doesn't matter."

"So where did the funding come from when the government monies ran out?" he asked as he poured her some lukewarm brew.

"About five years ago we became totally dependent on Metropolitan Hospital. From then on we had to fight for a yearly subsidy at the same time hospital funds were being drained as well. It meant we had to spend half our time polishing up our statistics—showing the effectiveness of our screening programs for TB, glaucoma, diabetes; all the figures on drug and alcohol programs, the teenage birth-control program, post-natal programs. But that fat little fart-face, Hobbs, and his like, would rather have spent a million on a CAT scanner than a few thousand on preventative medicine." She stubbed out her cigarette and lit up another. "He's the one to blame!" she spat.

"Who's the fat little fart-face, Hobbs? And what's a CAT scanner?"

"Elias Hobbs is the administrative director of Metropolitan Hospital. He's fat and he farts like a pig. A CAT scanner is a computerised diagnostic machine that picks up microscopic tumors in your nose and tells you what you probably know already—that we're all gonna die some day."

"So Hobbs is the one who axed the clinic?" asked Joseph.

"Yeah. But he didn't just axe it straight away. He made us suffer—the sadistic little creep!"

"What do you mean?"

"The yearly budget meeting was a few weeks ago. Hobbs had met Malcolm at the Cherry Blossom to discuss our current funding proposal. He told Malcolm that as far as he was concerned the People's Medical Clinic was through."

"What did he want to replace it with?"

"You got to understand these guys, Radkin. They come from business schools. They think that the country is built on profit and private enterprise and that's what makes it great. If you tell them this country has the worst infant mortality rate in the industrial world, they just don't believe you!"

"I know the type," said Joseph. "He's my managing editor . . ."

"Anyway, all that interests Hobbs is the survival of his hospital. And that means having 'sensible' programs that can compete with the Health Maintenance Organisations and the other private schemes."

"And I guess to people like Hobbs that means technology," said Joseph.

"Right! They have no idea in the world of the misery that goes on every minute of the day in homes not a block away from their beloved institution! Oh, it's fine to talk about state-of-the-art technology when you're well fed and plugged into the system. But idiots like Hobbs actually think they're being socially responsible by taking away the only programs that ever reach poor people and replacing them with a fucking machine!" Gerry's cheeks were glowing a bright red.

"So he cut the cord?" asked Joseph.

"Not as simple as that, Radkin," she said lighting up another smoke. "He made Malcolm an offer he couldn't refuse."

"What kind of an offer?"

"He said he'd give us another year's funds if Malcolm did

26

some dirty work for him. You see the hospital had been experiencing some salmonella outbreaks . . ."

"Yeah, I remember. They were almost decertified, weren't they?"

"In fact the State Accreditation Board had put them on probation. And guess what?"

"Another outbreak?"

"Right! So Hobbs makes a deal with the Board. If he can clean it up without any mortalities and if the media doesn't get wind, they'll let it slide."

"You're kidding! The Board actually colluded with him?"

"I thought you were a hard-boiled reporter, Radkin . . ." she said giving him a curious look.

"But what did this have to do with Malcolm Greene? You weren't actually part of the hospital, were you?"

"That's just it. Hobbs agreed to have an outside medical adviser head the investigation. And Malcolm had been a preventative medicine officer in the army."

"I see. So if Malcolm scratched his back, Hobbs would come up with the funds."

She shook her head. "Not so easy. Hobbs played hardball. We would get the funds only if Malcolm's investigation pinpointed the cause of the salmonella poisoning and if there was no leak to the media."

"So Malcolm became part of the cover-up?"

"As did I. He brought it up with the senior staff. We all agreed."

"That's terrible!" said Joseph. "Let me have one of those smokes, will you?"

She threw him the pack. "You think it's terrible? Better that our clinic was shut down?"

He lit up and inhaled deeply. "But that's the point, isn't it? Your clinic was shut down. You should have blown the whistle on him back then."

"It was a gamble, Radkin. The way we saw it we had nothing to lose and everything to gain. Malcolm was trained in tracking down food poisoning. And who the hell cared if the media

27

knew or not? We wanted the hospital to remain open as much as anyone . . ."

"So what happened, Gerry? You played the game. How come the clinic was shut and Malcolm is . . ."

She closed her eyes. "Malcolm died before the accident, Radkin."

"What do you mean?"

"I don't know what I mean." Her face looked drawn and tired.

"Come on, Gerry . . ."

She stood up. "Look Radkin, I've told you as much as I can right now. I'm trying hard to hold back on my emotions. You don't seem to appreciate that my best friend died last night."

Joseph stood up, too. "I don't want to upset you, Gerry, but it seems to me that this is a story that's got to come out."

"Maybe, but now's not the time," she said walking over to the door and opening it up. "Why don't you phone me later?"

"I'll phone you tomorrow," he said. "OK?" He stood by the door waiting for her to reply.

She nodded. "OK . . ."

Set in the shadows of Portrero Hill, the Metropolitan Community Hospital stood at the edge of the Mission district, the Latino section of town. The People's Medical Clinic was hidden away among the dour, fortress-like buildings, at the far end of the complex near the hospital chimney that rose into the sky like a dark finger of doom, belching out the foul smoke which over the course of years had given a grey and somber appearance to the hospital facade.

Joseph stood by the sculptured iron entrance gates looking in. A wooden road-barrier was being moved by a uniformed special policeman allowing a truck to pass by.

Once the truck had moved on and the barrier was replaced, Joseph went up to the cop, an older man who looked like he would have been on skid row if he hadn't been dressed in uniform.

"What's going on?" asked Joseph.

The cop looked at him suspiciously at first and then, probably because he wasn't the suspicious sort, said, "Hospital's closed down, son."

"Closed down? How can they close Metropolitan Hospital?"

"Can't rightly say how. But they did it."

Joseph glanced over at the adjoining green that led up to the buildings. Files, equipment, storage boxes had all been piled outside.

"What'd they do with the patients?" he asked, turning back to the cop.

"Sent 'em elsewhere, I suspect."

The cop wasn't the most talkative person he had ever met, thought Joseph as he fished out his wallet and got out his crumpled press-card. Some of them could talk your ear off if they were bored and standing alone like that.

"I'm a reporter," he said.

The cop inspected the card that Joseph handed him. "Good job, is it?" he asked, handing it back.

"Not really. You gonna let me in?"

"Nope."

"Why not?"

"Press ain't allowed."

"Who says?"

"Them's my orders, son."

Joseph reached for his cigarettes and then realised that he left them with Gerry. "You got a smoke on you?" he asked the cop.

The cop fished around for his pack and handed a cigarette to Joseph. "They don't let me smoke on duty," he said. "Wish they did."

"All this because of the explosion last night?" asked Joseph lighting up.

"They started closing down a few days ago. 'Cause of the strike."

"Strike? What strike?"

The cop gave him a strange look. "You sure you're a reporter, son? Where you been for the last week?"

"On assignment. They sent me to cover the cactus festival in the Mojave Desert. What's this about a strike?"

"Nurses' strike. Taken over by outside agitators. You should have been here a couple of days ago. That's when you would have had your story. Not much happening now."

"Lots of action, huh?"

"Action? Pitched battle just about ten feet away." He shook his head. "Some of those women are real hellions, all right. Wouldn't want to have any of them givin' me an injection."

"They set up a press office?" asked Joseph.

The cop pointed across the street. "In that Chinese restaurant over there."

Joseph glanced in the direction of the cop's thumb. A sign on the plate-glass window read: "Cherry Blossom Restaurant—Vietnamese and Chinese Cuisine."

"Guess I'll saunter over and see what they got to say," he said to the cop. "Thanks for the smoke."

"Don't know if anyone's still there," the cop replied. And then he turned back to let another waiting truck through the wooden barrier.

A notice posted on the door said: "Restaurant Closed By Order Of The Department Of Public Health."

Joseph tried the door. It opened.

There was a faint odor of spices as he walked in. The aromas of garlic and chilies and sesame oil still clung to the air even though the woks had cooled and now sat empty in their trays.

The tables were still there, though pushed to the side to form an aisle which led to the kitchen. Joseph stood for a moment and looked around. The decor was simple and unpretentious, but it had a certain charm. It was the kind of restaurant he wouldn't have minded frequenting as much for the ambiance as for the food.

"Anyone home?" Joseph shouted out.

A voice replied. "In here . . ."

He walked through the swinging doors into the kitchen and from there into a back room.

30

The back room contained a smaller dining area, probably a meeting place, he thought. On the walls were hangings of peaceful oriental scenes and in the center of the room was a sculptured rock made into a tiny lake with aquatic plants and flowers. A row of tables had been turned into desks and were piled high with papers.

A woman with a dark complexion and jet-black hair set in tight ringlets looked up from the table where she was sitting and said with some annoyance, "Who are you?"

"Joseph Radkin. I'm a reporter."

"You're a little late, aren't you?" she said with a trace of sarcasm in her voice. "The blood's already dry."

"I wanted to get some information on the strike." He liked her looks even though she obviously hadn't taken to him.

She pointed to the stack of papers. "Help yourself," she said.

He walked over and started taking some sheets. "How come they closed down?" he asked.

"You want the official reason or the truth?"

"Both."

"The official reason is rampant, uncontrollable salmonella poisoning that already caused three deaths and probably several more in the next day or two."

"And the real reason?"

She stared at him as if she were trying to make up her mind about something. "The truth is that they just wanted to close it down," she said.

"Why?"

"Because they want to get rid of public health hospitals," she replied simply.

"Sounds a bit drastic, doesn't it?" said Joseph. He pointed to a chair. "Mind if I sit down?"

She shrugged. "Help yourself."

"You're not saying they started a salmonella epidemic on purpose, are you?" he asked as he eased himself into the straight-back chair.

She shook her head. "You don't have to plan for it to happen. All you have to do is cut back on staff and loosen up

31

certain hospital regulations because you don't have any funds to enforce them, and just let nature do the rest."

"Did you know Dr Greene?" he asked her.

"Yeah, I knew him . . ." She looked down at the table.

"What do you think happened last night?"

She glared at him. "How the hell should I know?"

"I'm sorry," he apologised. "I wasn't trying to step on your toes."

"At this moment," she said, with an angry look on her face, "I wouldn't have minded if every fucking doctor in the hospital had been in that lab!"

"I thought Greene was different . . ." Joseph began.

"I did too," she said without waiting for him to finish. "It turned out he was just like the rest of those ego-inflated bull-headed snobs. Give them an MD and they think they own the world!"

"Are you referring to anything specific or is this just a general observation . . . I'm sorry, I didn't catch your name." Joseph resorted to option 33-A in the journalist's advice manual.

"You didn't catch it 'cause I didn't throw it, Mr Reporter."

"Mine's Joseph Radkin," he said, quoting option 34.

"Good."

"You don't like reporters?" he asked.

"Not much . . ."

"Neither do I." Option 36.

She laughed. "You're one hell of a newsman!"

"Well, you're one hell of a publicity woman," he shot back.

"I'm a nurse!" she said. "At least I was, once."

"I thought this was the union's public information office," he smiled.

"It is; take all the public information you want!" She pointed again to the multicolored sheets on the table.

"Look," he said, "I don't know what kind of experience you've had in the last few days with the gentlemen of the press, but, frankly, I detest them as much as you. I'm a freelancer. I just want to find out what's going on here. I don't even know

32

whether it's a story I want to write yet. I'm just trying to find out, that's all."

She sighed. "Mr Radkin, I trust you guys about as far as I can throw you and I can't throw you very far. But if it's that important to you, my name's Janet Baker. I worked across the road up until a few days ago. I was a chief ward nurse. I didn't know Dr Greene very well. I just assisted him in his enquiries and ended up getting the sack for my troubles."

"Because of what you told him?"

"What else? He was in charge of the investigation, wasn't he?"

"Was he?"

"Yes! And it was his report that done us in!"

"What report?"

"The one about the Vietnamese birthday cake!"

"What's a Vietnamese birthday cake?" Polly asked him that evening over dinner.

"How should I know?" he said. "You like the quiche?"

She picked at the crust with her fork. "If you have to throw our money away on take-out, how about going down market a little?"

"OK, next time pizza. Why didn't you tell me about the nurses' strike?"

She stared at him. "Tell you? Criminy, Joseph, it was blasted over the front page for days!"

"You know I wasn't reading the paper . . ."

"Or watching TV or listening to the radio or talking to me."

"I wanted to get the novel finished by the time Spinach was done."

"So why blame me if you weren't abreast of current affairs?"

"Anything else of importance happen while I was away?"

"You knew that Manhattan Island was sold back to the Indians didn't you?"

"No kidding?"

"No kidding. Also Vesuvius erupted, a new Dead Sea Scroll

33

was found, Martians invaded a local radio station, and some nut just taught a pig how to fly."

"It was bound to happen sooner or later," he said.

"So tell me about the birthday cake."

"It's a very weird story, Polly . . ."

"The weirder the better as your editor likes to say."

"Well, the best I can make out, Malcolm was on the trail of the salmonella bug . . ."

"That's the food poisoning virus, right?"

"Bacteria, Polly. It's a common staphylococcus that's pretty easy to keep under control if certain rigid precautions are enforced. But once it starts multiplying in large numbers it can run rampant in an institution like a hospital . . ."

"Is it fatal?"

"Not to a healthy person, usually. But the elderly and the infirm can get awfully sick. A bad epidemic can knock off an entire ward, I understand."

"OK, so Malcolm was on the trail. I guess he started in the kitchen?"

"Right. According to Janet Baker, the nurse I was talking to, the kitchen was an awful mess. Most of the food handlers were immigrant workers who hardly spoke English . . ."

"So was your grandpa."

"Yeah, but he didn't work in a hospital, Polly. These people were barely trained and probably couldn't read the rule book on hospital standards."

"That's racist propaganda, Joseph."

"Janet Baker is black, Polly."

"Doesn't make it any the less racist."

"Come on, give me a break! I'm not saying that these people were incapable of being trained. I'm saying that because the hospital chose to pay a menial wage, they got the most desperate workers; workers who couldn't care less about hospital procedure since they were being treated like scum. They could have been any color. In this case they happened to be brown."

34

"Look, we can argue this all night, Joseph. But what's your point?"

"Well the point is that the kitchen was a tinderbox for food poisoning. But the irony's that Greene didn't find any hard evidence for the salmonella starting there."

"So Malcolm Greene didn't find any bugs in the soup. Where did he look next?"

"According to Janet, salmonella bacteria can be anywhere, even in the dust on the floor. The trick is trying to find the common elements. Everybody, of course, eats the hospital food. So if you've ruled that out, you start looking for something environmental."

"Or something everyone ate that was brought in from the outside," said Polly.

"Right on the mark," said Joseph. "I think you're about ready to join the Great Detectives Club, Polly old girl."

"Is that what it was?" asked Polly.

"Well, that's what Malcolm suspected. And he started questioning the nurses to see if anything had been brought in from the outside that might have been the cause . . ."

"And that's how we get to the Vietnamese Birthday Cake?"

"One of the patients had a birthday. It seems he had been there for a while and he didn't have a family. So the nurses got together and chipped in to buy him a birthday cake."

"One with a kick, no doubt."

"The problem was that some of the people who had eaten the cake got sick and others didn't."

"But that must happen all the time," said Polly. "A group of people are exposed to a virus or bacteria. Some come down with something, others don't."

"The sticky point, however, is that some people who came down with the symptoms didn't eat the cake."

"So I suppose that rules out the cake as the culprit. Why bring it up in the first place?"

"Because Malcolm didn't rule it out. His theory was that the people who didn't eat the cake and came down with the symptoms were like the control group in a clinical psychology experiment who take placebos instead of a pill that makes you stand on your head, and end up standing on their head anyway . . ."

"Yeah, well the symptoms of food poisoning aren't the same as standing on your head."

"No. But have you ever been around anyone throwing up?"

"Last time you got drunk."

"Made you kind of queasy, didn't it?"

"Made me puke myself, Joseph. But that's because I was a little tipsy, too."

"Anyway, stomach disorders have a lot to do with the mind. At least that's what Janet said that Malcolm told her."

"That sounds like pretty flimsy evidence to convict anyone with, your honor."

"That ain't the half of it, kiddo. You know where they got the cake?"

"From a Sears and Roebuck catalogue?"

"Nope. From a Vietnamese restaurant. The chef baked it for them for free."

"The place across the street where you met Janet the Nurse?"

"And the place where Hobbs and Malcolm struck their deal. The Cherry Blossom Restaurant. It was the hangout for the staff. Seems that the guy who owned it was a Vietnamese refugee and a good friend of Greene's. Now there's a sign on the window saying it was shut down by order of the Department of Public Health."

"Well, that's friendship for you!"

"That doesn't sound like the Malcolm Greene we knew, does it Polly?" asked Joseph in a serious tone of voice.

"No, it doesn't. Did you talk to the guy who owns the place—the Vietnamese refugee?"

"Not yet. He lives upstairs. I knocked on the door and a little barefoot kid came down. Cute as a button! I asked for her daddy but she didn't seem to understand. Finally she shut the door on me and ran upstairs."

"She probably thought you were a cop, Joseph."

36

"Oh, come on, Polly. I don't look anything like a cop! No one would ever suspect me of looking like a cop!"

"I'm just teasing you. You tease me all the time. Now I'm teasing you!"

"Well I never tease you by saying you look like a cop!"

"You know, Joseph . . ." Her voice trailed off.

"What?"

"I don't think I ever heard of getting food poisoning from a cake."

"Neither have I, Polly. But there's a lot of things that don't make sense. Gerry Saunders, for instance. You know what she said when I made a stupid reference to Malcolm's death?"

"No, what did she say?"

"She said that Malcolm died before the accident."

"She could have been speaking figuratively, Joseph."

"I assume she was speaking figuratively, Polly. But even so . . ."

"Anyway, I don't understand what all this has to do with the genetic engineer—what's his name?"

"Professor Krohl . . ."

"Yeah. And why the hell did they close the hospital? I mean there must have been salmonella outbreaks before, Joseph."

"Janet claims they just used it as an excuse to get rid of the only public hospital in town."

"Well of course they used it as an excuse. But even in this city things are usually done with a little more finesse. You just don't close a huge municipal institution like that in a day."

"The other thing is why the police have the place cordoned off."

"Have you gotten the police report?"

"Not yet."

"What did the papers say?"

"That it's an explosion of unknown origin and it's under investigation."

"Maybe the explosion released some noxious substances."

"It was a laboratory, wasn't it? I wonder what kind of a lab it was?"

"What kind of labs do they have in public hospitals, Joseph? Usually ones where they do tests on things they take out of unlucky people, right?"

"Metropolitan was also a teaching hospital. The university might have been doing some research."

"If we go through our list of friends, I bet we come up with two or three who worked there."

Joseph drew in a deep breath. "I hope we're not opening a can of worms, Polly."

She took his hand and smiled. "I'll let you in on a secret, my friend. I think the can's been opened already."

Chapter 3

"Coffee?" he asked. "Tea? Milk?"

"We're going on an airplane flight somewhere?" She hauled her package to the breakfast table. "What are you doing up so early?"

"Lots to do today," he replied, flapping a jack. "You take syrup on your pancakes, don't you?"

"Are you all right, Joseph? I mean I sense a gleam in your eye. I say 'sense' because I can't see a damn thing until I've had my morning coffee."

"Coming up, madam," he said. "Fresh ground, mocha blend, just the way you like it."

She watched him pour and then add a dollop of milk (for Spinach, he said). She looked at him suspiciously. "You didn't win the Pulitzer or anything while I was asleep, did you?"

"Not yet," he said going back to the stove and pouring some more batter on the griddle. "Not yet . . ."

"Your mother moved out?"

"No."

"What then?"

"I just felt like it, that's all."

"Oh," she said, suddenly realising. "It's the story, isn't it? You're on the scent. The game's afoot."

He turned around and grinned.

"I knew it! You just love playing detective!"

"Don't complain. At least you're getting breakfast out of it."

She watched with wonder as a heap of perfectly formed buttermilk flapjacks arrived before her. She used the edge of her fork to cut into the pile and then speared the wedge. "Not bad!" she said, tasting the morsel. "Not bad at all!"

"Wait till you see what I've got planned for tonight!"

She gobbled up the rest of the pancakes, gulped down her coffee and then wiped her mouth. "Oh, didn't I tell you?" she

39

said, struggling to get out of her chair. "Your mother invited us up for dinner tonight. She wants us to meet Morris."

"Morris?" He glared at her. "Who's Morris?"

She grabbed her briefcase. "Her new friend. See you tonight," she said giving him a juicy kiss on the cheek.

"Morris?" he said, watching her go. "Sounds like the name of a cat."

He debated with himself whether to try the police. It wasn't his style and, besides, he didn't trust their information. What facts he needed could usually be gained through the daily papers and by interviewing people the press had ignored.

This time, however, he would have liked to have gotten his hands on the police report. The articles in the press had been sketchy to say the least. In fact, he had the feeling the story was being deliberately played down.

He tapped his pencil on the desk, thought a bit and then decided. He dialled a number and waited.

"*Daily News!*" said a singsong voice after five rings.

"City Desk!" he replied, trying to mimic her rhythm.

"Hold on please!" she said.

"I'm holding as tight as I can, lady!"

He heard her groan.

Then, some moments later, a rasping voice came on the line. "City desk!"

"Seamus Magee," said Joseph.

"He's not in . . ."

"Off today?"

"Don't I wish!"

"You know where I can find him?"

"You tell me," the rasp said with a note of disgust. "Maybe try his office . . ." it offered before disconnecting itself from the telephone.

The Temple Bar was located in an alley off Powell, not too far from the editorial offices of the *Daily News*, but far enough. In former times it served as the trading post for news items which eventually found their way into the score of rags hawked on the city streets. Most of the scandal sheets had long since passed away (no funerals were held, no tears were shed); nowadays most of the newsmen drank alone in front of their video display units.

Seamus Magee, however, was a man with traditions to uphold. And he upheld them well—as long as he kept a firm grip on the railing of the bar.

"What are you drinking?" asked Joseph when he found him already half-stewed at the ten o'clock bell.

"Jameson's," said Seamus. "What else is there to drink in this effing place?"

"A Jameson's and an orange juice," Joseph called out to the bartender.

"Who the hell ever heard of drinking Jameson's with orange juice? Who taught you how to drink? Liberace?"

"The Jameson's for you, Seamus. The orange juice is for me."

"Things are that bad, are they?" asked Seamus as the drinks were served.

"I'm having a kid," said Joseph. "Gotta watch what I put in my stomach."

Seamus gave him the once-over lightly. "You don't look pregnant to me."

"You're not a very good judge of those things, Seamus," said Joseph. "You never were."

"I beg to differ," said Seamus. "I was pregnant several times myself."

"What happened?"

"They grew up and started asking for money. That's when I took to drink."

"I thought you took to drink when Connolly died."

"Then too."

Joseph brought the drinks over to an empty table and motioned for Seamus to follow.

"I try not to sit down here," said Seamus coming over and reluctantly taking a chair.

"Why not?"

"Because once I'm down, it's usually too hard to get back up."

"I'll help you, Seamus."

Seamus patted him on the back. "You always were a good lad."

"So give me a run down on what happened at the hospital," said Joseph not wanting to waste any more time.

"They took out my spleen and put in an extra bladder. I can go forever now without having to take a piss."

Joseph sighed. "No, Seamus, I meant about the explosion at Metropolitan. Two of the doctors were killed in a lab, remember?"

"We all have to die sometime, Radkin, me boy, what difference does it make where it happens? You want another— uh—drink?"

"All right," said Joseph, closing his eyes.

Seamus came back moments later trying to balance a glass in either hand. He handed the orange one to Joseph. "Juice . . ." he said, with a trace of disgust in his voice.

"Thanks," said Joseph and he took a quick, nervous gulp. And then, suddenly, as his stomach erupted into flame, he said, "What the hell did you give me, Seamus?"

"Juice . . . You wanted juice, didn't you?"

"And what else?" Joseph felt his eyes begin to glaze.

Seamus lowered his voice and leaned towards Joseph. "I can't be seen with someone drinking sarsaparilla, Radkin. After all, I've got a reputation to uphold."

"Jezus!"

"I look to God meself sometimes in these days of trouble and sorrow."

"Seamus," he said, looking at him as seriously as he knew how, "I need some help."

"Don't we all, me boy. Don't we all."

"Seamus, cut that drunken Irish crap. I know for a fact you never stepped foot on the Emerald Isle. You were born on the Lower East Side of New York. Your mother was born in

Lithuania. Your father was born in London and was brought over to America at the age of three."

"How the hell do you know that?" asked Seamus angrily.

"You told me!"

"I told you?" Seamus let out a laugh. "The first rule of journalism—the very first one they teach you in kindergarten— is to consider the credibility of your source!"

Joseph held up a hand for him to stop. "OK, OK. I'm not asking you to show me your pedigree. Just tell me what you know about the closure of Metropolitan Hospital. How come they have it sealed off?"

Seamus ran his fingers through his hair and his tongue licked around his teeth as if he were trying to moisten his mouth. "Nobody's talking, Radkin. Maybe nobody knows, but I got the feeling that someone's trying to keep the lid on things . . ." As Seamus spoke, his Irish brogue began to fade away.

"How come?"

"You tell me."

"What's the police report say?"

"Lab explosion of undetermined origin. Probably caused by a gas leak."

"What were Greene and Krohl doing there?"

"Who knows? They were both doctors. They had a right to be there."

"At two in the morning?"

"The hospital's open twenty-four hours a day, Radkin. It's not a shoe store."

"Come on, Seamus. You're not talking to your editor!"

Seamus grinned and took another drink of whiskey. "I'll tell you what I think's going on. I think they were doing some secret work in that lab. Krohl's a genetic engineer, right? He was probably working on a university project heavy with government funds. He mistakenly mixed batch 'A' with batch 'B' instead of batch 'C', blew the place up and in the process let a virus out of its cage that will probably turn us all into tadpoles."

"What was Greene doing there?"

"Watching."

"Come on, Seamus!"

"OK. Maybe he was helping Krohl by holding a beaker."

"Cut it out, Seamus! There was a coincidence of events: the nurses' strike, the salmonella scare, the lab explosion . . ."

Seamus shrugged. "I could name you three other events: my editor's halitosis, you coming here to bother me, and a severe pain in my head. They may be coincidental, they might also just be symptoms of the various plagues in my life."

Joseph stood up. "Thanks, Seamus. I always enjoy our little chats."

Seamus held up his glass. "Likewise."

As Joseph was walking out he heard Seamus call. "Hey, Radkin!"

He turned around and looked at Seamus.

"I'll give you buzz if I hear anything. OK?"

Joseph winked, turned on his heels and left.

He called Gerry from a phone box. She answered immediately.

"Yeah?" Her voice sounded hollow to him: tired and wasted.

"It's Joseph Radkin. You said to call you today."

"Not a good time, Radkin. I'm about to go out . . ."

"When will you be back?"

"Don't know. Maybe next week sometime."

"Next week? Wait a minute, Gerry. You can't run out on me just now!"

"Run out on you? Hey, Radkin, are we living in the same world?"

"Gerry, listen, I know there's something going on. I just want to talk to you a while. I promise not to write anything without your OK."

"I need some time to think, Radkin . . ."

"Gerry, there isn't much time left!"

"Why not?"

"I'm going to have a baby in a couple of weeks!"

"Congratulations, Radkin, but I don't see what that has to do with me . . ."

"Just a little help, that's all I'm asking."

"I don't know how I can help you . . ."

"You said Malcolm died before the explosion. What did you mean by that?"

There was a moment of silence on the other end. Then Gerry said, "He'd lost everything by then. I'm not sure he wanted to live anymore."

"But the fight wasn't lost, Gerry. You could have continued the clinic somewhere else."

"It's more complicated than that, Radkin."

"Like how?"

"Listen, I really do have to think about things. I'm going to hang up now. Call me in about a week."

"Wait, Gerry! Please! Just one more question. OK?"

He could hear her sigh. "What is it?"

"Did Malcolm have any relatives here? Any close relatives?"

"His parents are both dead. He's got a sister. Her name's Robin. His only friends I know of were the people at the clinic."

"Where does Robin live? You got a phone number for her?"

"Robin lived with him . . . that is up until a few weeks ago."

"Where does she live at the moment?"

"I don't know, Radkin. She disappeared . . ."

"Disappeared? Did you say she disappeared, Gerry?"

"That's what I said. I'm going to hang up now . . ."

"Wait! Where are you going? You got an address I can reach you in case of an emergency?"

"I'm going to the Sierras. I'm pitching my tent under a redwood tree."

"Which redwood tree?"

"How the hell should I know, Radkin? For Christ's sake! I'm going to hang up . . ."

"Wait! Gerry, my number's in the phone book. My name's spelled R-a-d-k-i-n. You got it? Call me if you want to talk."

"If I wanted to talk I'd see a psychiatrist. So long, Radkin."

*

45

He took the bus down to the Mission district and then hopped off at 17th where he grabbed a quick enchilada at a neighborhood café. Then he continued walking till he reached the hospital.

He watched for a while from the other side of the street. The barricades were still in place and trucks were still being loaded with crates of equipment and supplies. The same cop was still standing guard. Joseph caught his eye and signaled to him with a slight wave of his hand. The cop nodded.

Joseph walked across the street. "Not a bad life," he said to the cop. "Not too much traffic down here. No thugs or pushers. Must beat the Tenderloin, huh?"

"Still tryin' for a story, son? Them nurses kick you out on your butt?"

"Came over to return the cigarette you loaned me yesterday," Joseph said taking out a pack and offering one to the policeman.

"Save it," said the cop. "You never know when you'll be panhandled."

Joseph took the cigarette and lit it. "You gonna let me in?"

"Nope."

"Why not?"

"No can do."

"Feds in on this?"

"Maybe. Maybe not."

"They giving you hazardous duty pay?"

The cop threw him a strange look. "Why you askin' that?"

"Didn't they tell you about the danger?"

"What danger?"

"From the explosion. They didn't say anything?"

The cop narrowed his eyes. "They didn't tell me nothin'. Hey, what are you tryin' to pull?"

Joseph put up his hands in a supplicating gesture. "No offense, man. Just wanted to know whether they told you what kind of decontamination work was going on."

"You hacks got bullshit comin' out of your ears," said the cop shaking his head.

Joseph shrugged. "Can't kill a guy for askin'."

The cop grinned and patted his holster. "You wouldn't want to try me, son."

"No," Joseph agreed. "I guess not."

He crossed the street again and went inside the Cherry Blossom Restaurant.

"Anybody home?" he called out.

"Back here!" came the reply.

He walked through the swinging doors into the kitchen and then into the back room. Janet Baker was there as before, sifting through the literature packets.

"Oh, no," she said, putting a hand over her eyes and peering at him through splayed fingers, "not you again!"

"Yep," he replied, trying to put on a charming smile. "Sweet little old me. Tell me something. If you guys are going to all the trouble of putting out this literature for the press, how come you cringe every time I come in?"

She made a dour face. "Because your paper is a load of cow droppings on a hot day!"

"Which newspaper isn't?" he asked.

"You sure you're a reporter?"

"Sometimes I ask myself the same question," he said, pulling out his pack of cigarettes and offering her one. "You smoke?"

"Only when I'm on fire," she replied.

He sat down in one of the chairs and crossed his legs as if he were planning to stay for a while. "Hey, I thought we sorted all this out yesterday."

"That was before I read today's *Defender*," she said glaring at him and then throwing him a copy. "You guys blame the hospital closure on us!"

Joseph glanced through the article. "That sonofabitch!" he groaned. "I'll kill him!" And then, looking at her apologetically, he said, "Janet, I'm no more responsible for what's printed in this rag than you are when a hospital denies responsibility for a botched appendectomy. Anyway, I wouldn't write crap like that!" He handed her back the newspaper.

"You might not put it in, but, baby, that's what comes out!" she said pointing to the story again.

"Look," he said, trying to explain, "I'm an independent freelancer. What I write is mine. If the *Defender* buys it and wants to print it, they do it under my by-line and my copyright. If they want to change anything they have to negotiate with me first. Believe me, I'm on your side. And the way I see it, you need all the friends you can get."

She stared at him for a minute as if trying to make him out. Then she said, "Tell me, macho man, what are you after?"

"A story."

"Yeah, you and a hundred other two-bit, lop-eared scribblers. All you want's a story. It doesn't have to have a beginning or an end. Just a little tickle. So you write your piece, have your fun, and add to all the fluff that people have between their ears!"

"You sure you're in the right business, kid?" he asked. "I mean did you nurses draw straws for this job or what?"

"We all do our bit, buster. None of us ever ran a strike before. But we're learning . . ."

"Well, I'll give you a hint to help you on the road toward good PR. The first thing you have to learn is how not to antagonise the press. You can curse them, spit at them, tear 'em into shreds if you want. But wait until the reporter leaves the room, OK?"

"You telling me how to run this place?" she asked defiantly.

"Yep. I guess I am."

She stared at him and slowly her anger melted. Finally, she let out a sigh and sat back down. "Maybe I do need a little help," she said in a quieter voice. "I sure ain't doing much for our cause as it is."

"The next thing you have to learn is to set up your publicity in the front of the shop, not in the rear."

"Well this is the room he let us use," she said in her own defense.

"Who?"

48

"Mr Lim. The guy who owns the restaurant. It's pretty sweet of him to let us have the space at all."

"Real sweet," said Joseph. Did you ever wonder what he's after?"

She threw him an angry glace. "Mr Lim's a refugee from Vietnam. He's got a wife and four kids. He ran a pretty fine restaurant until your Dr Greene came along and shut him down!"

He held up his hand. "I'm sorry, Janet. I apologise. I was letting myself get carried away."

"You do that, don't you?"

"Maybe I do. My wife says that all the time . . ."

"She ever try a woman's shelter?"

"Not yet. She's pregnant. She wants me around to watch the kid."

"Poor kid . . ." Then, despite herself, she let out a laugh, "OK, Radkin, what is it you want?"

He smiled back at her. "Call me Joseph. All right?"

She had a look that he interpreted as acquiescence. "So how can I help you . . . again."

"I want to meet Lim."

"He lives upstairs. Try knocking on his door."

Joseph shook his head. "I tried that yesterday. He just sends his kid down to say he's not at home."

"Maybe he wasn't at home."

"I think he was. Anyway, the family seems suspicious of strangers."

"Can you blame them?" she asked.

He shrugged.

"So you want me to introduce you, is that it?"

"Yeah. That's it," he nodded.

She looked down at her hands and thought for a moment. Then she said, "Give me a chance to talk it over with him. Come back tomorrow . . ."

"What time?"

"About ten. He comes down in the morning and putters around a bit. I'll talk to him then."

*

"Jezus!" said Polly in admiration. "You used real saffron in here!"

They were seated at the table upstairs in Rachel's apartment. The kitchen was just big enough for four if you didn't mind tight squeezes.

"Saffron," said Morris, "is essential. Without saffron you might as well not call it paella."

"Morris learned to make paella when he was in Spain," said Rachel, doing nothing to disguise the admiration in her voice.

"Probably from a Spanish anarchist," said Joseph under his breath, as he forked out a broken clam shell.

Polly jabbed him in the ribs with her elbow and then smiled. "It's absolutely delicious. What did you put in here, Morris?"

Morris made a dance with his hands. "A little of this, a little of that. Basically it's a stew . . ."

"A stew?" Rachel was aghast. "A stew is some meat and potatoes, a carrot, some vegetables, a little stock. This," she said, pointing to the huge bowl on the table, "is not a stew!"

"A stew is anything you throw together and let cook a while," said Morris.

"Well," said Polly, trying to mediate, "if it's a stew it's a pretty elaborate one. What do you have in here? Chicken, sausage, shellfish, artichoke . . ."

"All the ingredients for a great midnight stomachache," Joseph muttered.

"He likes to joke, my son," said Rachel, glaring at the young man across from her.

"So, Joseph, I hear you're working on an article about the hospital closure," said Morris, trying to change the course of the conversation.

"It's a shame," said Rachel. "They should all be ashamed of themselves! Instead of closing hospitals they should be building new ones!"

"They are," said Joseph. "For private patients."

"A room in one of them costs $250 a night! Imagine!" said Rachel in disgust.

"You could get a penthouse in the Hilton for that," said Polly.

"Well no one actually pays $250 a night," said Joseph. "Their insurance does."

"That assumes you have insurance," said Polly.

"Why aren't people marching in the streets?" asked Rachel. "In our day they would have been marching in the streets!"

"Maybe not marching in the streets," said Morris, "but there would have been more of a fuss."

Polly shook her head. "It's almost as if people have given up the struggle for public health."

"Perhaps it's the kind of health that's offered up as 'public'," said Joseph. "Who, in their right mind, would have gone to Metropolitan by choice? Unless, of course, they were going to the People's Medical Clinic."

"That's no reason not to fight to keep it open, Joseph!" his mother admonished, shaking her finger at him.

"Who said it is? Did I say it shouldn't be kept open? I'm just saying that the health system is in shambles and you can't expect people to fight for shambles."

"Joseph's right," said Morris. "People have to know what they're fighting for if you want victories."

"I'm saying more than that," said Joseph, not at all pleased to be defended by the elderly man: "I'm saying that the whole idea of hospitals as the basis of a health system needs to be re-examined."

"He's always hated doctors, ever since he was a boy," Rachel explained.

"That's got nothing to do with it!" Joseph said angrily.

"Where would you go to have your appendix taken out, Joseph?" asked Polly. "Max's garage?"

"Don't you people see?" said Joseph, suddenly feeling himself under attack from all sides, "Institutional care is a function of economic and social systems. The American economy is based on profit and loss; the government tries to run institutions like businesses. But people's bodies aren't machines, as much as the technocrats would like to convince us they are."

"Nobody at this table is going to disagree with that, Joseph," said Polly. "But I'm still glad I'm having my baby at a hospital and not at home."

"You're missing the point!" said Joseph, digging himself deeper and deeper into his hole. "I'm saying the models for health care can't be based on factories. You can't allow medicine to become controlled by the laws of capital, where expenditure becomes a function of gross returns, or we'll end up a nation of diseased people and healthy CAT scanners!"

"What's a CAT scanner?" asked Rachel.

"It's probably something that scans cats," said Polly.

Joseph got up from his seat. "Excuse me," he said. "I think I'm going downstairs to throw up!"

They watched him stomp out in silence. Finally Morris looked at the women and said, "You know what? I like that boy!"

"You'll never change!" said Polly as she struggled into her nightgown.

"You need to slit that thing down the middle if you want to fit into it anymore," he suggested.

"I mean, does it hurt you to be polite?"

"Pain is relative, Polly . . ."

"You mean for you pain is relatives," she said, letting herself fall into bed.

"That too."

"Turn out the light!"

"OK," he said, stretching out his hand and flicking the switch on the bedside lamp.

"He's nice, you know . . ."

"I told you before, Polly, nice doesn't describe anything. It's like saying something is interesting."

"He likes you."

"That's nice."

"Oh, Joseph!"

"Well, what does she have to bring him home with her for?

Why can't she just have her affairs in hotels or the back seat of cars like anyone else?"

"I just hope our child isn't a girl! You'll be interviewing the nurses at the hospital to make sure a boy isn't in the adjoining crib!"

"Child sex doesn't bother me, Polly. It's just I don't think it's decent for your mother to have an affair on top of your head."

"Affair? All she did was invite a friend over for dinner!"

"I didn't hear him leave, did you?"

"Who's listening? Besides, if she wants to screw around at seventy, more power to her I say!"

"Sure. Nooky from cradle to grave. You could run for congress on that platform, couldn't you?"

"What's really bothering you, Joseph? Why don't we get down to it, OK?"

"Nothing's bothering me that a knife at Lamont's throat couldn't cure!"

"So that's it! Lamont! What's he done now?"

"Oh, nothing. Just run one of those liberal, tear-jerking articles about the responsibilities of professionals to keep at their post no matter what the circumstances are. He blames the nurses for closing down Metropolitan!"

"Does he accuse them of purposely poisoning the food?"

"They've lowered their standards, so, in a roundabout way yes."

"Janet-the-Nurse must have loved that!"

"Didn't do much to endear me to her."

Joseph rubbed his eyes. He seemed to be drifting off into a world of his own. Then he looked at Polly. "He had a sister, you know."

"Who?" Polly said, confused.

"Malcolm. She disappeared."

"What are you talking about, Joseph?"

"Malcolm Greene's sister. Gerry told me she disappeared."

"You spoke to Gerry again today?"

53

"Yeah. She left for the Sierras. She's camping out under a redwood tree."

"She stayed just long enough to tell you that Malcolm Greene had a sister who disappeared?"

"I asked her if he had any relatives. She said he had only one—a sister. And that she had disappeared several weeks ago."

"This story gets weirder and weirder, Joseph. Why do you think Gerry cut out like that?"

"I wish I knew. Something's really troubling her."

"Well her life's work just went up in smoke. That would trouble me."

"If I had put my life into a project like that and it was shafted, I'd want to tell the world, wouldn't you?"

"Maybe she was in love with him, Joseph. Maybe Gerry lost more than her job."

"That may be, Polly. But she's running from something."

"What's she running from?"

"I don't know. But I'd sure like to find out."

"So who are you going to interview next?" she asked.

"I'm meeting Lim tomorrow morning. Then I think I'll try to get in touch with one of the doctors who used to work at the clinic."

"Well, good luck . . ."

"Thanks, Polly."

"Don't mention it. And Joseph . . ."

"Yeah?"

"Try not to be such an ass."

Chapter 4

It was different in the morning. Perhaps it was the light. Maybe
it was the emptiness: no cop across the street, no trucks. Just a
high metal fence that had been constructed overnight with a
jagged topping of barbed wire. To keep people out, he wondered to himself? Or to keep something in?

The Cherry Blossom was different as well. The place was full
of people: women, mainly, but a few men, too. Little groups
had collected in various corners, buzzing away like chatty
insects in a swarm.

His eyes darted around the room looking for a familiar face.
He found her at last, bursting through the kitchen doors like a
gust of wind, her arms heavily laden with stacks of leaflets.

He walked up to her. "Need a hand?" he asked.

She glanced at him as she swept by. "You want to help? Go
get a load of those pink jobbies in the back room and bring 'em
out here."

Obligingly, he followed her instructions. He found the pink
sheets easily enough. One could hardly miss them as they had
flooded the room like a blushing tidal wave. "Nurses Under
fire!" shouted the boldly printed headline. "Save our jobs!
Protect your health!"

He bumped into Janet coming in as he was going out.
"Arming the troops?" he asked.

"You see what those fuckers did last night?" she asked,
pointing in the direction of the barbed wire.

"Yeah—well at least they haven't brought in the moat and
crocodile crew as yet."

"What do they think? We're gonna storm the place?" she
asked ignoring his attempt at humor.

"Maybe it's not meant for you at all," Joseph suggested.

"You should have told me that ten years ago," she shot back,
completely misinterpreting his thought.

55

"Did you have a chance to talk with Lim?" he asked, transferring the leaflets from his arms to hers.

"Yeah. I said you were trying to set things straight. I told him you were OK. He's invited you up for tea."

"Thanks, Janet," he said, grabbing another armful of literature and walking back out with her.

"Sure, Radkin," she replied. "But do me a favour . . ."

"That's what I'm here for. What can I do?"

"Just don't prove me wrong!"

He rang the upstairs bell and waited. In a while the same tiny black-haired girl came down as before. She opened the door a crack and peeked out with her wide, innocent eyes.

"Hello, sweetheart," Joseph said. "Is your daddy home?"

She stared at him a minute and then closed the door. He heard the sound of her feet as she scurried up the stairs.

A moment later some other footsteps could be heard— heavier, this time. The door opened again. A middle-aged, round-faced man, appeared; his straight black hair was beginning to thin and his face was so shiny it could have been waxed.

"Mr Radkin?" he said, in a polite, almost ingratiating voice.

"Mr Lim?" Joseph said in turn.

There was a weariness on the face that gave Joseph to understand these were hard times for the wearer. "You are welcome to my home," he said, making a slight bow. "Please to follow me up the stairs."

At the top of the staircase was a dark landing from which a hallway led in either direction. To the left, an open door displayed a trace of light, a hint of steam; odors of cooking food wafted out. Lim turned right, leading him through to the front room where guests were entertained.

He pointed to a wooden couch. "Please," he said, "make youself comfortable, my friend."

"Thank you," said Joseph, sitting down and feeling the hardness stiffen his back.

Then, suddenly, Lim disappeared. Joseph looked around. The room was empty except for him. He shifted uneasily on the settee and glanced at the various furnishings. The room had a strange quality of being many things and yet, at the same time, very oriental. Some of the pieces, like a lacquered chest and an ornate vase, were obviously Chinese, though the couch he was sitting on was surely Salvation Army. But the mats on the floor, the preponderance of bamboo, and the delicate arrangement of the dried flowers, with their unique and purposeful placement, made it clear the origin of the hand at work.

Yet one wall was filled with children's art and the universal influence of Walt Disney. So, too, a battered television set gave some perspective to the cultural milieu.

Lim appeared again, out of the blue. He brought with him a tray loaded down with tea and little rice crackers of various shapes and sizes. He placed the tray on the mat and then proceeded to pour.

"You needn't have troubled," said Joseph, feeling embarrassed at having caused such a fuss.

Lim looked up at him curiously. "It is honor to serve a guest," he said. "Would you invite someone to your home and not offer tea?"

Joseph thought of Morris and then said, "Had you known Dr Greene for long?"

Lim took a sip of the fragrant jasmine and replied, "Dr Mac? Oh, I know him for long time." And a hint of sadness showed through his waxen face.

"What did you think of him?"

"He was a good man," said Lim. "I sorry he die."

"So you don't hold him responsible for closing you down?"

"No man is responsible for fate," said Lim.

That was a notion Joseph found hard to deal with. But he hadn't the time to suffer an existentialist debate right now. So instead of asking what fate had to do with betrayal of trust he said simply: "Could you tell me a little about what happened?"

"Dr Mac a good friend of mine. He and I spend many hours talking about Vietnam."

"He had been in Vietnam?"

57

Lim nodded. "He there during war. He work as doctor who look after whores."

"Excuse me?" Joseph thought that he perhaps had misheard.

"Most important job, Dr Mac tell me," Lim said with a smile. "If whores sick, army sick. If whores well, army well."

Joseph felt a trace of nausea. "Christ!" he thought to himself. "A fucking Green Beret!" But what he said was: "Did Dr Greene say anything else about his work there?"

"Dr Mac have many, many stories. But sometime he feel too unhappy to talk about them. He was man who like Vietnam but not like war."

"What did you talk about with him?"

"Food."

"Food?"

"Dr Mac a great eater. He love to watch me cook. He come in at lunch and stand by my wok sometime. I make him special dish and ask him to guess ingredients. He pretty good guesser. Not like Dr Hobb . . ." Lim made a face. "Dr Hobb ask me for catsup all the time."

"Catsup?"

"Catsup and chop suey and Lipton tea," said Lim with a look reserved for such heathens.

"Might as well send out for a pizza," Joseph muttered.

"That exactly what I tell him!" Lim nodded his head emphatically.

"So tell me about last week," said Joseph, trying to get back to business.

It was like asking someone to recreate the ancient past. "Last week," he said with a little smile, "I am refugee who make good. Last week I have restaurant and steady clientele. This week I have no restaurant and I am poor. Last week I on top of world. This week I on bottom . . ."

"Last week," said Joseph, "Dr Greene was alive. This week he's not. I'd like to find out why."

Lim refilled Joseph's cup with tea. "I like to find out why, too, my friend. When a good man die, many people want to find out why."

"Then tell me what happened last week," Joseph asked again.

"I see him several time last week," said Lim. "First happy, then sad."

"Happy? How so?"

Lim smiled. "He with woman. Very beautiful woman. I see his eyes. They all bright and shiny."

"Was it Gerry?" asked Joseph, to himself as well as to Lim.

"Miss Saunders? No. Someone else. Someone I not see before. But they talk very much and later, when I bring Imperial roll to Dr Mac, I slip note under lettuce."

"You put a note under the lettuce? What did it say?"

"It say 'I like this one, Dr Mac. You bring her back, OK?'"

Joseph laughed. "What did he say to that?"

"He not say much. She eat Imperial roll. Not him. She see note first." Lim made a sheepish grin. "My mistake."

"Did he ever talk to you about her, Mr Lim?"

"Things happen very fast after that, so he not say much. But one thing I tell you about her: she French."

"How do you know that?"

He smiled. "I come from Vietnam, Mr Radkin. I know French when I see."

"But he never came back with her after that?"

"He not come back to restaurant. He come see me at my home." Lim's expression suddenly changed. "Like you, Mr Radkin."

"To talk about the cake?"

Lim nodded. "At first I not know what he really want. He ask me what in the cake. I think he want recipe to make himself."

"What was in the cake?"

"Same thing as in all cake. Flour, water, eggs, butter. This one have some brandy. But it special cake, I tell him."

"What made it special?"

Lim's eyes lit up with pride. "Icing make it special. Icing made with special liqueur—Cointreu. And something else . . ."

"What?"

"Duck eggs. Fresh duck eggs."

"Duck eggs? Why duck eggs?"

"Duck eggs special. This special cake, so I use special eggs."

"You don't see many duck eggs around. Where'd you get them?" asked Joseph.

"That what Dr Mac ask me, too. He very concerned. He say people come down sick in hospital maybe from my cake. I get very upset. I say that all my ingredients fresh. No one ever get sick from my food."

"It does sound strange, Mr Lim. I never heard of anyone getting food poisoning from a cake. And like you said, it was fresh. I mean you baked it that very day, didn't you?"

"Everything but icing. Dr Mac tell me that duck eggs sometimes have disease from duck. You not smell it, but it there."

"So it was the icing he was suspicious of!"

"That why he say some people not come down with disease. He say that some people eat cake but not eat icing."

"Did he test the eggs for salmonella?"

"I not have any more eggs. So he can't test."

"So he never knew for sure?"

"He just suspect. Then he ask me where I get eggs so he can check the ducks."

"Where did you get the eggs?"

Lim was quiet for a moment as if this was a question he had pondered over before. Then he said, "I tell him that this difficult for me to say."

"Why would it be difficult? Certainly you don't forget where you buy something like duck eggs."

"It difficult because I not want to get my friends into trouble."

Joseph nodded. "I see. But if the ducks were diseased . . ."

"Yes. That what finally convince me. And Dr Mac say that no one get in trouble. He say he fix it himself." Mr Lim looked down at the floor. "That what he say to me, anyway."

"So you told him . . ."

Lim's eyes had a distant look. "It very strange. I have friend who also want to meet Dr Mac . . ."

"I'm sorry," said Joseph, "I don't understand."

"My friend name is Dr Minh. He a very educated man. He help in Vietnam refugee community with new people who just arrive. Sometime, he help write letter for people or fill out form. He very good man. One day he tell me he very worried about something. He tell me some people he work with start to disappear."

"Disappear? What did he mean?"

"I don't know. He work with tribespeople, mountain men. In Vietnam they called Moi—that mean 'savage'. Not many speak their language. But he say they disappear. Maybe die. Maybe run away. No one know."

"Didn't he go to the authorities?"

"He afraid to go to authorities because many refugee are on welfare. He can't say they disappear or money disappear too."

"So he wanted to meet Dr Greene? Why?"

"I tell Dr Minh that I have friend who run clinic and work with lots of refugee. He know if disease is killing people off."

"But what does this have to do with the cake, Mr Lim?"

Lim again had a strange look about him, as if he were marvelling at the irony or, perhaps, the hand of fate. "You see, Dr Minh is man who sell me duck eggs."

He stopped for coffee at a Mission café and then phoned the number information gave him for Philip Brewster. At first Brewster didn't seem as if he was nuts about meeting him, but when he found out Joseph was doing a story for the *Defender* he sounded eager to talk.

Brewster lived in the Marina district which was the other end of town. Joseph caught a bus that left him off at the yacht harbour. He stopped a while to sit on the green and watch the muscle men soak up the sun, wondering what they did for a living that allowed them to maintain such an expensive physique. Afterward, he strolled back to Chestnut Street, picked up some hot dogs at his favorite deli, and then continued on down the block till he came to an apartment building opposite the most exclusive porno movie house in town.

Joseph rang the bell. An intercom switched on and Brewster's metallic voice came through: "You the reporter who rang me a while ago?"

"Yeah. Radkin's the name."

"OK, I'll buzz you in. Number 10. Third floor."

Joseph climbed the three flights of stairs and then knocked at number 10. A man dressed in a jogging suit answered. He was tall and blond and looked like he'd be comfortable with a tennis racket in his hand.

"Come in, Radkin," he said, glancing at him somewhat askance, as if sensing all the smokes and junk food that gave Joseph his distinctive pallor. "What's your poison?" he asked walking over to the little mini-bar that was set up where the book shelves should have been.

"Not salmonella,"said Radkin.

Brewster looked at him for a minute and then laughed. It wasn't a very honest laugh, Joseph thought. In fact, it was like the canned stuff you sometimes heard on TV.

"OK, not salmonella. Whisky, beer, gin, wine, Bristol Cream, Perrier?"

"Beer's fine," said Joseph.

Brewster cracked open a German brew and handed it to Joseph along with a stein. He poured himself a large Scotch.

"You worked at the People's Medical Clinic how long?" asked Joseph.

"A couple of years," said Brewster, motioning for Joseph to take a seat on a plush, heavily upholstered chair.

Joseph did a quick scan of the room. It wasn't the Ritz but it was close. "Working with the poor must have its advantages," he said.

Brewster narrowed his eyes in a gesture of suspicion. "If I had to depend on that place for a wage, I'd be living in the Tenderloin," he said. "I've got a private income that pays the rent."

"I'm not here to check your taxes if that's what's worrying you," said Joseph. "I'm doing a story on Greene."

"Seems to me I recall your name, Radkin . . ." said Brewster, looking like he was squeezing his memory for a missing detail.

"I did a story on the clinic once," Joseph reminded him. "About a year ago."

Brewster snapped his fingers. "Sure. Now I remember." He smiled in a manner that Joseph thought was almost nasty. "Boy, did you have it all wrong!"

"What do you mean?" he asked, trying hard to figure out how a guy like Brewster could have possibly worked there in the first place.

"You made it sound like Malcolm was another Schweitzer returned from the grave."

"I wasn't writing about Alsatian organists," said Joseph, taking some offense at the remark. "But I do think it took a special kind of person to make a place like that work."

"Well that special person was Gerry Saunders," he said, taking a long drink. "Not Malcolm Greene."

Joseph rubbed his nose. "I'm not sure that's what Gerry Saunders would say."

"Maybe not," said Brewster with a note of annoyance. "It's true she really idolised Mac." Then, almost as an aside he added, "So did I . . . once."

"What made you change your mind?"

There was that grin again that made Joseph feel like someone had just dropped an ice-cube down his pants. "I got this thing against pushers . . ."

"Pushers?" Joseph shook his head. "If you're saying what I think, you might as well tell me that Santa Claus rapes little girls!"

Brewster shrugged. "That's your problem for believing in St Nick in the first place, Radkin. Mine, too."

Joseph held up his hand. "Wait a second, Dr Brewster, let's go back a few paces, OK? What happened to make you suspect Greene was a pusher?"

"A few weeks ago the cops were nosing around looking for evidence."

"What kind of nosing?"

"Inspecting our narcotics log. Checking medical records."

"What for?"

"Seems they had a notion there'd been some abuse."

"Listen, Dr Brewster. I've been around for a while. I know people who get involved with community work like Greene often come into conflict with the police."

Brewster stood up and walked over to the bar to refill his glass. "Maybe. But I got my own suspicions about Greene . . ."

"You want to spill it to me?" said Joseph.

"Depends on how you handle it," Brewster replied.

"What do you mean?" he asked, suddenly playing the innocent.

"Nothing attributed to me. Get it?"

"Why not? It's coming from you, isn't it?"

Brewster had a look of disgust on his face. "You reporters are nothing but a bunch of scum-bags as far as I'm concerned. You beg for a bite so you can write about some scandal and when someone finally throws you a piece of meat you got the nerve to balk at the conditions!"

"Look, the way I'm figuring it, if you want to tell me, you'll tell me. If you don't, you won't. I'm not begging for it, Brewster."

"I'll say it again: nothing attributed to me. OK?"

"I'll ask you again: why not?"

Brewster ground his teeth. "Because it's not considered professionally ethical to accuse a fellow doctor, no matter what he's done. Get it?"

"Yeah. I just wanted to hear you say it. That's all." Joseph smiled as charmingly as he knew how.

"You're a creep, Radkin. Did anyone ever tell you that before?"

Joseph nodded. "Many times, Brewster. Many times."

Brewster laughed. "All right. As long as we know where we stand."

"I think we know where we stand," said Joseph.

"So nothing's attributed to me, right?"

"What ever you say, boss."

"OK." Brewster locked his hands behind his neck and looked up at the ceiling. "It was about a week ago. There's this guy, Charlie, who's always coming into the clinic. I mean he comes maybe once, twice a month looking for Mac. Never has an appointment, just barges in. But Mac has a policy set up with reception that whenever Charlie comes, he's notified.

"Anyway, this time Charlie comes in bleeding like a turkey on Thanksgiving. I happen to be on call and I see the guy dripping juice all over the floor. So I shout out to Carmen to get him into my examining room and fast."

"Who's Carmen?"

"She's the receptionist . . ."

"OK," said Joseph, taking notes, "go on."

"Well, Charlie doesn't like it one bit. 'I wanna see Mac!' he shouts. I tell him Mac'll come after I bandage him up. He starts to holler. I try to calm him down. But he pulls out this blade— I mean a blade about two feet long—and he starts swinging it around . . ."

"Where was Malcolm at the time?"

"Upstairs in administration overseeing the empire. We have—we had—an intercom. We called up to Gerry, but it seems Mac was 'indisposed'. Anyway, we have a room at the end of the hall for situations like this. We call it the Crisis Chamber. The idea is to get the nut back there before he really flips out and starts slicing up our patients . . ."

"How'd you get him back there?"

"Carmen did. She had a bottle of Dos Equis beer she was saving for lunch. She held it out in front of him like a carrot and walked him over as easy as strolling a baby through the park. It's just that once he got there and Mac didn't show, he really got pissed and started throwing a tantrum.

"Eventually Mac comes, grabs the knife out of his hand and dresses Charlie down. 'I told you never to come in like this!' he shouts. Not a peep comes out of Charlie's mouth. Then Mac has me shove off. And that was that."

"So?"

"I was interested in what happened. So I inspected the patient report Mac wrote up later that afternoon. Mac had given him self-dosing syringes of morphine sulphate."

"To ease the pain?"

"Shit!" Brewster almost spat on the floor. "Those cuts were superficial. All he needed was some antiseptic and a bandage."

"You call that evidence for pushing? Brewster, you must really hate the guy!"

Brewster's face darkened. "Listen, Radkin. The man had let us down. The way I see it, I lost two good years of my life!"

"There's a couple of thousand people in this city who lost more than that," said Joseph, standing up to go.

"Hot dogs? This is a joke, right?" Polly looked at him and waited for the punch line.

"I'm sorry, Polly. But I just got in twenty minutes ago. I would have gone to the quiche shop but you said you hate quiche."

"But I hate hot dogs even more than quiche!" she said.

"Look, how about a quick spaghetti? It wouldn't take any longer than a half-hour."

"I'm hungry now, Joseph! I'm hungry! The baby's hungry! We're both hungry! And we both hate hot dogs!"

"I'm sorry, Polly. Really, honestly, I am. I just didn't have time . . ." he pleaded.

She pointed to her swelling. "And you think I do? I have to work all day carrying this thing around! You think I enjoy having a basketball for a tummy?"

"No, of course not. Believe me, Polly, if I could carry it around for you for a while, I would."

"Oh shut up!" she said.

He went over and put his arm around her. "Did you go to the doctor today?"

"Yeah."

66

"What did he say?"

"It could be a week. It could be three."

"Did you tell him that you're still working?"

She nodded.

"What did he say?"

"He wants me to quit."

Joseph sighed. "So everyone's in agreement, Polly. Everyone wants you to quit and stay home and rest and eat all you want and wait for Spinach to pop out."

"Everyone's in agreement except me, Joseph. Remember, I have a vote, too."

"But, Polly, it just doesn't make any sense!" he shouted, finally giving in to his frustration.

"Yes it does!" she hollered back. "It makes perfect sense! Someone in this house has to bring in an income!"

He closed his eyes. "So that's it . . ."

She realised she had gone too far. She took his hand. "No, Joseph, that's not it. I said that out of anger. I'm just not in control of my emotions any more." She shook her head. "I just don't know what's going on with me!"

"What's going on with you, Polly, is that you're about to have a baby. And you're so damned concerned about losing your fucking identity that you can't accept the fact that you're no longer in charge. There's a biological process that's taken over your bodily chemistry. You're just going to have to let go!"

"So what do you want me to do?"

"Quit your job!"

"I can't quit my job!" she yelled. "There are thousands of homeless people starving out on the streets! Some of them are having babies too!"

"God damn it to hell, Polly! They're going to starve with you or without you! Your personal suffering isn't going to feed anyone!"

She looked up at him, her eyes pleading for understanding. "Joseph, today I had to take care of a girl . . . she couldn't have been over fifteen. She's been living on the streets for over a year now. The other day she aborted at twenty-four weeks by sticking a clothes hanger up herself. She aborted all alone, in a trash can, in a dark alley. Alone, Joseph. She did it alone by sticking a fucking clothes hanger up her vagina! And today she took me to see the mess!" Polly's face reddened and then, like a crumbling wall giving way to a relentless tide, she dissolved into tears.

He cradled her head. "Polly, Polly, Polly . . . I'm so sorry . . ." Tears began to roll from his eyes, too.

Her words came out in gasps. "Have you ever seen a foetus at twenty-four weeks, Joseph? It's fully formed. It's a real person already. She showed it to me. It's tiny face contorted, covered in blood and slime, lying there in the trash with moldering, stinking, putrefying garbage left over from some middle-class plate!"

She looked up at him with swollen eyes. "Joseph, what kind of world do we live in that a fifteen-year-old girl would do such a thing?"

He shook his head. "I don't know, Polly. I don't know . . ."

Her eyes lowered to her belly. "I'm not sure I want it to come out, Joseph."

He kissed her on the lips. "Yes you do, Polly. You do. You've got too much faith in the future not to want it to come out."

He held her in his arms, rocking her gently back and forth as she cried, softly, and the tears rolled down her face on to his clothes making them damp.

And over and over again he kept repeating, 'Polly, I'm sorry. I'm so sorry . . .'

It was later that evening at the South China Café on the other side of Noe Hill in the Castro that he told her about his day.

"Lim?" she said, picking through the noodles of her chow mein to get to the beef. "That doesn't sound like a Vietnamese name."

"It's not," said Joseph, "It's Chinese." He tasted the chicken in black bean sauce and nodded his head with satisfaction.

"Hoa, I guess," said Polly.

"What?"

"Hoa. They're the Chinese minority in Vietnam. Part of the Chinese diaspora from ancient times. What's remarkable is that they were never assimilated into Vietnam."

"What's more remarkable is that the Viets were never assimilated into China. I mean, wasn't it just a province at one time?"

Polly took a bite of the shrimp in lobster sauce. "Yes. I don't know why some people like the Vietnamese were able to keep their national identity while other cultures were swallowed up." She motioned to Joseph with her chopsticks. "This is good, try some."

He poked at his bok choy. "We knew so little about it . . ."

"What?" she asked, pouring some more tea.

"Vietnam." He looked at her. "It dominated our lives for so long and yet we knew so little about it."

"Our generation was wrapped up in the present, not the past," she said. "You didn't need to know about the origins of Annam to understand that napalming a tiny village in the Central Highlands was wrong."

"Yeah . . . well that's what we said back then, anyway."

"History is a bottomless pit, Joseph. The more you think you know, the less you understand."

He smiled. "Spoken like a true historian."

She frowned. "Sociologist, Joseph. Please!"

"Spoken like a true sociologist with a minor in linguistics."

"Which brings us back to Lim," she said. "I still don't understand about the ducks."

"Well, Malcolm worked as a preventive medicine officer in Vietnam during the war. It's very possible he had an experience there with a salmonella outbreak caused by tainted duck eggs. I did some research and found that ducks tend to be carriers of salmonella and the bacteria is often transferred to their eggs. The back streets of Saigon, with all its raw sewage problems, must have been a real breeding ground. So it stands to reason that Malcolm would have been sensitive to the possibility."

"And Lim had used raw duck eggs to make the icing . . ."

"Right. And since Malcolm had suspected the cake anyway, he must have felt he was hot on the trail."

"But the trail led Malcolm to a man who wanted to meet him as well. That's very strange, don't you think?"

"Not too strange. Probably Lim doesn't have many friends in San Francisco. As one of the ethnic Chinese from Vietnam he wouldn't fit easily into either world. Dr Minh was his main contact with the refugee community. It's not too incredible that he would provide him with both speciality food and gossip. But what is weird is that bit about the refugees who disappeared— the mountain tribespeople. What do you know about that, Polly?"

"You used to see them all the time down in the Tenderloin scavenging for food," she said, looking down at the remnants of fried rice on her plate. "Mainly women in native dress, with huge wooden plugs fitted into their earlobes. The Montagnards were different to the others. They were forest people lost in a concrete jungle."

"Every once in a while I'd see them going through the rubbish bin in the park next door to our house. Not so often anymore. I still don't understand how they ended up here," said Joseph.

"After the war there was so much chaos the government started dropping refugees anyplace that would take them. Fishermen in Las Vegas. Clerks from Saigon in some Iowa farmtown. Dance-hall girls in a Southern Baptist community. There wasn't any logic. They just dropped them where they could, that's all."

"But what do you know about an illness or plague?"

She shrugged as she finished off the rice. "There's always talk about disease being spread by refugees. There probably was talk like that back when your grandparents were living in the tenements of New York."

"So what do you think Lim's friend meant when he talked about people disappearing?"

"Maybe just that. Maybe they left for parts unknown. They

were like ghosts here, anyway, Joseph. They weren't city dwellers. Nobody was going to train them for a job. Maybe they went up to the Sierras like your friend, Gerry. Did you ask Lim if you could meet his friend?"

"Yeah. He said he'd think about it. He's not too keen . . ."

"I suppose not," Polly agreed, "judging from what happened to him last time."

"But the trail led Malcolm somewhere."

"Somewhere beyond ducks, you mean."

"Right. Then there's this drugs thing that Brewster tried to lay on me."

Polly shook her head. "That's ridiculous. People like Malcolm aren't pushers."

"But this guy, Charlie, who used to come to visit him—Brewster claims there was a special relationship. And Malcolm did give him some morphine."

"That's what Brewster claims at any rate."

"You don't believe him?" asked Joseph.

Polly blinked her eyes. "I didn't speak with him, Joseph. You did. Did you believe him?"

"Why would he lie about something like that? What would he have to gain?"

"When you lose a hero sometimes you have to destroy him in your mind," she said.

They walked down 24th Street as Polly consumed a double scoop of Jamocca almond fudge. It was a shirt-sleeve evening with just a hint of breeze. People strolling down the boulevard would have tipped their hats if hats had been in style that year.

"Then there's the mystery woman," said Joseph as they stopped to look into the window of a magic shop.

"Excuse me, have I missed something?" asked Polly.

"Didn't I tell you about the Frenchie that Lim said Malcolm was making eyes with at lunch?"

"This is beginning to sound more and more like a dime-store novel," said Polly.

"OK," he said, shrugging his shoulders. "If you don't want to hear . . ."

She poked a finger in his side and said, "Come on! You know I love dime-store novels!"

Joseph grinned. "You're such an easy listener!"

"That's why you live with me, I suppose." She made a face.

"That and your fried potatoes. You make the best fried potatoes in the world!"

"I'm glad I'm appreciated," she said.

"Lim said he was having lunch with this fancy French lady right before the duck egg thing. He said he'd never seen her before or since. But, to hear Lim talk, they were more interested in other things than food."

"Well that tells me something," said Polly.

"What?"

"She wasn't pregnant or she'd have been more interested in food than other things. How did Lim know she was French?"

"He has a feel for it, he says. Can tell a Frenchie from thirty paces. On the other hand, maybe it came up in the conversation."

"Do you think it's significant?"

"Look in any basic investigative journalism book."

"I know," said Polly in the tone of someone who's heard a joke for the fiftieth time. "*Cherchez* etcetera . . ."

"Right!"

"So what are you going to do? Phone the French consulate? 'Hello, I'm looking for one of your *femmes fatales* who might have been in the vicinity of blah, blah, blah.'"

"Something like that. Yeah."

They started walking back home. He held her hand and recalled how nice it was when they were younger and used to make these promenades a daily event.

"So you'll quit your job?" he asked her.

"I already have."

"You did? Really?"

"Yes. I was angry at myself. I was angry at you. I was terrified at what happened to that girl. I told them I was

72

leaving, but I couldn't tell you. Not just then."

"I wish you'd trust me more," he said.

There was a touch of wistfulness in her voice as she said, "Maybe I will some day."

Chapter 5

"I thought you were going to sleep in today," he said, surprised to see her up. "What are you doing?"

She had a turban wrapped around her head and was wearing a long colorful smock. Her hand, which held a cloth that once may have been a T-shirt, moved deftly over the wooden furniture. She was humming an unfamiliar tune.

She smiled calmly. "I'm cleaning up," she said.

"I can see that, Polly. I thought you were supposed to be resting up."

"At the moment, I find it restful to clean." She began to hum once more.

He wasn't going to say anything, but he had never known her to find it restful to clean before. In fact, cleaning was a chore that she had put on her list someplace after building nuclear fallout shelters. Before, when cleaning had taken place, it was a somber game of drawing lots—whoever got the shortest straw started with the toilet.

"You want some coffee?" he asked going into the kitchen and putting the kettle on.

"Do we have any herbal tea?" she replied from the other room.

"Herbal tea? Did you say herbal tea? The last time you had herbal tea you used it to rub over a rash of poison ivy. You don't have poison ivy, do you?"

"No, I don't have poison ivy. I just wanted a relaxing drink."

He shrugged to himself and brought down a box of camomile, sniffed it and made a face.

"You sure you don't want a drop of whisky in it? Something to mask the taste?" he hollered.

She had started the vacuum cleaner. "What, Joseph? I can't hear you!"

"Forget it," he said, pouring the water and mixing in the

74

weed. He brought the concoction over to where she was vacuuming and stood for a minute while she swept around him.

Finally she turned off the machine and relieved him of the cup. "There," she said with a satisfied smile, pointing to her handiwork. "Doesn't that look better?"

"It doesn't look worse," he said.

"I'm going to start on the bedroom next," she said, taking a sip from the cup. "I was thinking of partitioning off a little space for the bassinet."

"Bassinet? I thought we were going to have it sleep in a dresser drawer?"

"What would you think of some polka-dot curtains? I was thinking of putting a little more color into the room."

"Polka-dot curtains?"

"You don't like polka dots? Well, how about just a bright design?"

He sighed. "I thought we agreed that Spinach was just along for the ride. It wasn't supposed to change things."

"I've always wanted to brighten the room up," she said. "It's not only for Spinach. The place is so drab, don't you think?"

He looked around at the ancient posters and the peeling walls. "I think it has atmosphere."

"Is that what you call it? Well, help me open up the windows. I want to air the place out."

He made her breakfast. Pancakes, again. And, sitting at the table, he was startled to see her looking like the dream of a typical American housewife: barefoot, pregnant, and glowing with some ill-defined sense of satisfaction.

"You don't have a pot to piss in yet, you know that don't you, Joseph?"

The dream evaporated in a gust through the open windows. "What do you mean?"

"Well, how long have you been working on this story?"

"A couple of days."

"And what have you found out?"

"That there's a story . . . someplace."

She poured some more syrup over the last three pancakes in her plate. "The way I understand it, you were supposed to find out what happened that night when Malcolm Greene and Dr Krohl were blown to pieces in a hospital lab."

"Yeah. So?"

"So you've succeeded in muddying the waters by creating more footprints than a centipede has toes."

"Centipedes don't have toes."

"You know what I mean."

"I will if you say what you mean."

She put down her fork and started ticking off the items on her fingers. "You've got two missing women—Malcolm's sister and his French croissant. You've got a knife-wielding, morphine-shooting weirdo. You've got a trail of duck eggs that lead from a plague of hospital salmonella to a Vietnamese scribe. You've got a tribe of Montagnards who've mysteriously disappeared. You've got a hospital ringed with barbed wire and closed to the public. But you have no more of a clue as to what went on in that lab than you did before you started this investigation."

"But I got the makings of a hell of a story if I can ever put the pieces all together," he said.

"Maybe so, but you've also got a time factor to contend with," she said pointing down below.

He grimaced. "What are you suggesting, then?"

"A deal." She was wearing the kind of smile he had seen on her before. His grimace became a cringe.

"What kind of a deal?"

"The way I see it, you need some help."

He narrowed his eyes. "What are you suggesting, Polly?"

"A temporary partnership. I'll help you research the story."

"But Polly," he said with some surprise, "what about the polka-dot curtains and the bassinet."

"I can do the curtains while I'm on the phone. The bassinet I can buy. Besides, this nesting thing was just a hot flash."

"I thought as much."

"There are conditions, though . . ."

76

"Conditions?"

"Yeah. I want to be included in the by-line."

"Polly . . ."

"Take it or leave it!"

"Well, who's going to do the cooking?"

She grinned slyly and said, "How about your mother?"

His study became the operations room for what was to be known by them as "The Big Story". Joseph had suggested "The Fat Tale", but Polly objected for obvious reasons.

Polly got a huge piece of butcher paper and tacked it on the wall.

"Don't take down my *Guernica*!" Joseph pleaded.

"Picasso wouldn't mind," said Polly. "Besides it's the only place it'll fit."

She took a felt-tipped pen and divided the paper in half. One side, she headed in bold caps: MALCOLM GREENE— HEAD OF PEOPLE'S MEDICAL CLINIC. The other side she headed: DR KROHL—GENETIC ENGINEER.

"Now," she said, drawing some vertical lines down from "Malcolm Greene" and turning to Joseph, "let's add in the cast."

"Well, first there's Gerry Saunders . . ."

"OK," said Polly, writing in the name. "What do we know about her?"

Joseph rattled off what he knew. "Co-founder of People's Medical Clinic. Dedicated to community health care. Going through a period of mourning and introspection because of death of clinic and friend."

"All right," said Polly, trying to abbreviate his remarks. "What kind of information did we get from her?"

"First, that Malcolm had made a deal with the hospital chief, Elias Hobbs, for another year's funding if he traced down the cause of the salmonella attack."

"OK. Let's put down 'Deal with Hobbs'," said Polly, her pen writing at lightning speed.

77

"Second, that the clinic actually was closed prior to the explosion. We didn't know that before."

'Right: 'Death of Clinic'."

"Third, that Malcolm was dead before he was blown-up. Or so she claims."

Polly stopped, her pen poised in mid-air. "How should I put that?"

"Say, 'Questioned state of Malcolm's mental health'."

"All right," she said, turning up her nose. "That'll do until something better comes along."

"Fourth, she brought up the sister, Robin, and said she had been missing."

"Fine: 'Robin—Missing sister'. Anything else?"

"Presently unavailable as she is living under redwood tree in Sierra mountains."

"Right: 'Living under tree'. OK, who's next?"

"Janet-the-Nurse, I guess."

"What do we know about her?"

"That she doesn't know beans about PR."

"Not relevant," said Polly, waiting impatiently with her pen. "Assisted Malcolm in salmonella investigation and introduced me to Mr Lim."

"All right. Let's make a line for Lim. He's the owner of the Cherry Blossom Restaurant, the maker of the poisoned cake and the friend of Dr Minh. He's the one who's worried about the Montagnards, right?"

"Right. He wanted Lim to ask Malcolm whether there was a plague. And he's the link to the salmonella ducks. By the way, before we forget Lim, he's the one who mentioned the French Croissant."

"OK. Let's have a line for the French Croissant," she said, marking it with a flourish. "Now then, who's next?"

"Philip Brewster, I guess. He was a doctor at the clinic—his brief fling with serving humanity, I suppose. Accused Malcolm of being a pusher. Told me the story about Charlie-the-Weirdo."

"A line for Charlie-the-Weirdo?" asked Polly.

78

"Might as well," said Joseph.

"That all?"

"I guess . . ."

Polly stepped back and inspected the sheet of butcher paper. "What do we have?"

"A mess," said Joseph.

She shook her head. "That's not good enough, Joseph."

Giving her a look of warning, he said, "Investigation is more than making charts on walls, Polly. It's an art. It works more on following hunches than listing facts."

"Maybe, but what do you see when you look at the chart?" she asked, pointing at the wall.

"A bunch of names and crisscrossing lines."

"You want to know what I see?"

"If you insist."

"I see half a sheet full and half a sheet empty."

"What do you mean?"

"Everything's under Greene. Nothing's under Krohl."

"Polly, I haven't had time . . ." he began.

She winked. "That's why I joined this expedition, pal."

It was later that day when he finally reached Lim.

"Have you thought it over?" he asked.

"I have thought it over," said Lim. "Meet me in half-hour where they sell day-old bread, OK?"

"Day-old bread?"

"Yes. On 17th and Folsom. You know where is?"

"I know it, Lim."

The Day Olde Bakery was packed from dawn to dusk. It used to be for down-and-outs or those whose welfare check made crusty rolls a luxury. Nowadays it served the growing army of the unemployed and others whose weekly budgets had been squeezed. An engineer who couldn't find a job felt as hungry as any drifter on the road. He may have eaten cake the year before; now he lined up with the rest for day-old bread.

He spotted Lim when he arrived carrying an armful of loaves and muffins to his car.

"Very cheap here," he said as Joseph greeted him. "You try the sourdough muffins. Very, very good . . ." He threw the stuff into the back seat of his ancient Ford coupé, and then turning to Joseph he said, "Hop in. It not far, but they go bananas if you keep car here when you not shop . . ."

"Go bananas?" Joseph thought what a strange expression that was for Lim to use. He wondered how much English Lim had learned from his TV.

They headed toward Harrison, down the smelly, oil-stained street that led through what was left of the industrial section of town.

"Have you known this fellow, Minh, for long?" asked Joseph as Lim drove his Ford over gaping chuckholes that trounced what was left of his suspension.

"I meet him when I first arrive. I not know English much then. He very kind to me. I see him sometime for beer. We talk about old days."

"Does he know we're coming?"

Lim shook his head. "He have no telephone. He very poor."

With a wheeze and a final blast from the red-hot tail pipe, Lim parked his battered Ford on the remains of what once was a garment factory.

It was a run-down district. Sometime before there had been light industry here: besides clothing, there had been tool and die plants, a tannery, and even a small metal works making pig iron for a nearby manufacturer. Now the industry had moved on, searching for new pools of cheap labor. Those buildings that still stood were just relics of the past, their iron frames, steel girders, like meatless bone, showing through the torn façades. Others were just rubble: here and there a crater—not from bomos, but peaceful dynamite.

The buildings that still stood between the lots of broken stone and twisted metal rod, were caked with soot from dirty air. Rats hid among the cinders and disused brick, waiting for a chance to leap out on unsuspecting prey. Their droppings festered in the stagnant pools that filled with sewage when it

rained. Little patches of poisoned soil grew only toxic weeds.
That is to say, it wasn't very pretty here. Perhaps it never was.

"People still live here?" asked Joseph, more to himself than
Lim.

"Redevelopment agency tell them all to go," said Lim. "But
they no tell them where."

"Sounds pretty familiar," said Joseph in response.

Lim took him to a narrow house. Joseph followed him up the
wooden stairs and stood back a step as Lim knocked against
the plywood which boarded up the hole where the glass should
have been in the front door.

They waited a while and when no one came Joseph said,
"Perhaps he's not at home."

"We wait a little more," said Lim. "He live upstairs. Sometime he very slow."

A short time later, Joseph saw the front-window curtain shift
a bit and two eyes stare out at them.

"Someone's there . . ." he began. But before he could
complete his thought, the door opened up and a young man
appeared.

The young man—he couldn't have been over eighteen
years—started to speak to Lim in Vietnamese. He looked
concerned and every so often would glance suspiciously at
Joseph.

Finally, after what seemed to Joseph as a great deal of
chatter, Lim turned to him and said, "This is Minh's son. He
say his father not come home last night or night before. He
very worried."

"Does he know where his father went?" asked Joseph.

Lim turned back to the young man and spoke to him again.
Then, looking at Joseph, he said, "He not know for certain.
He think father visit buffalo."

"The city of Buffalo?" Joseph asked.

The chattering began again. And once more Lim turned to
Joseph and said, "He not know. He just hear father say he visit
buffalo."

81

"Did he take a suitcase? Ask him if his father took a suitcase."

"No," said Lim. "He not take suitcase."

"I suppose he went to the zoo," said Joseph.

Lim asked the young man a question in Vietnamese and the reply was, again, garrulous.

"Is zoo open at night?" asked Lim, looking at Joseph.

"Not that I know," said Joseph. "Maybe." And then, motioning toward the young man, he asked, "What did he say?"

"He say he . . . nervous."

"It took him that many words to say he was nervous?"

"It very complicated to say you nervous in Vietnamese."

They were in the operations room. Polly was standing, pen in hand, in front of their "Big Story" chart.

"Did you ask him about Malcolm's meeting with Dr Minh? He was there, wasn't he?"

"I asked him about that while he was driving me back to the Mission in that clunker of his. He said that Dr Minh had invited them in for a drink."

"What kind of a doctor is he, Joseph? Did Lim say?"

"He's not a doctor doctor, if that's what you mean. Lim uses the word as a term of respect. He said Minh is a very educated man. I asked him to describe the room they met in. He said it was bare of furniture except for some wooden chairs, an old desk, a bookcase, grass mat on the floor. The bookcase, he says, was stacked with books and the desk piled high with papers. He also said there were some old photos on the wall of his family in Vietnam."

"Is his family still there?" asked Polly.

"Lim said his wife is dead. Some of his children remained. Of course, I met his son."

"Did Lim give you the gist of the conversation between Malcolm and Dr Minh?"

"He said Minh fed them a drink—sort of rice liquor—and they toasted their new friendship."

"Some joke," said Polly with a sour look.

82

"Anyway, Malcolm asked Minh about the duck eggs. Minh said he didn't keep ducks himself, but only distributed the eggs as a favor to his friends."

"His friends?"

"Yes—the Montagnards. You see, they were the source of the duck eggs."

"And the Montagnards—they're the ones Minh had said were disappearing! Right?"

"Right. According to Lim, Malcolm pressed him on this. He wanted to know what evidence Minh had—whether he had personally witnessed anyone die."

"And?"

"Minh said that it was very difficult to understand. In their language 'to leave' and 'to die' are often the same word."

Polly nodded her head. "Like many tribal societies. Death to them has a different meaning than it does to us."

"How so?" asked Joseph.

"It has to do with a spirit that departs, not the body itself. So if the spirit leaves, the body can remain and continue with its functions, but to the tribe, in their view, the person has departed. Likewise, the body could leave and the spirit could remain."

"Lim said that Minh was fascinated by these people. He said that they were very mysterious. 'Men of the forest' he called them. 'They remember things that perhaps we have forgotten about,' he said."

"I seem to recall reading about them in a social anthropology class, Joseph. The French sent teams of anthropologists to study them during the forties. They saw them as some of the last examples of fairly untainted tribal societies—though by the forties some cultural mix had already set in. But they were certainly one of the last groups of hunters and gatherers to survive the modern age."

"Do you remember anything else about them, Polly?" Joseph furrowed his brow as if he were working something over in his mind.

"I have a book somewhere. I'll search for it. It was a

83

wonderful book by one of the French anthropologists who lived with these people for several years . . ." Suddenly her expression changed.

"You remembered something?" he asked her.

"Yeah. I remember reading that during the war the CIA made an unauthorised translation of his book and passed it out to their men in the field. Later, when the French publishers found out, it caused quite a stir."

Joseph scratched his head. "Polly, weren't the Montagnards used by the CIA to fight against the National Liberation Front?"

"'Used' is the proper word, I think. The Montagnards were truly in the middle. In fact, their way of life was being destroyed. They were victims of the geopolitical struggle that was going on around them. But they were certainly armed and trained by the CIA as a means of disrupting North Vietnamese supply lines. And that's probably why some of their tribes were brought here after the war."

"And dumped," said Joseph.

"But the real damage done to those people wasn't from the shooting or the bloody struggle for territory."

"No? What was it then? Not being able to receive *Dallas* on their TVs?"

She ignored his sick attempt at humor. "It was the spraying of their forests, Joseph. It was the unrelenting, horrible, inexcusable spraying of their land with Agent Orange."

"Let's make a line for the duck trail, Polly," Joseph suggested. "From Lim to Minh to the Montagnards. Call it 'The Vietnam Connection'."

She drew the line and then stood back and observed. "Their life is one big tainted egg," she said, with a certain commiseration in her voice.

"The Montagnards?"

"Yes. All the people who suffered through that awful war."

"At least your egg isn't tainted, Polly," he said, looking at her kindly.

84

She stared back at him and suddenly he sensed her fear. "We don't know that for sure yet. Do we?" she said in a soft voice.

"Come on, Polly, I thought we weren't going to let those ideas eat at us. All prospective parents are worried, you know that. But most serious deformities work themselves out as spontaneous abortions. You're healthy. And Spinach has a kick and a half."

"I'm also thirty-eight years old," said Polly.

"And I'm over forty. But spiritually we're both still twenty-five, so don't let it worry you. OK?"

She smiled. "OK."

"So what did you find out about Krohl?"

"I've got a few calls out to people I know from the university. Nobody's got back to me yet. But I did find his obit in the newspaper."

"Yeah," said Joseph. "I read it, too. Seems the guy was up for a Nobel prize, huh?"

"Right. Molecular biology is hot stuff now. And he was there from the beginning. Besides a prestigious university background, Henry Krohl was a recipient of a couple of plum grants. He must have been some mover!"

"A real high-flyer," Joseph agreed.

"But they were pretty vague about his current project. Construction of viral antigens could mean anything."

"So there's no clue to the relationship between him and Greene?"

"Not yet. But I'm workin' on it. What's next on your side of the sheet?"

Joseph looked up at the chart. "I'd like to keep on the duck trail. But frankly, I'm stymied."

"You think it's worth interviewing Minh's son again?"

He shook his head. "The kid was obviously afraid of something. But I'm not going to get anything out of him myself. And I can't see dragging Lim down there a second time."

"I know a couple of people who work with the Vietnamese community," said Polly. "They might be able to help us out."

"How?"

"Well, maybe they know Minh. Or maybe they might give us some information on the Montagnards."

"Good," he said. "Check it out."

"So what are you going to do?"

He pressed his lips together. "I think I'm going to concentrate on Malcolm Greene. I want to know a little more about his personal life—what he was up to right before he was creamed . . ."

She studied his face. "How are you going to do that, Joseph?"

He winked and said, "Ve haff vays off finding out zos tinks!"

"All right, Herr Goering," she said; "just don't put anybody on the rack."

"Speaking of racks, what's for dinner? I'm starving!" he said, licking his chops.

She smiled. "Ask your mom. We're going upstairs to eat, remember?" She got behind him and began to shove him out the door. "Come on. We have to get changed."

"Changed? To go upstairs?" He turned around to stare.

"Yes. She's having company."

She had gotten him as far as the bedroom door but no further.

"Who?"

"Morris." She went inside the bedroom and opened the wardrobe. She was inspecting the contents.

He looked at her aghast. "Again? What's he done? Moved in with her?"

She took out a maternity dress and then stared down at her belly. "I bought this twenty sizes too big, Joseph, and now I can hardly fit into it!"

"You're not listening to me!" he said. "I want to know why I have to have supper with them! I had supper with them once this week. Isn't that enough?"

"Do you think I should change into a sari, Joseph? I also have a Hawaian muu-muu or a Japanese kimono I could wear. What do you think?"

"I think we should go up stark naked with an arrow painted on the point of my thingamajig and a bull's eye on your tummy."

"That's a thought," she said. "I do have some polka-dot material left over from the curtains. Maybe I could just wrap it around me."

"Or how about dressing ourselves in diapers with a gigantic safety pin. You could have a little bow in your hair and I could do up mine in a rubber band . . ."

She looked at him sternly. "Hurry up, Joseph! You haven't even put on your socks!"

Chapter 6

He left early the next morning, before she was awake. He
wrote a note and put it under the coffee-pot. "Early interview,"
it said. "Back whenever."

There wasn't any interview, just a minor crisis of spirit and a
major one of intent. He had come to the point in his story
when he had to decide whether it was any use going on. It had
happened before, but never with such emotional incendiaries.
It meant that an important decision needed to be made. But,
at the moment, most important decisions seemed to be out of
his hands. He knew that in a few weeks, or even a few days,
his entire life would change and he would be a father. Whatever
else that implied, it marked a new beginning. It also meant an
end.

He stopped in at his neighborhood café and ordered a coffee
and a roll. Despite Polly's academic penchant for lists and
organisation, he knew that in his line of work it was instinct
that counted. It's what made him a good investigative journalist
and, despite his disgust with the trade, gave him the confidence
to continue when others would have tossed in the sweaty towel.

And he had a feeling about this story. He couldn't put his
finger on it yet. But he did have a feeling.

"Sometimes you gotta take a chance," he said to Marie, the
waitress.

"Don't I know it!" she said. "That's why I put my last ten
bucks on the lottery."

He drank his coffee and gave Marie a dollar bill. She brought
him back a quarter change. He flipped the coin.

"Heads I do it, tails I don't."

It came down tails.

"Fuck it!" he said. "I'll do it anyway!"

"That's the spirit, Joey boy!" said Marie encouragingly.

He tossed her the coin. "Buy yourself a piece of a lottery
ticket with this," he said. "It might be your lucky day!'

*

It was mid-morning by the time Joseph arrived at the narrow street perched atop Portrero Hill. The old wooden houses, once the refuge of the working classes looking to escape the stink of chemicals and putrid fish, rose from the cleansing fog of Mission Bay like cottages for a race of dwarfs.

The address he had copied from the phone book was on Perne. It wasn't hard to find. The place was a little larger than the rest, a gingerbread miniature of what San Franciscans liked to call "Victorian". A row of hedges on either side gave it a bit of privacy; in the back, the terraced garden plunged down a steep ravine, and then was lost forever in the mist.

He stood in front and tried to imagine living in these heights. It was quiet. There was a sense of seclusion up here amongst the clouds. And yet, the wisps of fog that swirled with the winds gave it an eerie feel.

The chill air made him shiver as he walked over to the porch and peered inside the front window. It was too dark inside to see. He pulled up the collar of his shirt and tried the door. It was locked.

Breaking and entry wasn't really something he felt comfortable with. It smacked of burglars or the CIA. But he knew he hadn't time to pussyfoot around. And with Malcolm dead and his sister disappeared, he felt the end (whatever that was going to be) would simply justify the means.

He walked around the side, searching for a ventilation pipe to show him where the bathroom would be. A junky he had once interviewed had told him bathroom windows were the best. "No one wants to gas themselves to death," he had said to Joseph, "so they leave it open just a bit thinking guys like me won't notice." He had smiled and patted the warty thing underneath his eyes. "I just follow my schnoz."

As it turned out, Joseph didn't need his expertise. A window at the side couldn't have been more inviting if it had a notice posted on it reading: "Wide open! Thieves and Investigative Reporters Welcome To Come In!" Joseph seized the opportunity, heaved himself up and, wriggling through the opening, climbed inside.

There was a mighty crash, like an explosion, which echoed throughout the silent house. For a moment, he supposed he was in the throws of a fatal heart attack. Gasping for breath and trying to slow the mad rhythms in his chest, it suddenly occurred to him that he had ended up on top of a desk which had been set flush against the wall. Looking down at the floor, he saw the remains of a picture frame that had been pushed off in his wake.

He sat there with the papers and the pens, next to an electric typewriter, wondering whether there was anyone around to hear. And then he thought, maybe sister Robin had come home. He pictured having to phone Polly from jail: "Hi, I won't be home for a while. I'm afraid you'll have to raise Spinach alone . . ." Boy! Would she be pissed!

But no one came, perhaps because no one was there. Or maybe they were cowering under the bed. In any case, he lowered himself down.

The glass from the picture frame was scattered all over the floor. He picked up what was left and inspected the photograph. It was a young woman, pretty, blonde, and blue-eyed—the All American girl next door, if you happened to live in a WASPish neighborhood, he thought.

He put the photo back and then he noticed that all the drawers of the desk had been opened and ransacked. At least it appeared that way. Someone hadn't taken the time to stuff the contents back inside.

"Well, well! I'm not the first!"

Even at this hour in the morning, the room was still quite dark. He went over to the doorway, found the light switch and turned it on.

"Too soon to have been disconnected by the electricity company. Doctors probably pay their bills in advance."

It was a comfortable room, though somewhat cold. An old couch took up one wall, the desk another, and a bookshelf a third. A group of posters, mounted under glass, provided the decorative theme of motion with its ships and boats and planes.

"This guy must have done a lot of travelling. Either for real or in his mind."

He sifted through the desk drawers and came up with ordinary odds and ends: stationery supplies, medical papers, some doctoring equipment.

"Nothing much of interest here. Or if there was, it's been taken."

There were some files, income tax, insurance, bills, things like that. Nothing really personal. Joseph flipped through them quickly and then went on to the bookshelves finding nothing more than texts and reference books—not much to keep you warm on a stormy night.

"God, what a bore! The most exciting thing this guy probably ever did was get blown up in a lab!"

He went out through the door into a darkened hall. He turned right and walked a few steps, emerging into the front room.

It was nicer here, he thought—warmer, somehow. Maybe that was because of the fireplace which projected a sense of cosiness even though the fragrant logs were stacked, unused, neatly to the side. There was an expensive stereo system that was built into a nook. Above it were shelves with records. Joseph looked through the titles: Mingus, Parker, Bix Beiderbecke. There was a coffee-table in the center of the room that had some art books—French impressionism seemed to be his style, since that's what was also on the walls. There were also books on tools and basic home-repair scattered around on the end tables. But nothing more.

"Didn't this guy read anything interesting?"

Then he noticed there wasn't any television in the room.

Shrugging his shoulders he went back into the hall and walked its length, heading toward the rear of the house. This way, the hall opened up into a large kitchen and dining area. To one side was a professionally laid out workspace built of butcher block. A large double sink filled with pots and pans and stinking, putrefying food.

He went over and sniffed. A cast-iron fry-pan was thick with a creamy goo that was beginning to mold. He made a face. "How disgusting! And him a doctor!"

Taking the pan out of the sink, he dumped the contents into the trash bin. Then he filled the sink with soapy suds and let it soak. "One thing's for sure, the guy didn't have a maid." He wiped his hands on a dish towel. Then he looked over at the dining table. "But he did have company."

He walked over to the place settings and looked them over. "It mustn't have tasted too bad, 'cause they really licked the platter clean." He noticed an ashtray which was next to one of the plates. He inspected the stubs. "And one of them was a woman by the looks of things. Or else Greene wore lipstick."

Something felt mushy under his feet. He looked down and saw that the floor was covered with a thick layer of spaghetti. In the mess, a bit of material caught his eye. He bent down and picked it up. It looked to be a piece of a dress. "Maybe they had a spaghetti fight. Who knows what people without television do for enjoyment."

And then he smiled and asked in a mannered voice. "You think it might be the French Croissant, Watson, old boy?"

"Perhaps it is, Holmes!"

A double glass door opened on to a verandah. A circular metal table was on the wooden deck. Two folding chairs faced out toward the bay. On the table were empty coffee cups and two glasses, still half full.

He made a huffy sound. "What do you think they were doing out here, Holmes? Staring out at the moon? Ha, ha!"

He stuck his finger into one and tasted. "It's obvious, my dear man. This drink is a sweetened brandy. Probably Drambuie, I'd wager. When do you drink Drambuie, Watson?"

"Never if I can help it. Can't stand the stuff, myself, Holmes."

"Yes, but try to picture the scene, Watson. It's a beautiful starlit night. You've just dumped spaghetti all over the floor and now you're sitting out here on the verandah. You've had your coffee and you're drinking some liqueur. You look over into her eyes and she smiles. What do you say?"

92

"Well, Holmes, I guess I say, 'How about another spaghetti fight?'"

"What if she doesn't want to have a spaghetti fight, Watson? What do you say then?"

"I ask her if she plays whist."

"No, Watson, you bloody fool! You ask her if she wants to roll in the hay! Why else would somebody leave a perfectly good glass of liqueur half full?"

"I don't know, Holmes? Why would they?"

"Because they were all sexed up and ready to go, you nitwit!"

He finished off one of the glasses of Drambuie (if that's indeed what it was) and walked back into the kitchen, then down the hall until he came to a door on the right-hand side. He opened it and walked in. It was an ordinary bedroom: a double bed with night-table on either side; a dresser with a few knick-knacks; and some free-standing bookshelves.

The bed was unmade, the covers rumpled. He sat down on the mattress edge and opened up a drawer of the night-table closest to the hall-side of the room. It was empty.

"Empty, Holmes. Can you deduce something from that?"

Joseph got up and walked around to the other side.

"It's elementary, my dear Watson. He slept on the far side of the bed." He opened the drawer on the other table and peered inside. "Aha!"

"You found something, Holmes?"

"Yes, Watson," he said pulling out a lacquered box. "Whoever went through this place didn't use a fine-toothed comb."

"Well come on Holmes, don't keep me in suspense! What's inside?"

Joseph opened the box.

"God Damn!" He emptied the contents on to the bed. There were nine disposable syringes. He picked one up and examined it. "Morphine sulphate! Well, I'll be a monkey's ass! The guy was a junky after all!"

He took the syringes and stuffed them into the pocket of his jacket.

He got up from the bed and walked over to the bookshelves. "Let's see what you read, Malcolm old boy, while you were going off into your dreams."

The books were stacked randomly, one on top of the other. There were histories of Asia and South America; some classic works of literature—the likes of Balzac, Proust, Turgenev, and Dostoevsky; and some travel books and adventure stories.

"Malcolm, Malcolm . . ." He whispered in quiet wonder walking out into the hallway again. "My image of you changes each time I go into a different room!"

There were two doors left to open on the other side of the hall. One led to the bathroom where Joseph stopped for a moment to relieve a swollen bladder and to check the cabinet for its contents—which from its array of colognes and hair oils led him to believe that Malcolm had a streak of vanity which he must have pampered now and then.

The other door led to the second bedroom. This room was truly different from the rest. It quite clearly belonged to a woman. The coloring—a sort of rosy pink—and the furniture were distinctly feminine: there was a dressing table with a triptych mirror, some assorted makeup, and a seat to use while a disguise was being forged. Also, there was a lavish wardrobe with a full-length mirror as one of its doors.

But on the other side of the room, in what he saw as a schizophrenic reaction to all the puff and powder, were rows of radical ecology and antimilitary posters tacked on to the wall. And the books, arranged neatly here in perfect rows, told another story yet again. There was Mao side by side with a book on Petra Kelly and the German Greens; an international symposium on nuclear wastes leaned up against Regis Debray's study of Che; The Swedish Tribunal on Vietnam came next, and then a book on the Paris Commune, and on and on and on.

There was also another photo on the shelves of the same woman whose picture Joseph had seen in the study. But she was no longer the blonde-haired, blue-eyed kid. This time she looked older, more mature. She was standing arm in arm with

94

another woman, some years older by her looks, before the entrance of a baroque stone building. There was a look about her that Joseph found appealing.

"Stranger and stranger."

He turned and looked down at the bed. "Seems like this is where all the action took place."

He picked up a silken dress that lay amongst the rumpled mess. He noticed it was ripped almost in half.

"Looks as if someone couldn't wait, Watson, my man."

"Or maybe something else."

He searched around for signs of struggle or injury.

The battle or frantic love-making (whatever the case may have been) was confined to the bed, however. Everything else seemed to be neatly in place.

"Check the drawers, Watson!"

"Right you are, Holmes!"

"Find anything?"

"Only this book: *The Men Who Built The Bomb*. Do you think it might be a clue?"

"Everything is a clue, Watson. Haven't I taught you anything yet?"

He opened the cover. There was a dedication dated two years before which read, "Stockholm, Sweden. To Robin, in comradeship and trust. From Nadine Poiret." Further on he came to the table of contents. One chapter was circled in red. He turned to that section and, pulling out a pillow from the pile at his side, he lay down on the bed to read.

Suddenly, as he was turning through the pages, he heard the doorbell ring. The sound shot through him like a high-voltage jolt, freezing him in position.

He pictured a heavy rock soaring through the silence toward a plate-glass window. His muscles tensed as he waited for the crash.

"Do cops ring doorbells, Holmes?" he whispered.

"Not unless they're collecting for a benevolent fund, Watson."

"Maybe they'll go away, then, Holmes."

He walked quietly to the bedroom door and opened it. But as he did he heard the sound of a latchkey and then the opening of the door.

"God damn it, Holmes! Look at the mess you've gotten me into!"

"Don't panic, Watson!"

He heard footsteps growing louder as they neared the room.

"Don't panic, you say! What now?"

"Quick Watson, under the bed?"

He tried to squeeze himself under, but he couldn't fit. The footsteps stopped outside the door to the bedroom. Joseph leapt up and lightly danced over to the wardrobe, concealing himself inside just as the door to the room opened.

He held his crotch. "Holy Shit, Holmes! I'm gonna piss in my pants!"

"Hold on, Watson! I gotta piss, too!"

The footsteps moved heavily around the room.

"It's not a woman, Holmes."

"It could be a fat woman, Watson."

"It could be a fat anything, Holmes."

"Maybe it's Polly, Watson."

"It couldn't be Polly, Holmes. She doesn't know I'm here. If she knew I was here, she'd kill us!"

"Then I hope it's not Polly, Watson."

"Well then, who do you hope it is, Holmes? A burglar?"

"If it's a burglar, Watson, he'll look in here for certain!"

"Why's that, Holmes?"

"Because, you cretin, this is where she'd keep her minks!"

"You know what Holmes? I never really liked you much. In fact, I think you're an arrogant son of a bitch!"

"Watson—I always thought you were a nincompoop."

The footsteps stopped in front of the wardrobe.

"Well, Holmes, you smart ass! You better think of something pretty quick!"

"Don't worry, Watson," he said to himself with the bravado of a soldier about to be blindfolded and tied to a stake. "Have I ever let you down?"

The wardrobe door opened. A tall man in a pin-striped suit towered before him.

"Hello," said Joseph as loud as he could manage, stretching his mouth into a wild, contorted grin. He stuck out his hand. "Glad you could come!"

The man's face drained of blood, like a sink whose plug was pulled. The pupils of his eyes seemed to disappear into his head just before his body collapsed like a leaky bagpipe and crumpled to the ground.

Polly was sitting on the couch, watching him drink his third whisky. "I still can't believe you did such a dumb thing!"

"I can't believe I did such a dumb thing either, Polly." He gazed at her with a helpless expression. She was always a sucker for his little-boy looks.

"But you must have known you were taking a pretty big chance! I mean you could have been thrown in jail!"

He stared down at the floor, repentantly. "I know." He looked back up at her, wide-eyed. "Can you ever forgive me?"

She shook her head in frustration. "Oh, Joseph!"

He smiled meekly. "But you have to admit, I did get some good information."

"At the risk of your life, yes."

He shrugged. "What's my life compared to 'The Big Story'?"

She looked at him angrily. "I told you before, I'm not going to raise Spinach alone!"

"You could always put it up for adoption."

"We have our agreement, Joseph. I expect you to stick by it. I haven't gone through eight and three-quarters months of this to give it away!"

He finished his whisky and held out his glass. "Pour me another, would you?"

She took his glass again and refilled it. "Well, at least your hand isn't trembling anymore," she said, giving it back to him.

"Another couple of drinks and maybe I'll be able to say the same thing for my insides. You know, they say that when you're really, truly scared, your ass starts to pucker . . "

97

She made a face. "Who says that?"

"I read it somewhere. But it's true, Polly. I can tell you from experience, it's true!"

She rolled her eyes and sat down in the chair across from him. "OK, so go on with your story. What happened after he revived?"

"Well, I had managed to get him up on to the bed and loosen his tie when suddenly he opened his eyes. Then he pops up like a jack-in-the-box and shouts: 'Who the hell are you?'"

"What did you say?" Polly stared at him in amazement.

Joseph shrugged. "When confronted with a question you can't answer, just ask it back. I learned that from a politician. So I shouted: 'Who the hell are you?'"

She laughed, despite herself, and shook her head.

"The guy was so flustered he answered me. 'I'm Robin's fiancé' he yells. 'What are you doing in her closet?'"

"Well, you couldn't very well ask him that back, could you?"

"No," Joseph agreed. "So I told him."

"You told him what?"

"I said I had heard someone open the door and that it frightened me so I jumped into the closet."

"Didn't he ask you what you were doing in her room?"

"I told him that I was looking for a book."

"A book? You told him you were looking for a book?"

"Yeah," said Joseph, pulling out a book from his jacket pocket. "This one."

"And he fell for it? I mean the guy couldn't have been that much of an idiot!"

"People in a state of emotional crisis believe many things we'd find hard to swallow, Polly . . ."

"Come off it!" she said, throwing him one of those looks which meant she knew better. "What did he say?"

"He wanted to know how I got into the house and why I was there."

"Two very reasonable questions. Just what I asked you myself."

98

"I jingled some keys at him and told him that Malcolm had given them to me and had asked me to pick up some stuff . . ."

"What stuff?"

"He didn't ask for specifics, thank God, 'cause I couldn't very well have shown him these," Joseph said, emptying the syringes from his pocket and putting them on the coffee-table.

Polly walked over and picked one up. "What are they, Joseph?" she asked, holding it up to the light.

"Morphine. Read the label."

"Morphine?" Her voice expressed her shock. "Where did you find them?"

"In Malcolm's bedside table."

She looked at him in horror. "Well, why didn't you leave them there?"

"Would you have left them there?"

"Damn right!" she shouted. "You think I want morphine in my house? Besides, it's his not yours!"

"He doesn't need it anymore, Polly."

"We don't either! Get rid of them!" She went back to her chair and let herself down with a thump.

"I will, I will. But don't you want to know what happened next?"

She looked at him reproachfully. "OK. What happened next?"

"I asked him if he wanted any coffee. Made it seem as if I really belonged there. I tried to look as if I knew my way around the place."

"By that time you probably did!"

"Yeah, I had already started doing the dishes. What burglar does that?"

"Wish you'd do more of that at home!" she said under her breath.

Joseph ignored her mutterings and went on. "So I make him coffee and he begins to tell me his story. His name's Roger Gasser, by the way. Turns out he's an attorney for Consumer Affairs. Said he was really concerned about Robin. Hasn't seen

99

her for a couple of weeks. He's been coming by every once in a while to check Malcolm's house."

"To see if she had returned?"

"Yeah. He looks through her stuff to see if anything's missing, like underwear and socks."

"How sad," said Polly. "Has he gone to the police?"

"He said that he and Malcolm had discussed that right before Malcolm died. But they decided against."

"Why?"

"Because of the circumstances. Seems she's done things like this before. In fact, as it turned out, she and Gasser had grown pretty distant since she came back from Sweden."

Polly held up her hand. "Whoa, Trigger. You've lost me. What's this about Sweden?"

"Gasser told me that Robin had gone there for a conference—something to do with her PhD. I think he said she was a biologist. Gasser said that ever since she's come back she's been a different person. About six or seven months ago she moved in with Malcolm again."

"So what's the problem?" asked Polly. "The woman obviously wants to be on her own."

"Gasser said they never really split up. In fact, he agreed with her decision to move out. He thought they both needed some space away from each other to think things through. Anyway, about the same time she moved in with Malcolm she started a new job at the hospital—Gasser says that Malcolm fixed it for her."

"Doing what?"

"Working as a medical records clerk."

"With a PhD in biology? That doesn't make sense, Joseph."

Joseph shrugged. "Maybe she couldn't find a job in her field, Polly. Things like that happen all the time."

"Maybe."

"Whatever. The point is that she left about a couple of weeks ago. She gave no notice or anything. She just didn't turn up at work."

"Then it does sound like a case for the police."

100

He rubbed his chin and thought a moment before he started speaking. "Except for one thing. Gasser ran into somebody who saw her a few days ago—or so they claim."

Polly sat back in her chair and studied his face. Then she said, "Joseph, why was he telling you all this? I mean, Christ! You're the guy who popped out of her closet!"

He grinned. "You think I made the whole thing up?"

"Maybe you did . . ." She looked at him suspiciously.

"Of course I didn't. You think I have that kind of imagination?"

"Yes. You probably spent the entire afternoon at a cafe . . ."

"And that's where I picked up the morphine, I suppose?"

She looked worried again. "I told you, I don't want it in my house!"

"I heard you, Polly . . ."

"So why was Gasser telling you the story of his life, Joseph?" She tried to stare him into submission.

He shrugged. "I'm a professional. I could get a story from a can of beans."

"Come on, Joseph!"

He made a face of annoyance. "Look, the guy had his defenses down. I scared the shit out of him coming out of the closet like that. Then I helped him get back on his feet and made him coffee. I convinced him I was Malcolm's friend. And I was a sympathetic face. Besides, I'm a good listener . . ."

Polly shook her head and sighed. "Talk about brainwashing!"

"Brainwashing?" He looked positively hurt. "I didn't wash his brain!"

"I'm not talking about his brain, Joseph. I'm talking about mine. I've almost gotten to the point that I believe you!"

"Thanks," he said, wrinkling up his nose.

"OK," she said. "Help me up from the chair."

He walked over to where she was sitting and gave her a hand. "Where are we going?"

"To the operations room!" she said, marching in front of him.

He followed her and stood before the chart. "What are we doing here?" he asked.

"Hand me that pen!" she ordered, pointing to the desk.

He gave her the pen and then watched as she took charge.

"Under 'Robin' we'll put the information you gathered in your own little Watergate way."

"Watergate was a botched up burglary. I didn't botch mine up."

She placed the marker under "Robin". "Let's fill this in, shall we? I'll write 'Had PhD in biology' and 'Went to international conference in Sweden'."

She turned to him and said, "Why Sweden, I wonder?"

He shrugged. "This is your game, Polly. Not mine."

"I thought it was our 'Big Story'?"

"We have different ways of working," he replied.

"It's true I don't hold up banks," she said, "but if you bear with me, I think we'll get somewhere."

"You might put down that she worked as a medical records clerk at the hospital then."

"Right," she said. "And we'll make a line from her to this Gasser fellow. What did you say he does?"

"He works at City Hall. He's an attorney with Consumer Affairs."

"Of course, how could I have forgotten?"

"So," he said, "is that it? Can we leave the war room now?"

"Not yet," she said. "I have some information, too. Except I used a telephone instead of a crowbar!"

"Like I said, Polly: We all have our own way of working."

Polly took her marker and pointed to the side of the chart that was blank. "If you recall, one of us was going to try to get some information about the other party who was liquidated."

"Yes," he replied. "We had a rather large female volunteer."

"Well, this rather large female volunteer got a response to her query today. An old chum called her back and said that he indeed knew one Henry Krohl and said Henry Krohl had been very elusive of late."

"Can't you stop beating around the bush, Polly, and say what you have to say?" His face showed his impatience.

Under "Krohl" she wrote: "Working on secret government project."

"What does that mean?" he asked, reading the words.

"It means what it says. My contact claims that Krohl had been the recipient of a large grant from the defense department."

"Polly," he said with a sigh, "eighty percent of the scientific research done in this country is funded either directly or indirectly by the military . . ."

"Yes, but this was different," Polly went on. "My friend said that he's never seen such strict security precautions in the biological sciences before. He says it's more like what you see up at the radiation labs. He says people are under surveillance twenty-four hours a day."

"Does he have any idea what the project is about?" asked Joseph.

"He says there're rumors of a new generation of biological warfare experimentation going on, but he'd be surprised if that type of stuff would be done in a populated area. Usually that kind of experimentation is done in seclusion—in places like the Mojave Desert."

Joseph took out a cigarette and lit up. Then he stared at the chart. "Did he say anything else?"

"Only that there seemed to be a good bit of panic after the explosion."

"He hasn't picked up on any other rumors?"

Polly shook her head. "He said everyone's clammed up."

"Can't he ask around?"

"There's an inner circle, Joseph. Sometimes it's loose, sometimes it's tight. This one seems to be as tight as hell!"

"Then I guess you'll need to look for another source." said Joseph.

"There is one other thing," said Polly. "My friend said there was a guy hanging around trying to pick up some info on Krohl's project."

"Did he know him?"

She shook her head. "No. But he described him for me. Said he had a strawberry patch on his forehead—just like Gorbachev."

Joseph let out a sigh. "I suppose you'll have to put Gorbachev's name down, too.'

Chapter 7

'It's for you," she said. He was still in bed. She had been up for hours.

"Who is it?" he asked, rubbing his eyes.

"Didn't say . . ."

He sat up and looked at her. "Man or woman?"

"Woman."

"Young or old?"

She put her hands on her hips, making a defiant stance. "How the hell am I supposed to know, Joseph? It's the telephone not the door!"

He dragged himself out of bed and stumbled into the study. He picked up the phone. "Yeah?"

"Radkin? Listen, I'm out of coins. The number is 8245531. Got it?"

"Gerry! Is that you? Hello! Gerry?"

It was too late. She had already been cut off by the insidious greed of the telephone empire.

"Polly!" he shouted. "Do you know where she was calling from?"

Polly came in with a hot cup of coffee in her hand. "Who?"

"Gerry!" he shouted. "It was Gerry! Where was she calling from?"

"Didn't she say?" asked Polly handing him the cup.

He ran his hand nervously through his hair. "She was calling from a pay phone, Polly. She said she ran out of change. She gave the number and asked me to call her back. Then she was cut off! Why didn't she just call me collect, damn it?"

"So what's the problem? Phone her back."

His eyes were wild. "I can't phone her back! She didn't give me the area code!"

"Sit down, Joseph," she instructed. She had lived with him long enough to know when he was about to blow it. "Don't you know where she was camping?"

He sat down in his desk chair and took a sip of coffee. He shook his head. "No." He looked up at her. "The redwood trees aren't provided with address numbers, are they?"

"She's probably at a café or a gas station, Joseph. If she is, she'll be able to get some more change and phone you back."

"But she might be on the highway!"

"Look, why don't you call the operator and tell her the situation. Maybe she'll be able to match the number with an area code," Polly suggested.

"If she's still in the Sierras!"

"It's worth a shot."

Just then the telephone rang. Joseph leapt for it. "Gerry? Of course I'll accept the charge!" He winked at Polly and grinned. "Eureka!"

Polly gave him a poke. "I'm going to write down some questions for you to ask her as well."

He held up his hand for her to be silent. "Gerry!" he shouted into the mouthpiece. "Where are you?"

"You needn't yell, Radkin," she said, "I can hear you fine. I'm still up here, camping out. Not too many people around. I'm calling you from a phone box on the road."

"I'm really glad you called, Gerry."

"Yeah. Well, I've had a lot of time to think things out . . ."

"Good."

"How's the story going?"

"Not too well. I really needed to ask you some questions."

"That's why I phoned you, Radkin. There's a lot of stuff that doesn't make sense. I want to talk to you about it when I get back."

Polly held a sign in front of his face. "ASK HER ABOUT ROBIN!" it read.

Joseph shooed her away with his hand. "Uh . . . Gerry, tell me about Robin."

"You mean Malcolm's sister? He was really worried about her."

"She was working in the medical records department of the hospital, right?"

"Yeah. He had gotten her that job a few months before. I never understood why. I mean, that kid was destined to be a fantastic scientist, not a clerk."

"So why do you think she wanted the job?"

"She claimed she wanted to understand the workings of the hospital from the bottom up."

"I guess you can get a bird's-eye view from reading all the records, huh?"

"Yeah, but a distorted one. She was always pestering Malcolm with things she thought she discovered. It used to drive him mad."

"Like what?"

"Lots of things. She kept finding statistical aberrations in certain kinds of diseases—like carcinomas. Malcolm had to point out to her that this was a teaching hospital and that deviations were bound to exist."

"Did she give him any details?"

"I know she was really concerned by a university research program that was going on."

"What research program?"

"It had to do with cancers in female reproductive organs."

"Who was in charge, Gerry? Do you know?"

"In charge of the research project? Henry Krohl . . ."

"Krohl! But, Gerry, that's the guy who . . ."

"Yeah, Radkin, I know. But Krohl was doing some really important work in tumor research. Everybody was expecting him to make a very important breakthrough."

"What did Malcolm think of Krohl? Did he ever say?"

"Ever say? Are you kidding? He idolised the guy! Krohl was one of his professors in medical school. Malcolm always looked to him as a source of inspiration."

"Wait a minute, Gerry! I thought Krohl epitomised everything Malcolm fought against!"

"You mean bioengineering? Malcolm was excited as anyone about the new research into the structure of genes. What he opposed was misdirected priorities. He didn't want research and technology at the expense of basic medical needs."

"But that's the whole point, isn't it?"

"Maybe. But Krohl was Malcolm's biggest ally on the hospital board. You know, he's the one who helped us get the clinic started in the first place."

"Really?" said Joseph, giving Polly a startled look. "I'll be damned!"

Polly tugged his sleeve and mouthed the word, "What?"

He brushed her off. She took a piece of paper and penned: "ASK HER ABOUT THE FRENCH CROISSANT!"

He shook his head and made a face. "Uh . . . Gerry, tell me about the French Croissant."

"What are you talking about, Radkin? Croissants? I'm on a diet. Just eating fruit and nuts for a few days."

"No . . . uh . . . listen, Gerry, I understand that right before the shit hit the fan, there was this French woman."

"Oh, you mean Nicole. She's a reporter from some French paper who came to interview him."

"Interview him? About what?"

"The clinic."

"Are you saying she came all the way from France to interview him about the clinic?"

"She was doing an article on the crisis in Western medicine, she said. Part of the article was about how wealthy nations like America deal with health problems among the poor."

"That could be summed up in three words: not very well."

"She wanted some examples of alternative approaches. That's why she came to us."

"Isn't it sort of suspicious—her turning up just then?"

"Not really. She had written us about a month before, setting up an appointment." She chuckled.

"What's so funny, Gerry?"

"Oh, I was remembering the confusion. We were in the middle of our crisis—fighting to save the clinic. Malcolm was desperately trying to track down the salmonella thing—and suddenly she turns up! Anyway, I phoned Malcolm at the hospital and told him there was a reporter here and before I can say anything else he shouts; 'That Robin! I'll kill her!' And then two minutes later he's huffing and puffing and standing in front of my desk whispering; 'You didn't say anything to him, did you Gerry?' As if I would . . ."

"I'm sorry, Gerry, you lost me."

"Oh, don't you see? He thought Robin had blown the whistle on the hospital about the salmonella outbreak and the reporters were lining up to confront him with the cover-up. Then he turns around to see this dishy Parisian woman who's come to make a hero of him! It was really funny!" Her laughter trailed off. Then, in tones that had a trace of sadness, she said, "He was so straight, you know."

Joseph thought of the morphine he had found in Malcolm's bed table and tried to figure out whether Gerry didn't know or if she were just trying to protect him.

Polly looked down at his notes and gave him a nudge. "MAKE SURE TO GET FRENCHY'S FULL NAME AND THE NAME OF HER NEWSPAPER!"

"Yeah . . . Gerry, do you know Nicole's last name?"

"Proust . . ."

"Like the writer?"

"I guess . . ."

"What newspaper did she work for?"

"Let me think . . . it was something like 'Liberty'. . ."

"*Libération*?"

"Right! That's the one!"

"Listen, Gerry. When are you coming back?"

"Tomorrow or the next day, Radkin. I still have a few things I want to think about."

"Can I get in touch with you at this number?"

"You can try. Maybe the chipmunks around here have an answering service."

"Well, give me a call tomorrow, Gerry."

Polly hit him over the head with her notebook to get his attention. She held out a sign: "REMEMBER TO ASK HER ABOUT CHARLIE-THE-WEIRDO!"

"Oh, yeah, before you hang up. What about Charlie-the-Weirdo?"

109

"Charlie-the-who?"

"I spoke to one of the doctors who worked at your clinic—Philip Brewster. He told me about this guy named Charlie who used to hang around. He said that Malcolm had some sort of relationship with him."

"You spoke to Brewster?" she asked. Her tone of voice made her feelings about him quite clear.

"I thought he might tell me something about Malcolm."

"Brewster has a jaundiced view, Radkin. Don't take anything he says too seriously. The guy was one of those upper-class do-gooders who try to ease their conscience by spending a few years doing missionary work. Malcolm was getting pretty fed up with him toward the end. I was, too."

"What about Charlie, though?"

She hesitated a minute. "What did Brewster tell you, Radkin?"

"He said that he suspected Malcolm of passing him morphine."

"That son of a bitch!"

"You don't think it's true?"

Her voice was quieter, as if she were struggling with herself to keep control. "Listen, Radkin, Charlie was Malcolm's albatross. He was a link to a period that Malcolm was trying hard to forget."

"Vietnam?"

"Yeah. Something happened between them—I don't know what. Malcolm would never really speak about it. He kept referring Charlie to Veterans organisations, but Charlie always came back to him. He was big trouble. But Malcolm felt he owed him something."

"Something like morphine?"

Her voice had a hard edge to it now. "Whatever that jerk, Brewster, says, Malcolm didn't deal in drugs!" Her voice began to crack. He could almost see the tears begin to run down her cheeks. "He was about as close to an American saint I think I'll ever see!"

"I'm not trying to upset you, Gerry," he said. "I just needed to know, that's all."

"Listen to me, Radkin. I don't want his name slandered, do you hear?"

"I'm not into slander, Gerry."

"I know what sells papers, Radkin."

"I think this story runs deeper than that, Gerry. Honestly, I'm not going to betray your trust."

"You better not!"

"Give me a call tomorrow, OK?" he said.

"I'll see how I feel."

Polly jabbed him in his ribs. "MAKE SURE YOU GET CHARLIE'S LAST NAME!"

"Oh, Gerry, one more thing . . ."

It was too late. She had already hung up.

"That was real smart," she said. "You had it on a plate and you let it slip right off!"

"What could I do?" he said, putting out both palms like a pauper. "She hung up on me."

They were standing in front of the chart. Polly was writing in all the new information.

"I had the sign up in front of your nose. All you had to do was look and read!"

"I was concentrating on what I was saying and listening to her. It's not that easy."

She made a "humphing" noise. "I could do it better and with less sass!"

"You got enough sass to fill a barrel of parilla!" he shot back. "Anyway, I did find out that the French Croissant is named Nicole Proust and that she works for *Libération* newspaper in Paris," he said, picking up the phone and starting to dial.

"What are you doing?"

"Calling the international operator to get the number."

"You're calling Paris?" she asked in disbelief.

"Right."

"You know how much that costs?"

111

"I'll put it on expenses."

"What expenses?"

"The expenses for the story."

"Who's going to reimburse you, Joseph? Not Lamont!"

"The Pulitzer prize committee—they'll reimburse me, Polly."

She slapped her forehead and shook her head. "Jezus Christ!"

He held up his hand for her to be quiet. "Operator, I'd like to make a call to France. . . .'

"So what now?" she asked. They were sitting at the dinner table. He was eating a ham on rye—mustard, pickles, no mayo. She was nibbling on an egg salad with a side order of sardines.

He kept staring at his plate. "Maybe she got the paper wrong. Maybe it's not *Libération*."

"Maybe you don't speak French well enough to know the difference," she said.

He looked up at her. "I speak French well enough to ask for 'Nicole Proust'. And I can understand when someone says they never heard of her—especially when they say it in English!"

She shrugged her shoulders, took a sardine by the tail and let it drop into her mouth.

He stared at her in amazement. "I saw a penguin do that once, but never a real person."

"Penguins don't have hands," she said.

"Real people don't swallow sardines whole."

"Are you saying I'm a figment of your imagination, Joseph?" she smiled sweetly.

"Make sure you drink your milk," he ordered. "Remember what the doctor said about the importance of calcium during pregnancy. You'll want to be able to show me your ivories after Spinach is born, won't you?"

She poured herself a glass of milk. "So, back to square one."

"Not exactly," he said, tapping his fork on his plate, "we'll just have to hold the French Croissant for later."

"So what now?"

He shrugged. "Not many leads, Polly old gal."

"I guess this is where reporters have to play their hunches," she said.

"Yeah. But you were right. I should have gotten Charlie's last name."

"You're playing the Vietnam card, huh?"

"Guess so."

"Let me look at those notes again," she asked, pointing to the papers he had written on.

He passed them over to her and she paged through the scribbles.

"You did find out that Malcolm sent him to some veterans' organisations. It might be worth a few phone calls. You must know some of those people from the story you did on job discrimination."

"I know Harper—he runs the Veterans Resource Center."

"Call him. It's a shot in the dark, but we're just sitting here anyway."

"It's not a shot in the dark, Polly. It's a shot into another world."

The store-front office was located in the heartland of despair; where the urban refuse lay redundant like rusted machines in a microchip age.

Joseph had been here some years before when the pressure was on to refurbish the image of Vietnam vets. He had interviewed hundreds of them back then and they all had given him a similar story: "Nah, we never say we were in 'Nam when we go lookin' for a job. That's like tellin' 'em we were locked up on a murder charge . . ."

In the end, he had written: "They came back drugged and disillusioned, these men of war. They found a nation willing to ship them off to die in some exotic land but reluctant to give them a dignified job when they came limping home. Somehow, it seems, we've transferred all our guilt for that rotten war. We sent them there to kill and now we can't forgive them for what they've gone and done . . ."

113

It didn't win him a Pulitzer, but he got a few pats on the back from some of the guys at the Veterans Center.

Now, some ten years later, the store-front looked much the same: still littered with unread pamphlets printed by an insensitive, word-spewing governmental press. There was a raw, unkempt feel to the place—mirroring, perhaps, the men who wandered in and out through the revolving door.

"Hey, Radkin!" Jack Harper stood up as Joseph walked in. He transferred the chicken leg he was eating to his left hand, and stuck out his right. "What's happenin', man?"

Joseph shook Harper's hand and then wiped his palm on his pant leg. He glanced around. "You sure live your life in a time warp, Jack. Don't you ever want to chuck it in and start a greasy spoon café?"

Harper grinned and tossed the chicken bone into a nearby can. He held out the box it had come from as an offer: "You want a piece of 'finger lickin' good'?"

"Not unless you provide a stomach pump in the back room," Joseph replied.

"Hey, man! I live off this stuff!" said Harper, feigning outrage. "Without the chicken burger industry this country would be down the drain!"

"Maybe you're right," said Joseph. "I just read that they make more from fast foods now than automobiles. MacDonalds has more branches overseas than General Motors."

"Chicken burgers rule the world, man!" said Harper in a whisky voice. He pulled out a pack of Camels, lit up, and then tossed the pack to Joseph. "Once it was the pepper trade—you know, back in the days of Marco Polo. Now it's chicken burgers. The whole fuckin' world wants our chicken burgers. If we had just let 'Nam have a few more chicken burgers, we wouldn't have had to fight that shitty war!"

"I told you before, Harper, that war was fought for drugs. You guys were sent there by the Mafia to make sure the poppy harvest wasn't tampered with." Joseph took out a smoke and threw the pack of cigarettes back to Harper.

"Well if that's why they sent us, they sure made some

114

mistake. I personally consumed fifty or sixty acres myself and I wasn't half as wasted as some guys in my unit."

"No kidding," said Joseph, lighting up. "And you're still alive to tell about it?"

Harper laughed in his husky way and slapped Joseph on the back. "That's what everybody wants to believe, so why should I deny it? Shit, you know, everyone from 'Nam has their war stories."

Joseph shook his head. "I never know what to believe when I talk to you. I thought I was a bullshitter, but you take the Kewpie doll as far as I'm concerned."

"How do you think I kept this place alive?" asked Harper. "Man, you got to heap it on with a trowel if you want to get any bread from those tight-ass financiers. But I never joke around about drugs with money men or newspaper hacks. They think we're all hop-head freaks and mass murderers anyway. I don't want to reinforce their views."

"In case you've forgotten, Jack, I'm a newspaper hack," said Joseph.

Harper took a drag on his cigarette and let the smoke run slowly from his mouth. "I figure you got a little more sophistication than your ordinary pen-pusher." He stared at Joseph with penetrating eyes. "Those two-bit bureaucrats and churchy types got a one-track mind as far as drugs are concerned. They got no understanding that those same drugs that keep us in the gutter here, back in 'Nam they saved our God damned lives!"

"How do you mean?" asked Joseph.

"Fuck it, Radkin! They were our escape from hell!"

Joseph glanced out the window at a youthful wino crashed out on the streets. "Not much of an escape from the looks of things."

Harper sat back down in his chair and put his boots up on top of his cluttered desk. He grinned at Joseph, showing him his nicotine-stained teeth. "Hell ain't so bad, sometimes. Shit, I could have a job on a newspaper like you. Then I'd really be a mess."

Joseph gave him the once over, glancing at his tattered

115

clothes and grizzled face. "You're mess enough for the *Defender*, Harper," he said. "Any messier and you'd be pickings for the Salvation Army."

"My army days are over," said Harper. "And I ain't lookin' for salvation."

"Not for you,' Radkin nodded outside at some pasing junkies. "For them."

Harpers face grew tense. "I ain't lookin' to save nobody's soul, either. And after a dozen years of beatin' my head against the wall it's a good thing I ain't. Those kids who left the army back in '72 are pushing middle age by now. If they ain't found themselves yet, they never will."

"You're not giving up on them, are you?" asked Joseph.

Harper leaned forward. His voice was softer, like a man resigned to his fate. "You know as well as I do, Radkin. It suits their purposes just fine that those guys are drugged out of their gourds half the time. If they're spaced out, they ain't marchin' on the White House and threatenin' to burn it down like they ought to be."

"I don't think it suits their purposes for junkies to break into middle-class homes to support their habit, Jack," said Joseph.

Harper sat back again and put his hands behind his head and then looked up at the ceiling. "Yeah. Well if they could sweep 'em up and dump 'em all into an incinerator, they'd do that instead. Maybe someday they'll invent a pill to make 'em all disappear. Until that time, drugs'll have to do."

"Can I quote you?" asked Joseph with a sly grin on his face.

Harper pointed to him with a threatening finger. "Man, don't forget! I got your address!"

"I moved," Joseph said. "Didn't I tell you?"

"We'll find you, man," replied Harper. "We got our network."

Joseph laughed. "Yeah, that's why I'm here. I'm looking for someone. A guy named Charlie."

"That's what we called the VC back then." said Harper, twisting his rough face into sort of a smile.

"Well that's what this guy calls himself now. He was a patient at the People's Medical Clinic. He knew Malcolm Greene, the chief honcho there."

Harper gave him a look of suspicion. "What you want him for, Radkin?"

"I'm doing a story on Greene. I think this guy Charlie might help me. He knew Greene in 'Nam."

Harper rubbed the bald spot on the top of his head. "I need more than a first name, Radkin. It's a tight world here, but not that tight."

"I don't know too much about him. He's got no fixed address—the people I talked with said he lives on the streets. And he likes morphine."

"Morphine?" said Harper. "That's not an easy fix to get . . ."

"Yeah, I thought it was pretty unusual myself. I wouldn't think much of that would be going around even in 'Nam."

"More than you think," said Harper. "Medics had access to the stuff, they carried morphine and atropine in their combat bags. But there was a pretty strict accounting done. Heroin was an easier high. You could get that on any street corner in Saigon."

"So why would someone get hooked on morphine?" asked Joseph.

Harper shrugged. "You don't always have the chance to choose your poison, Radkin," he replied.

Joseph pondered that for a moment and then said, "I also know that Greene referred him to some veterans' organisation. I don't know which one."

"Probably one of the adjustment centers if he was referred from a clinic," said Harper, going over to his files. "There's a couple that deal with stress-related problems . . ." He let out a hoarse chuckle. "That's the buzz word now—'stress-related'. You get a punch in your groin and it's 'stress-related'." He pulled a couple of index cards. "Here's one that works specifically with homeless vets," he said, copying down the number. "You want me to give them a call?"

Joseph nodded and while Harper dialled the number, he walked over to the water cooler, pulled a paper cup from the receptacle and filled it, watching the bubble in the giant bottle rise to the top and then explode in a burp like a stomach reacting to a spicy meal.

He drank the liquid and crumpled the cup in his hand. Then, turning back, he saw Harper motion him over with his hand.

Harper held out the receiver. "Her name's Sandy Grey," he said. "She's got somethin' to tell you."

Joseph took the phone. "Hi," he said. "You know something about Charlie?"

It was a woman's voice on the other end: a low soprano, but strong and clear. "You're asking about Charlie Johnson?" she said. "The vet that Malcolm Greene referred to us?"

"Yeah," said Joseph. "He's the one. You know him?"

"Yes, I do . . ."

"Great!" said Joseph. "I need to talk to him about something."

"I'm afraid that's impossible . . ."

"Nothing's impossible, Sandy."

"In his case it is 'cause Charlie Johnson's dead.'

It was half-past two. He was sitting in a booth at Bob's Café on Polk Street nibbling at an apple pie when she came in. He didn't notice her until she was standing over him saying "Are you Mr Radkin?"

He wasn't expecting someone so tiny. She reminded him of a petite social worker he had known in Chicago who ran a home for retired seamen.

He stood up. "Hello, Sandy," he said, motioning for her to sit down opposite him. "Thanks for coming." Then he asked, "How'd you know who I was?"

She smiled. It was a hard smile on a prematurely lined face. "I've been around," she said. "I know a newsy when I see one."

"I'm not so sure how to take that," he said. He pulled out a pack of cigarettes and made her an offering. She shook her head.

118

"Take it any way you like," she replied as he lit up a smoke for himself.

The waitress came over and Sandy ordered a coffee. The waitress pointed to a tattered sign saying there was a dollar minimum in the booths between noon and three so she ordered a piece of pie as well.

Joseph took a long drag on his cigarette and let the smoke drift slowly from his mouth as he contemplated the face across from him. She was a tough cookie, he thought. But then, he figured, if you're baked in a hot oven you're bound to be a little crusty around the edges and soft in the centre.

"Tell me about Charlie," he said.

She was trying to size him up, too, it seemed. "Harper says you're doing a story on Greene. What's the deal?"

"You know he was killed in a lab accident at the hospital?"

"Who doesn't?" she asked, taking the coffee from the waitress who had just come over. She started to spoon in some sugar.

"I'm doing a story on him and the closure of the clinic," said Joseph, watching as she put four sugars in her coffee before she stirred.

"What's this got to do with Charlie?" she asked, finally putting the cup to her mouth and taking a drink.

"Charlie knew Malcolm in 'Nam. Something happened there between them, I think. I was hoping he'd be able to tell me about it."

Sandy put in another spoon of sugar. "I don't expect he'll be able to tell you much of anything anymore," she said, tasting the coffee again.

"Better watch it. Sugar stunts your growth," Joseph advised.

She stared at him. "The coffee here smells like sewer water and tastes like shit."

He nodded. "I know. Why'd you want to meet here then?"

She motioned toward the window. "'Cause it's close to the bus stop."

"Makes sense . . . how'd Charlie die?"

"He was stabbed in the belly about fifteen times," she said as

119

casual as you please. "His guts spilled out on the pavement. They tried to stuff 'em back in, but he was a goner before he reached the emergency room."

Joseph looked down at his pie and saw a few raisins poking out from the crust. He pushed it away with the edge of his hand.

She grinned. "A squeamish newsy! Well, I'll be!"

"I'm not a newsy," he said somewhat defensively. "I'm a journalist."

"There's a difference?"

"Yeah. I'm not after trash."

She shrugged and took a forkful of pie. "Sounds to me like you're in the wrong business then."

He rubbed his eyes. "You might be right at that. You got any suggestions for another career?"

She let out a boisterous laugh that caused a few customers to turn around and stare.

Joseph smiled back at her. "They know who did it?" he asked.

"Did what?"

"Killed Charlie . . ."

"He was a streety, a down-and-out, a junky, a bum. Guys like that don't have police investigations. They're put into a bag and dumped into the morgue. Then they notify the next of kin that the body needs collecting and would they kindly pay the storage fee. Since a guy like Charlie ain't got no next of kin, or anyone who'd admit to being one, they take his wallet and call some number that they find. In this case, they found mine."

"Yours?" Joseph gave her a curious look.

"My office. He had my card . . ."

"You know him long?"

"Not long. But long enough to know he was unemployable, uncurable and unmanageable."

"That's a lot of uns."

"And paranoid to boot."

"How so?"

She narrowed her eyes. "He kept saying they were out to get him."

"Who were out to get him?"

"Paranoids aren't specific about who, what, where or when." Joseph stubbed out his cigarette and lit up another one.

"You smoke too much," she said.

"You use too much sugar," he shot back. "Anyway, I've got an excuse. I'm going to have a baby."

"Then you're a little paranoid yourself," she replied.

"You know he was hooked on morphine?" he asked, looking into her eyes to see what her response would be.

"I wouldn't be surprised. He was hooked on everything."

"Everything?"

"There's plenty of everything on this street," she said. "But you got to pay for it . . ."

He cringed. "I'd like to know what his paranoid fantasies were about . . ."

The expression on her face changed. She held out her hand. "I'll take one of those weeds now . . ."

He held out the pack. She took one and lit up. She inhaled deeply and then tilted her head back and blew the smoke toward the ceiling. "He said they were being kidnapped . . ."

"Who?"

"The bag ladies. You know, the refugees, the ones who wear those strange costumes and who always rummage in the trash. You must have seen 'em around."

"Yeah. Did you believe him?"

Sandy shook her head. "I heard those rumors before, though. But I also hear rumors that children are being sold into white slavery and that pensioners are being hacked up in butcher shops for meat."

"But he claims he saw some actual kidnappings. Did he describe them?"

She showed her annoyance by making a face. "Have you ever listened to the ranting of a junky, Radkin? Try it sometime before you ask me to make sense of their paranoid dreams!"

"Indulge me," he said with a charming smile.

121

She sighed. "He said he was sleeping it off in an alley behind some trash sacks. He heard a ruckus. He saw some toughs grab this elderly woman. I remember he called her a 'gook', the racist sonofabitch!"

"Did he describe the toughs?"

"Said they were dressed in white like ambulance drivers. Said they stuffed her in the van with blacked-out windows . . ."

Joseph studied her expression. Beneath it all, he thought that somewhere there was the remains of a sensitive young woman. "You hear of any strange illnesses going around? Especially in the Vietnamese community?"

She put another sugar into her cold cup of coffee and stirred. "I wouldn't be surprised if we all died of some weird disease in another year or two.'

Polly took a red marker and drew a line through Charlie's name. She was standing before the chart, looking very expectant. "What do you think of that kidnapping story?" she asked.

"I don't think it's a drug-induced delusion, if that's what you mean," Joseph replied, seated at his desk. "But the same event could be seen in many ways. A guy like Charlie lived in such a violent world that he probably projected his own fears into innocent situations."

"For example?" asked Polly.

"For example a woman being put into an ambulance could be disoriented. Maybe she didn't want to go to hospital."

"Why would they be putting her into a van, though, Joseph? And one with coated windows at that!"

"Maybe they weren't, Polly. Maybe a delivery truck was parked next to the ambulance and his drugged-out mind made it into a montage."

She put down her marker. "It could be anything," she agreed. "It's just weird that we're picking up on so many stories that relate back to the Montagnards . . ." Then she looked up at the chart. "Did that Grey woman say anything else?"

"I asked her if Charlie had any friends that she knew of. She said guys like that don't tend to keep friends for long."

122

"She's probably right," said Polly. "That's what makes it all the more strange that Malcolm kept seeing him for so long."

"He probably didn't have any choice," Joseph responded. "But the way Sandy described him, he was too messed up for Malcolm to have done business with him."

"But you didn't believe that anyway, did you?"

"Believe what?"

"That Malcolm was a pusher . . ."

He shook his head. "No. He wasn't a pusher. But he did pass the stuff. And for the life of me, I don't know why."

She put down her pen. "Well, the answer can wait. Right now we have to practice."

"Practice what?" He looked at her curiously. "Right now we can't even answer a census questionaire."

She took his hand and pulled him from his chair. "I have to practice my breathing techniques and you have to practice your effleurage."

"Oh, yeah," he said, allowing himself to be extracted from his seat. "That hippy-dippy birth class where they were trying to convince us to launch Spinach under water like a submarine."

"No one was trying to convince us of anything. They were just suggesting that underwater birth was a option . . ."

"Some option," he grumbled. Then looking at her haggard face, he said more sympathetically, "How do you feel?"

"I feel like a bomb ready to explode," she replied as they walked into the bedroom.

"Just hold your fuse for another couple of days," he said.

Chapter 8

A hand reached out and touched him on the shoulder. He screamed.

"Joseph! What's wrong?"

He opened his eyes. Polly was standing over him. She looked worried.

He rubbed his sweaty forehead. "It was nothing, just a dream," he said, trying to get up from his chair. "What time is it?" he asked.

"It's nearly ten," she replied.

"In the morning or night?"

She pointed to the window. "It's light outside. Figure it out for yourself."

He managed to pull himself up and stumble into the bedroom.

She watched him with amazement as he tried to change his clothes. "Where are you going?" she asked.

"City Hall," he replied, tying the laces of his shoes.

"How come?"

"I want to find out about a missing bird . . ."

"A missing bird?"

"Yeah. A robin red breast . . .'

If one could have viewed them looking down from the splendid dome, the crowd of people in the rotunda of City Hall might have seemed like an endless trail of ants scurrying along the spokes of a grinding wheel.

Joseph crammed himself inside an elevator and then got off at the third floor. On his way down the hall, following the numbers on the doors, he came to one marked "Men" and decided to pay a call. Inside, he found a vacant cubicle and sat down to do his business while noting the graffiti etched into the toilet facade. They were mostly vulgar and humorless, leaving him to wonder about the civil service mind.

124

When he was finished, he flushed and belted up. Then, after smoothing down his shirt and putting on his jacket, he reached for the latch. He opened the door just as someone else was starting to come in.

"Hi!" said Joseph with a wide contorted grin. "Nice of you to meet me here!"

The tall man in a vested suit stepped back a pace, his eyes as wide as empty porcelain plates. "Christ almighty!" he shouted. "This is the second closet I've opened up this week to find your Goddamned mug grinning out at me!" Gasser stared at him in amazement. "The Mafia's given you a contract on my life, am I right?"

"If they had, you'd be dead by now," said Joseph, stepping out of the booth.

"I'm close enough as it is," said Gasser, putting his hand over his chest. "I think one more nut popping out of a closet and I'll be pushing up the daisies."

Joseph went over to the basin and washed his hands while Gasser locked himself inside the cubicle.

"What are you doing here, anyway?" Gasser called out. "Did Malcolm leave something of yours in a City Hall toilet, too?"

"Not that I know of," said Joseph.

"Oh, I get it. You're one of those perverts who gets his kicks by crapping in strange places."

"Actually, I've come here to have lunch with you," said Joseph.

"Sorry," said Gasser from inside his retreat. "I usually make it a habit not to eat where I shit. Besides, I'm busy today . . ."

"Too busy to talk about a murder?" asked Joseph.

"Mine?" Gasser's voice sounded strained.

"In a manner of speaking," Joseph replied.

They were sitting in Max's Delicatessen just up the street. The brunette waitress, who looked as if she were auditioning for a part in a chorus line, had brought them both corned beef on rye.

"You paying for this?" asked Gasser, digging in.

125

"Me? Hell no! I don't have an expense account."

Gasser stared at him over the top of his corned beef sandwich. "I thought you said you were taking me out to lunch?"

"I said I came to have lunch with you," Joseph replied, dipping into the coleslaw. "You think I got the dough to splash ten bucks on a sandwich? Besides, you're the one who wanted to come to this place!"

"They got the best corned beef in town here," said Gasser. "It's the only place in Frisco you can get anywhere close to a New York-style sandwich."

"For these prices you could fly back and have the real thing." Joseph replied.

"All right," said Gasser, shaking his head. "It's on me. Just let me enjoy my lunch!"

"Thanks," said Joseph, showing his teeth.

"And don't grin at me any more!"

"Anything you say, chief. How about a malted milk?" Joseph motioned to the waitress who ignored him and walked away.

"So what's up?" asked Gasser. "Why have you chosen me to pester?" He seemed to be getting more annoyed as his sandwich grew smaller.

"I want to know why you lied to me."

"Are you a priest or just a nut? Or maybe you're a nutty priest . . ."

"I'm a reporter."

"I knew you were either a reporter or a cop," said Gasser, looking like he was having an attack of heart burn. "You seemed too dumb to be a legitimate thief."

"The cops are after her, aren't they?" asked Joseph.

"Who? Bonnie Parker? I think she was caught a few years back."

"Come on, Gasser," he said. "I'm trying to find out why Malcolm was killed. I think you can help me."

He shook his head. "I think you've got the wrong man . . ."

"You want me to write the story without you? OK by me. I'll just have to tell it the way I see it then . . ."

126

"How do you see it then?" Gasser asked, giving Joseph an angry look.

"The way I see it, Robin was a terrorist."

Gasser wiped his lips with his napkin and glared at the man across from him. "Listen, Radkin, I got a career to think about!"

"So do I," said Joseph.

"Well what the hell do you want from me?" he said.

"Just some information. I won't involve you, Gasser, I just want to know whether I'm on the right track. The cops think Robin's involved in something, don't they?"

Gasser made a tiny nod with his head. "Who did you talk with?" And then, probably realising he didn't want to get involved, he said, "Forget it. Don't tell me."

"I always protect my sources, Gasser. Do you think she's tossing cocktails?"

"I think she's a sweet kid who's a little mixed up right now. But she's got too much respect for human life to be a terrorist."

Joseph thought he saw a trace of sentiment in Gasser's eyes. But then he decided it was probably the spicy mustard. "When did the feds contact you?" he asked.

"A couple of weeks ago. Right before Malcolm . . ." His voice trailed off.

"Have you seen her since then?"

Gasser shook his head.

"You know where she is?"

"I don't want to know," he growled.

This time it wasn't the mustard, Joseph thought. "Tell me about Stockholm," he said.

"What do you want from this, Radkin?" Gasser asked, furrowing his brow. "I told you, I got my career to think about . . ."

"I said I'm not going to involve you, Gasser," Joseph replied, realising, once more, that first impressions usually are the best.

Gasser let out a short laugh. "Why should I believe that?"

"Because I'm an honest guy," said Joseph with one of his endearing smiles.

"I warned you about that grin!"

"Look," said Joseph, exchanging the smirk for a serious face, "something's going on that's more important than your fucking career. I think you know that, Gasser!"

"More important than your fucking career, too, Radkin?"

"More important than my fucking career, too. But at least my fucking career might help shed some light on this mess . . ."

"If you can get anyone to print it . . ."

"What do you know about what's going on?" Joseph threw him a hard look.

Gasser shrugged his shoulders. "Probably no more than you. I know there's shit flying fast and furious at the highest levels. And I know that there's a heavy lid on the pot."

"Tell me about Stockholm," Joseph said again.

"There isn't much to tell. It was a convention of scientists concerned about ecology, germ warfare, nuclear energy, man-made plagues. She met some people there who influenced her more than me . . ."

"She talk to you about it?"

He shook his head. "Not much. But she came back with that gleam in her eye. She was ready to save the world."

"And you're not."

"I'm older than her, Radkin. I went through my messianic stage in the '60s."

"Was she concerned about anything in particular?"

"Genetic engineering."

"What about it?"

Gasser unwrapped the cellophane from a complimentary toothpick and began probing his teeth. "She thought the military had some interest in the field. She kept talking about viral bombs . . ."

"Viral bombs? I don't understand . . ."

"It's just speculation, as far as I'm concerned," said Gasser. "Think tank stuff. But she was convinced that the military was manufacturing viruses that are the equivalent of 'smart' missiles—ones that can home in on specific targets.'

"And you were dubious about it, huh?"

"I'm not saying it isn't possible. It just sounded pretty far-

128

fetched to me." He pointed in the direction of City Hall. "Back there you wouldn't believe the number of wild stories I hear every day . . ."

"I'd like to know more about her concerns," said Joseph.

"I think I've told you too much already," Gasser replied. "I've got to get back . . ." He motioned to the waitress to bring over the bill.

Joseph put a restraining hand on Gasser's arm. "It's only half-past noon and you still haven't told me about Malcolm yet.'

He spent the afternoon at the downtown library, doing some research. By the time he got back home it was already after dinner.

"I saved you some food," Polly told him. "It's upstairs."

"I'm making some coffee," he said. "You want some?"

"All right. As long as we're not making another night of it."

"We're on the brink, Polly," he said, putting on the water. "I feel it in my gut!"

"Maybe what you're feeling is all the caffeine you consume," she said.

"That's coming out more as heartburn. This is lower down."

She patted her belly. "I know what you mean."

He dumped some ground coffee into the filter cone and doused it with boiling water. "Gasser said that the cops thought Robin was a terrorist."

"You saw Gasser today?" she asked.

Joseph nodded. He brought the aromatic brew to the table. "I met him in a toilet. We had a corned beef sandwich together."

"In the toilet?"

"No, at Max's . . ." He poured her a cup and one for himself. "Boy, is that place expensive!"

"I thought we were economising," said Polly.

"You don't think I'd pay, do you? Christ, that guy makes at least fifty grand a year."

"Who does he think Robin is terrorising?" asked Polly, taking a sip of coffee and then deciding to let it cool.

"He doesn't. But he did tell me about the Stockholm conference. He said it was a meeting of radical scientists."

"What's a radical scientist?"

"People concerned about the misuse of technology, I guess. The way he put it, they were trying to do something about man-made plagues."

"Like nuclear dumps?"

"I suppose. He said Robin's special interest was genetic engineering. She was talking to him about viral bombs—new biological research for military purposes."

"That's nothing new," said Polly. "That kind of work has been going on for years . . ."

"Robin thought that the advances in bioengineering were opening up possibilities for a new kind of warfare. I found some back issues of *New Scientist* in the library. There were a load of articles on military adaptations of genetic research. They made it sound pretty terrifying . . ."

"Like what?"

"If you can adapt a virus to attack cells with a certain genetic combination, you have the means for a kind of genocide that would make Hitler's ovens seem like a Hansel and Gretel story."

"That sounds a little science fiction to me, Joseph . . ."

"I'm not saying it's definitely happening right now, Polly. But according to those articles, ideas are being floated . . ."

"How would something like that work, Joseph? And why would someone want to do it, anyway?"

"Think about it, Polly. The cellular structures of certain groups of people are almost like fingerprints. In theory, you could easily create a virus that would attack these cells like a heat-seeking missile and kill them off."

"But why?"

"Why? Maybe for population control or social cleansing or getting rid of aberrant, uneconomic groups. Or maybe just to keep America clean and white."

130

Polly shook her head. "Listen, Joseph, you can postulate anything and make it sound possible. But we're trying to figure out what happened not too many days ago in a lab here in San Francisco. We're not trying to take a time machine to Brave New World. It doesn't sound to me like you came back with much hard information."

He put down his cup and glared at her. "You want hard information?"

"Yeah." She patted her belly. "We don't have the time to play space cadets."

"Well, a couple of days before the lab explosion, Malcolm had been busted by the cops. Is that hard enough for you?"

Polly's eyes popped open like rice shot from a gun. "Did Gasser tell you that?"

"Yep. You want some more hard stuff?"

She nodded.

"He was busted on suspicion of dealing in the narcotics trade."

"No kidding?"

"No kidding. More?"

"I don't know if I can stand it."

"He was arrested with a woman."

"A woman?"

"That's what I said."

"You going to give me a name?"

"How's Nicole Proust?"

"The French Croissant?"

"Yep."

She looked at him suspiciously again. "How does Gasser know all this, Joseph?"

"Because he bailed Malcolm out."

"What happened to Nicole?"

"He doesn't know. There wasn't any record of her arrest. And when Gasser took him to her hotel, they found she had left."

"Checked out?"

"They asked around and found someone who remembered her. She was in the company of two very large men."

"Jezus! How weird! Where did the cops bust them, Joseph? Did Gasser tell you that?"

"Inside the park."

"Golden Gate park? What were they doing there at night?"

"Good question, Polly. Malcolm didn't say. Gasser dropped him off at home. He never saw him after that."

Chapter 9

He had another bad night. He kept dreaming of viral bombs. They came in all colors as well as basic red, white and blue. They came in packs, like M & M's, with a guarantee not to muss your fingers. They had little tadpole tails that wiggled and squirmed. They seemed quite content to eat a cell for breakfast, lunch or dinner. They weren't choosy, like pregnant Pol. They didn't care about the sauce.

He felt a hand shake him once and then again.

He opened up his eyes. "You're not a viral bomb," he said.

"No. I'm on a short fuse, though."

He sat up. "Why's that?"

"Because I'm tired of answering all your phone calls."

He ruffled up his hair and opened and closed his eyes once or twice, just to make sure they worked. "It wasn't Gerry, was it? You should have woken me if it was Gerry . . ."

"No, it wasn't Gerry. The first one was somebody named Magee. Do you know someone named Magee, Joseph?"

"Yeah. I know Magee. Who was the other?"

"The other was weird. It was someone you don't know . . ."

"How do you know that?"

"Because he mispronounced your name. He sounded tough . . . uneducated . . ."

"Did he leave his number?"

"No. He didn't say who he was either. I tried to wake you, but you were sound asleep."

"Next time throw a bucket of water on my head," he told her as he struggled into his clothes.

"I'll remember that," she said. "Coffee's hot. It's in the kitchen . . ."

Magee was at his office when he phoned. Joseph was thankful that he was still sober enough to talk.

"What's up?" he asked.

"Got a story for you, Radkin. From an anonymous source . . ."

"Shoot!"

"Dateline: San Francisco. A reporter from the *Evening Blatter* has scoop. Certain documents have come into his hands regarding secret work in genetic research going on at university. Documents are given to editor at *Evening Blatter* and then are mysteriously lost . . ."

"When did this happen, Seamus?"

"Word started leaking the other day before the plumbers came in and fixed the pipes. Now we got a flood of speculation that they're busy trying to mop up."

"What's it about?"

"Nothing hard. But the term 'genesis' keeps cropping up. They say·something's been constructed and then let out of its cage. But what's interesting is how fast the iron curtain fell and how many lips have been zipped shut. Something big is going on—big enough to send in the tough guys to muzzle up our freedom-loving publisher."

"Who's the reporter, Seamus. Do I know him?"

"He's the science writer. A guy by the name of Draper— George Draper. I don't think you know him. He's only been here for six or seven months."

"Well what's he got to say about all this?"

"That's the strange thing, Radkin. He hasn't been seen for a while now. Nobody seems to know where the hell he is.'

Josephine Draper lived in a small flat on California Street, situated in an area that wasn't nauseatingly trendy, but wasn't the slums of Filmore either. She looked haggard and unkempt when she answered the door: a washed-out scarf was wrapped around her head; she had on a well-used housecoat.

"Sorry for the way I look," she said, excusing herself in a manner that made him understand she didn't really care what he thought.

"Thanks for letting me come over," said Joseph. "You should see the way I look in the morning."

134

"It's afternoon," she reminded him. And saying that she nervously lit a cigarette which had been hanging, virgin-like, from her mouth.

She ushered him into the living room and picked up some laundry from the sofa in order to make room for him to sit.

"You want something to drink?" she asked. She was already heading toward the kitchen. "Coffee or a beer?"

"Coffee will be fine," he said. He hadn't tested out his kidneys yet that day.

He glanced around. The place looked like her; slovenly, but underneath the mess a sense of former care. Knick-knacks were placed artistically on a row of shelves and, in between, an ashtray filled to overflow with half-used smokes. Fine prints sitting under polished glass were hanging crooked on the walls as if someone had come by and given them a shove. On the plush beige carpet were some dirty socks and a week's worth of scattered news. It all added up, he thought, to mental disarray rather than the purposeful disorder that existed in houses like his own.

He spotted a photo on the mantelpiece and went over to examine it. The picture was of her and some man, obviously in happier days.

"That photo on the mantelpiece—is that of you and George?" he called out.

"Yeah, back when he had hair. He looks different now. A little fatter, a little balder. He used to comb his hair down to hide the birthmark on his forehead . . ."

"Birthmark?"

"People mistake him for Gorbachev now." She came back in and handed him a cup of brownish brew. She had a glass of foam that she had kept for herself.

"How long has it been . . ." he started to say.

"Since I've seen him? About a week," she replied, sitting down in a chair flicking the ash from her cigarette into a nearby vase.

"I understand he was working on a story . . ."

She laughed abruptly. "He was always working on a story!"

135

"But this one, I think, was different."

"They were all different, Mr Radkin," she said, taking a drink of foam and then wiping her mouth. "You're a reporter. You should know."

He nodded. "Yes, but some are more different than others. Do you know what he was working on?"

She extinguished her cigarette by grinding it on to the glass of the coffee-table. Then she immediately lit another. She stared at him and said: "Maybe you should be asking who he was working on."

"All right, who was he working on?"

"She was about five-foot eight, blonde hair and blue eyes. She was young and pretty. I don't know her name." She took another drink of foam and then continued to stare at him in a combative way.

"I'm . . . sorry . . ." Joseph murmured.

She let out a humorless laugh. "Why? Wouldn't you jump at the chance to ditch an old bag like me?"

"I'm married to a woman who's as big as a house and growing bigger every day. We argue like cats and dogs. I wouldn't have it any other way," he said.

Her eyes had grown more sympathetic. "In that case, Mr Radkin, you'll never amount to anything in the newspaper trade."

"Maybe you're right," he said. "I don't like the business much anyway."

She laughed again. This time with some mirth. "You sounded pretty eager on the phone."

"Oh," he said, "don't get me wrong. I love the game. It's the papers and the people who run them I can't stand."

"Then maybe you should start one of your own," she suggested.

He shook his head. "That's like starting your own brewery," he replied. "Newspapers aren't much different. They just trade in stories instead of beer. It's pretty much the same thing."

"And you wouldn't buck the system, is that what you're trying to say?"

136

He reached for his own cigarettes and lit one up. "No, I buck it all the time. That's why I end up with such little work."

She got up from her seat and started back for the kitchen. "I'm opening up another beer," she said. "Why don't you join me this time?"

"What the hell? Why not?"

She came back in carrying two steins of foam. He half thought of explaining to her the intricacies of pouring a can of beer into a glass.

"What kind of articles had your husband been writing?" he asked.

She lit up the next cigarette in her chain and said, "I thought you knew. He was writing a series on obstetric issues. Anyway, in the course of his interviews he kept picking up on concerns about all the spontaneous abortions and births of children with deformities that's been happening lately."

Joseph put down his glass and stared at her. "Wait a second, I haven't heard about anything like that! Don't you think if stuff like that was going on there'd be a lot of publicity?"

"That's what the public health department said, too. They said they keep records and if there was a major statistical increase, they'd know about it."

"So he was obviously wrong . . ." said Joseph, feeling a sudden sense of relief.

"George didn't think so. He talked with too many people who were giving him the same story. They were concerned there was a major ecological problem that was being covered up."

Joseph nervously brushed his fingers through his hair. "It sounds pretty ridiculous. I mean things like that can't be covered up so easily. It's not like you can hide a bunch of deformed babies." His voice trailed off. He tried to light a cigarette and found his hand was shaking.

"Is there something wrong with you?" she asked, looking at him with a concerned expression.

"My wife's pregnant," he explained. "We're expecting a kid any second now."

She let out a sigh. "I see . . ." Then, after a momentary pause, she said, "He didn't mean that every baby was being born with two heads; the vast majority of births, he said, are normal. It's just that there's a statistical increase in abnormal births. But 'abnormal' can include things as minor as harelips or cleft chins." She smiled. "There's some famous actors with cleft chins. It hasn't done them any harm."

"I don't want my kid to be an actor," said Joseph, looking down at the ground. And then, lookng back up at her, he said, "What happened to the articles he was writing? How come I haven't read any of this in the paper?"

"Not many doctors are willing to go on record saying there's something like that going on. Sometimes there are statistical blips that make it seem like there's an epidemic on paper when, in actual fact, it's just a curious bunching of cases—like throwing dice and getting a series of sevens in a row."

"Maybe that's what it was," he said.

"Maybe it was. Anyway, George wrote his stories in a very low key and they were buried on page thirty-eight."

"But what did he think was going on?" he asked.

"A cover-up. Something like the thalidomide case where pregnant women took a drug that caused severe birth defects and the cause was withheld for fear of throwing a major company into bankruptcy."

Joseph puffed at his cigarette and felt a strange tightness in his chest. "Did he have any evidence?"

"I think so. But I didn't know it. Not until a week ago that is."

"What happened then?"

"That . . . woman . . . came by."

"The blonde?"

"She came to get some documents."

"What documents?"

"The Genesis Files. At least that's the name George had written on the packet."

"Do you know what they were about?"

She shook her head. "The woman did, though. She even

knew where George had hidden them. I didn't know they were here."

"She didn't offer any explanation?"

"No." She looked at him with a curious smile. "She seemed to be someone possessed . . ." Then she stopped for an instant and studied his face. "Rather like you, Mr Radkin."

He caught a bus down to the ocean and then walked along the beach. He took off his shoes and socks and let them dangle over his shoulder while he strolled into the surf and felt the ice-cold water send its shocking message to his brain.

Something bad was going on. He knew it now. Polly was nine months with child. Perhaps this evil, so terrible to comprehend, was in her too. And, if it was, what could he do about it except wait and pray that it wasn't?

He looked out into the ocean, into endless sea and thought about coming here some months before—with her. They had walked together, arm in arm, thinking of the future, no longer alone, but with their child. Joseph thought of running with her in the sand. They pictured what it would be like when they were three. Spinach would be on his shoulders, he imagined, laughing as they ran. Laughing . . .

He kicked the sand. "I'm frightened," he said to no one. "I'm frightened and there isn't a fucking thing I can do!"

He called her from a telephone box on Ocean Highway. He waited and counted each ring. When it reached ten, he told himself something was wrong. Then she answered the phone.

"Hello?"

He knew it from her tone of voice. "Polly, are you OK?"

"Oh, Joseph! Something terrible happened!"

"Polly! What is it?"

"I was on my way to hospital . . ."

"My God! You're going into labor!"

"No, Joseph! It's not me! It's your mother!"

"My mother? She's not pregnant, Polly. You are!"

"She fell down the stairs with a pot of hot chicken soup!"

139

"What? What are you talking about, Polly? What's chicken soup got to do with anything?"

"Listen to me Joseph! She fell! We called an ambulance. She's in hospital!"

"Is she OK?"

"I think so, but you never know with someone her age . . ."

"Where did they take her?"

"Mount Rushmore."

"But that's where you're going to deliver!"

"Yes. Oh, Joseph! I feel so guilty!"

"Guilty? Why do you feel guilty?"

"The chicken soup, Joseph! She was bringing it down for me!"

He stopped by the hospital to check on his mother and then he went back home.

Polly was in the kitchen brewing up a pot of coffee. She caught the look in his eyes when he came in.

"You mother will be all right," she said. "They'll just keep her in hospital a couple of days for observation."

"I know she'll be all right," he said. "She said her dying wish was that I feed you chicken soup and be nice to Morris. But if you want to know the truth, I think she decided to book a room there so she'd be the first to see her grandchild when it arrived. It's not my mother I'm worried about . . ."

"What is it then?"

Looking at her belly, he said, "Polly . . . what would . . . I mean, have you ever thought of . . ."

"What are you trying to say, Joseph?"

"What if Spinach wasn't quite right?"

"Quite right? I don't understand."

"Well, what if something went wrong. What if Spinach had a cleft chin or a harelip or something like that?"

She looked befuddled. "What of it, Joseph? What if it had blond hair and blue eyes?"

He took a deep breath and said it. "What if it had two heads?"

140

"Two heads?"

He nodded.

She smiled at him. "Don't worry, Joseph. I know expectant fathers are concerned about these things, but Spinach is going to be a perfect baby. Trust me."

"You're not concerned anymore?"

She shook her head. "I suddenly feel very calm. I'm not sure what happened, but suddenly I came to understand that everything was going to be all right."

"But what if it wasn't?" asked Joseph.

She took his hand and held it. "I need you to believe as well, Joseph."

He tried to smile. "I do," he lied.

"Good," she said. "Because it's going to happen soon."

He suddenly felt his heart skip a beat. "Really, Polly? How do you know?"

"I've been having contractions all evening."

"Why didn't you tell me? You should tell me when things like that happen!"

She looked unruffled. "There wasn't any reason to tell you. Sometimes you start having contractions and then they go away. It's just the uterus beginning to practice, that's all."

"It's happened before?"

"Yes."

"How do you feel now?" he asked nervously.

"They've gone away. But they lasted for almost three hours and they were getting quite intense."

He rubbed his head. "What does that mean, Polly?"

"It means that it could happen tomorrow or next week. False labor is a common phenomenon. Remember, they told us about it in birthing class."

He got up from his chair and shook himself as if trying to get free from a mass of cobwebs and said, "I think I want to go to sleep."

Chapter 10

It was the middle of the night. Joseph suddenly sat up in bed like a man who had just seen a snake in the sheets.

"Polly!', he shouted. "I got it!"

Her eyes popped open. "You really had it? Is it here?"

"Is what here?" He looked at her curiously.

"The baby! I dreamt that you were having the baby instead of me!"

"Polly, if guys could have babies do you think we'd put up with this nine-month thing?"

"I guess not," she agreed. She rubbed her eyes. "Why did you wake me up then?"

"Because I know what happened to Nicole Proust!" he gave her a wild look of sweaty midnight dreams.

"Can't it wait?" she asked.

"No! Don't you want to hear?"

His voice sounded so disappointed that she turned back over and said, "All right, Joseph. Tell me: what happened to Nicole Proust?"

"She was deported back to France!"

"How do you know that?" she asked.

"It's the only thing that makes sense!" He leaned closer to her and slapped his hand on the mattress for emphasis. "Why else wouldn't she be in prison?"

"Maybe the cops didn't think she was involved?" Polly suggested.

"That's nonsense! Two people caught in the park on suspicion of passing drugs? They're not going to let one of them go even if they don't think they are involved."

"They would if the other one was an undercover agent, Joseph."

For a moment it seemed as if Joseph was frozen in mid-air. Then, finally, regaining control of his voice he said, "No, not

Nicole. She wouldn't do a thing like that." He looked at Polly. "Would she?"

"You don't even know the woman, Joseph!" Polly said with exasperation.

He rubbed his chin. "Oh, yeah. Somehow, I thought I did . . ." Suddenly his eyes lit up again. "Then what about the bruisers who escorted her out of the hotel? Who were they if not Federal immigration men?"

"They could have been fellow undercover officers, Joseph. Did you think of that?"

"I'd prefer to think of them as immigration men."

Polly sighed. "Joseph, if someone is being held on immigration offenses, they're put in jail. They go before a judge and they have a hearing. They're not just carted off and put on a plane."

"They ship Mexicans back over the Rio Grande without batting an eye, Polly."

"They might do it to the Mexicans," said Polly, "but they don't do it to the French."

"Maybe," Joseph replied, sinking back into his thoughts, "maybe not."

"Can I go back to sleep now, Joseph?" she asked, turning on her side again.

"Yeah . . . sure." He got out of bed and put on his robe.

"Where are you going?" she asked.

"Go back to sleep, Polly. I want to look for my thinking cap."

She found him asleep in a chair by the telephone with an empty bottle of whisky in his hand. He was snoring loudly. She pried the bottle loose and then found a light cover to put over him.

The telephone rang. She picked it up quickly so as not to disturb him.

"Hello," she said.

"Hi," came the voice. "Is Radkin there?"

"Not enough of him to do you any good. Can I take a message?"

"Yeah, this is Rosen down at AP. He asked me to do a little checking for him. Tell him there's no record of any immigration order on a Nicole Proust. You got that?"

"Yes. Thank you. I'll tell him."

She hung up the telephone and went inside the kitchen to start the kettle. Then she sat down at the table and while she waited for the water to boil, she picked up the book she had been reading and opened it again.

Suddenly something clicked in her mind. She got up from the chair and went back to Joseph's study and rummaged around the mess on his desk looking for his phone book. When she located it, she paged through the listings until she found the one she was searching for. Then she went to the telephone and dialled the number.

Somewhere in his head a ray of light filtered through a crack. He wondered, for a moment, whether this fissure was permanent or temporary, Like a peek-a-boo hole in a soap bubble. He rubbed his bloodshot eyes and saw a blurry Polly standing over him. She was smiling—or so it seemed.

"You were right, you know," he heard her say.

"Right about what?"

"Your friend from AP phoned . . ."

Suddenly the world came into focus again. "I knew it! She was deported, wasn't she!"

"Before you get too smug, there's something I should tell you . . ." she began.

"What?" He was still high on the pleasure of solving at least a tiny mystery.

"Your friend said that there's no record of anyone named Nicole Proust having been deported . . ."

Her bucket of water quenched his flames. "Then what are we talking about, Polly? Why did you say I was right?"

"You were right in a way, Joseph. I phoned him back. There was no record of a Nicole Proust having been deported, but there was of a Nadine Poiret . . ."

"The inscription in the book I found at Malcolm's house!"

said Joseph, slapping the side of his face. "I knew I was on to something!"

"Don't I deserve a little credit?" asked Polly.

"I told you," he said, rushing to the telephone, "you'll get a mention in the by-line.'

They all spoke some form of English at *Libération*, even if they liked to pretend they didn't. At first the woman who finally took his call was reluctant to give him any information.

"But who are you?" she asked.

"I'm the editor of the *San Francisco Gazette!*" he shouted. "For crying out loud, lady, this is urgent! Does she work there or not?"

"She sends us the article from time to time," said the woman. "I give you an address if you wish to write . . ."

"Write? Are you kidding? We might all be dead by the time the postman rings her bell! Listen, have you ever heard of Godzilla?"

"I don't think so."

"Well he's a Japanese dinosaur who came out of a nuclear waste dump. If I don't get hold of Nadine in a hurry, it's very possible he'll climb up the Eiffel Tower and irradiate the entire city of Paris as well as the Palace of Versailles!"

In the end, she finally give him the phone number which he copied down with a triumphant flourish.

It was then that Polly came in with some coffee. "You got it?" she asked.

He sat back and tossed her a satisfied smile. "Polly, I could get the head of the American Cancer Society to give me a smoke and light it for me in a wind storm."

"Too bad I missed the master at work," she said, drinking the coffee.

"I thought that was for me," he said, in a voice teetering on caffeine deprivation.

"Ask me politely," she said.

"Polly, may I have some of your coffee?" he asked sweetly.

"No," she replied, drinking the rest down in a thirsty gulp.

He looked at her in disbelief.

"But since you asked me so nicely," she continued, after putting down her empty cup. "I'll bring you one of your own."

She left and he shook his head. "Meshugana woman . . ." he muttered to himself as he dialled the number he had written on his note-pad.

It took a while for the connection to get through. Then he heard the ringing of the telephone somewhere across the wide Atlantic.

Polly came back in with his coffee. "You calling her?" she asked, placing the cup down next to him.

He took a sip. "Yeah. No answer."

"Try again later," she suggested.

He looked at her. She was standing. What he saw was her bulge. And he remembered the two-headed baby and the stories about deformities Draper had so convincingly told to his wife.

"I've got to get through to her, Polly!" he said, clutching the phone tighter, as if that would help in some strange way.

She gave her belly a circular rub. "Suit yourself, Joseph," she said. "I'm going to lie down."

As she walked out of the study, Joseph suddenly heard a receiver being lifted somewhere in Paris.

"*Oui?*" A feminine voice came through as if it were in the other room.

"Hello! I'm calling from San Francisco to speak to Nicole Proust!"

There was silence on the other end. And then the voice said softly, "Who are you?"

"This is Joseph Radkin. I'm a friend of Malcolm Greene . . ."

"He's alive?" The voice was tremulous, as if wishing yet not daring to hope.

"I'm sorry . . ." said Joseph.

Again there was silence.

"I need to talk with you, Nicole," he said. "It's crucially important!"

146

"I'm afraid it is too late," she said. "I was on my way out. I must catch a plane."

"A plane for where?"

"Who are you?" she asked again, this time with more suspicion. "I have never heard Malcolm speak of your name."

"I'm a reporter. I did a story on his clinic."

She let out a short, ironic laugh. "That is what I told him, too."

"Nicole, Nadine, we must talk," he repeated. Then, looking up at the chart on the wall, he started reading off names. "I know about Robin and Dr Minh and Gasser . . ."

"Who is Gasser?" she asked.

"I know about the Genesis Files . . ." It was like throwing darts without knowing where the target was.

"I'm sorry, I must go," she said. Her voice sounded urgent. "I will miss my plane."

It was a last desperate step. He had to resort to honesty. "Nicole, please understand. My wife is pregnant. I need to know what's going on. It started as a story. Now it's my life!"

"But how can I help you?" she asked. Her voice sounded as pleading as his own.

"Just talk with me. That's all I ask."

"I tell you truly," she said. "My plane, it leaves for Vancouver in forty minutes. I will be back in one week's time. If you wish, you may call me then."

"One week is too late, Nicole. Isn't there somewhere I can call you in Vancouver?"

"I do not know my hotel. The arrangements have been made by the organisers."

"The organisers?"

"Of the convention where I will speak."

"What convention, Nicole? Please tell me!"

"I'm sorry . . ." Her voice sounded tearful. And then, suddenly, she hung up.

"Shit!" he hollered out.

"Joseph!" Polly called from the bedroom. "Is something wrong?"

147

He dialled the number again and waited for it to ring. Polly came into the study. "What's happening? Did you get a hold of her?"

"The fucking bitch hung up on me!" he shouted in anger.

"I'm sure she isn't the first one," said Polly. "Did you speak to her at all?"

"Yeah," he said. The phone was still glued to his ear. It was ringing now. "She came back to answer it. She said she was on her way to catch the plane."

"Did she say where?"

"Vancouver . . ."

"Vancouver, Canada or Vancouver, USA?"

"Canada, I guess. She was kicked out of America, remember?"

"So why are you calling her back, Joseph? If she left, she left."

"I was hoping she'd reconsider," he said. He slammed down the receiver, let out a curse, and buried his head in his hands. His voice was more a moan: "Polly, what are we going to do now?"

She smoothed back his hair, gently, as if she were stroking a cat. "We'll have the baby, Joseph. There'll be other stories, but there won't be another Spinach."

He looked up at her and she could see the tears in his eyes. "Polly . . ."

"What is it, Joseph?" She was becoming concerned at the violent change in his moods.

"Polly, I'm frightened."

She stroked his hair again. Her voice was calming. "You had a bad dream," she said. "It's over now."

"It's not a dream."

"Then I don't understand . . ." She gave him a questioning look.

What could he say, he wondered? What could he tell her?

He took her hand. "Polly," he said, "I have to go somewhere . . ."

"Will you be back for dinner?" she asked. And then she realised he wouldn't.

Chapter 11

It had happened so fast he hardly knew he was no longer in the US of A.

Several hours before, he had been poring over the airline schedules at Pippa's World Wide Travel office in what was once a neighborhood salami shop.

Pippa, who formerly had been a pre-school teacher but had decided after ten years of leaky noses and smelly bottoms that her talents would be better served by sending people on long journeys to strange and distant lands, looked at Joseph suspiciously and said, "If you want to go now, there's a flight out of Oakland that leaves in an hour and one from SF International that leaves in two."

"Can I be back by dinner-time?" Joseph had asked her.

"Why don't you just go home and smoke a joint?" Pippa had suggested. "It's cheaper and it takes less time."

Now he stood waiting at the Air Canada gate for flight 941 to arrive. It was the only direct flight from Paris that day. If she wasn't on this one, chances were she had told him what was known in the trade as a "cock and bull".

He didn't really know how he'd recognise her, but he was sure he'd think of something. He remembered the time he had to interview the draft dodger who was coming back from Sweden after fifteen years of exile. He knew it was him because he was whistling an old Phil Ochs song.

The passengers from the Air Canada flight out of Paris had just started to unload when Joseph saw a man running up to the arrival gate. He was young and wore a chauffeur's cap and was carrying a tiny blackboard on which was scrawled the name: "Nadine Poiret".

Joseph moved fast. In a moment he was by the young man's side. "Hey, you looking for Nadine Poiret? I saw a guy with a sign like yours pick her up just ten seconds ago . . ."

"No shit?" said the chauffeur.

149

"No shit. He had a hotel cap on . . ."

"Did it say Vancouver Hilton?" the kid asked.

"Yeah. Vancouver Hilton."

"Well that's where I was supposed to take her. Man did they get their wires crossed!" And letting out a stream of curses, the young chauffeur walked way.

Quickly, Joseph got a sheet of paper from his briefcase and scribbled Nadine's name in bold letters. He held it aloft, waving it back and forth as the passengers began to stream from the restricted passageway.

And then he saw her. He knew her at once. It was as if he had seen her somewhere before.

She came up to him and smiled pleasantly. She had a certain charm, he thought, the kind of self-possession that puts chauffeurs at ease.

"I am Nadine Poiret," she said.

He returned her smile with a grin. "Yes, I know . . ."

"Excuse me?" She glanced at him strangely.

"You look very French," he explained. And he winked. Then he glanced around, trying to decide in which direction to go.

"But aren't you the chauffeur?" she asked. She kept looking at him, as if she were trying to figure something out.

"Yes," he said, as he helped the cabby load her baggage. "But my car broke down."

"Then why didn't they send another car?"

"I was already here when it happened." He held the rear door open for her. "Please get in."

She hesitated a moment and then smiled. "I hope I'm not being kidnapped."

"In a taxi?" He laughed as he slid into the cab after her.

"Where to?" asked the cabby, a smouldering cigar stub sticking out of his mouth, as he twisted his head toward the rear.

"Take us to the Hilton," said Joseph.

"Which one?" asked the cabby.

He was suddenly flustered. Wasn't one of them enough?

How greedy could Conrad get, he wondered. "The Vancouver Hilton," he replied. "We are in Vancouver, aren't we?"

The cabby made a face and spat a piece of tobacco out the window. "I know you want the Vancouver Hilton," he said with a growl. "I'm asking you which Vancouver Hilton you want? The one by the airport or the one in town?"

"The one in town," he said, guessing that's where a convention would be held—unless the one she was going to was about skydiving.

As they sped off, Joseph turned and looked at her. She had a worried expression on her face. Perhaps she was thinking of the last time she was in North America, he imagined.

"How was your flight, Nicole?" he asked, unconsciously using her other name. And then he realised his mistake.

Her face suddenly became tense. She stared at him without speaking.

"Better than mine, I hope," he said quickly. If the jig was up, he thought, the only thing left to do was to talk fast. "Christ! Was it bumpy! I'm sure glad Polly didn't come or she would have definitely dropped the kid ten thousand feet in the air . . ."

"Who are you?" she asked, still staring at him intently.

"Joseph Radkin. I spoke with you earlier today—remember?"

Her face was still tense. She tried to speak. "Did you . . ." Her voice dropped off.

"Did I what?"

There was a look of distaste in her eyes: ". . . hurt the man who was to meet me?"

"Hurt him? Why would I hurt him?"

"That's good," she said with some relief.

Joseph let out a chuckle. "Say, who do you think I am, Nicole?"

It was as if she could barely say the words: "The FBI? The CIA? The secret police? They are all the same to me."

"Someone once accused me of that before and I got so angry I did something I regretted later," he said with annoyance.

151

"Did you shoot them?" she asked, looking at him with some trepidation.

"No," he replied, smiling at her accent. "I didn't shoot them. I squirted mustard from a plastic jar . . ."

"Squirted mustard from a plastic jar?" She made a face. "I do not understand . . ."

"Into her eye, Nicole. Into her eye . . ."

"Oh," she said as if it all made sense now. "I see."

"Well she didn't—the woman I squirted mustard at, that is. Not for a while, anyway."

"Then you are really a reporter?" She said it without much conviction.

"Yes," he assured her. "Really."

Her brow became creased in thought again. "How did you find me?" she asked.

"In the Yellow Pages."

"The Yellow Pages? What are you talking about?"

"I'm just joking," he said, pulling out a pack of cigarettes from his jacket pocket. "Do you mind if I smoke?"

She shook her head. "I am very confused, Mr . . ."

"Radkin . . . Joseph Radkin. I'm confused, too, Nicole," he said, lighting up. "That's why I wanted to meet with you." He held out his pack. "You smoke?" Then he suddenly remembered. "Of course you do. You left a trail of cigarettes all over Malcolm's dinner table."

"Then you are the police!" She crossed her arms and looked away.

"I'm not the police, Nicole, and I think you know that. I was in Malcolm's house hoping to collect some clues to his murder before the cops got to it. Unfortunately, I was too late . . ."

She stared straight ahead, not looking at him. But her face had begun to flush.

"What did you want from him, Nicole?" he asked.

She didn't answer.

"Nicole," he said in a quieter voice, "I came all the way from San Francisco to talk with you because I think you're the only one who knows what happened to Malcolm before he . . ."

152

Her face was red. Tears had started to well from her eyes.

"I don't want to upset you, Nicole. But it's not only you. Many lives are at stake, I think . . ."

There was a strange sort of lighting in the hotel bar; it came through rose colored filters and was made to shine directly on the ferns. Like many drinking holes it was designed to ease ones passage into inebriation without hurting the eyes—a fact the liquor industry knows quite well: bright lights and alcohol don't mix.

They found a corner table and sat down. The pre-recorded music in the background was playing an old Gershwin tune. A dolled-up waitress took their order with a syrupy smile.

"So, what can I get you two lovebirds to drink?" she asked.

"We're not lovebirds," said Joseph. "Just friends."

The waitress gave him a knowing wink. "OK, just friends."

"May I have a Martini?" asked Nicole.

"Sure, honey. You like it dry?"

"Oh, no!" she said. "I mean Martini and Rossi. Red. With a little ice and lemon."

"Gotcha," said the waitress. "Red vermouth on the rocks with a twist."

Joseph ordered a whisky. No ice. No twist of lemon.

The waitress left. Joseph turned to her and said, "Thanks, Nicole."

"What are you thanking me for?" she asked.

"For having a drink with me."

"We haven't had our drink yet," she replied.

"I mean, thanks for agreeing to talk with me."

He thought it strange that she looked less vulnerable here in this den of iniquity than at the airport.

Nicole lit up a cigarette and drew in some smoke. "I'll tell you what I know," she said. "But in the end you may understand even less than you did before."

"I understand nothing now," Joseph replied. "Anything you tell me would be like giving coins to a pauper. When you're as broke as me, even pennies seem a lot."

153

"When we spoke on the telephone you said you knew about the Genesis Files . . ." she said, looking into his eyes.

"I know they exist. I know they connect Malcolm to Krohl. But I don't know what they are."

"And what do you know about me?" There was a tiny smile on her face: it had a mixture of intrigue, irony and pathos.

What did he know about her? he wondered. He took a puff at his cigarette and said; "I know you were posing as a writer from *Libération*."

"I do write for them occasionally," she interjected.

"Yes . . . well, you told Malcolm you were doing an article on world health."

"That was true . . ." she put in.

"But that wasn't your main reason for seeing him, was it?"

"Perhaps not," she said. And her eyes grew sad again.

"I know you met his sister Robin some years before at a scientific convention held in Sweden and that you gave her a book on the making of the first atomic bomb. You signed it Nadine Poiret. Is that your real name or is it Nicole Proust?

"They are both my real names," she replied.

"I don't understand," he said. "Do they give children two first and last names in France?"

"I was a war orphan," she explained. "I did not know my parents. The family who raised me gave me their name. Later, when I grew up, I found out I had another name as well."

"I see," he replied, without truly understanding what she meant. "But getting back to Robin, what was she like when you met her?"

"She was so young and innocent then . . ." Nicole said. She gazed across the room into the soft light. "She had come to a lecture I had given on the nature of scientific discovery. She had never really considered the question of ideology before."

"What do you mean?" asked Joseph.

"The idea that the scientific process does not happen in a vacuum, but flows from currents of thought associated more with the political world than that of science itself."

"As both a woman and a scientist," said Joseph, "how could she not have known that?"

Nicole pressed her lips together. "It doesn't seem unreasonable to me. Young scientists want very much to believe in the objectivity of their field. And in their limited experiences, perhaps they are right. They haven't felt directly the powerful tide of grants and funds which push everything in certain predetermined ways."

Joseph took a drink of whisky, then flicked the ash from his cigarette into his cuff. "It's really no different than anything else," he said. "We all live with the axe hanging over our heads."

"Science is different because of the time in which we live," she replied. "If technology has become our religion, Mr Radkin, then scientists have become our priests. They have been given temples in which to perform their acts of deliverance. They believe they have been blessed by God, but, in fact, they often end up working for the Devil."

She looked and sounded very sure of herself, he thought. "I'm sort of partial to stereo and TV, myself. And, frankly, I wouldn't mind a dishwasher if I could afford one."

"I'm not talking about uninventing electricity, Mr Radkin," she said crossly, as if accusing him of sloppy thinking. "I just don't want it to be hooked up to people's genitalia."

"That's the work of sadists, Nicole, not kids doing their post graduate studies on the workings of electrons."

Her voice was calm again, but she was obviously making great efforts to keep her patience. "I might remind you, Mr Radkin, that the atomic bomb was made by people you would have been proud to have known. They were kind, gentle and very naive."

Joseph raised his eyebrows. "Are you a scientist, Nicole?"

"I am an anthropologist."

"What do you do when you're not chasing around the world lecturing young graduates on the evils of their profession?"

"Do you mean what did I do before I became involved in trying to save the earth from total annihilation?"

155

"Yes, that too."

"I was an ethnologist."

"I'm sorry to be unclever, but what exactly is an ethnologist?"

"I studied the origin and structure of certain societies. I was especially interested in the few tribal groups that managed to last into our century without having been affected by what we like to call 'the modern world'."

"You mean there are some left?"

"A few. Some in Amazonia. Some in the South Pacific. My interest was French Indochina."

"Vietnam?"

"Yes—Vietnam, Cambodia, Laos."

"That area not affected by the modern world?" He let out a short, ironic laugh. "You must be joking!"

"Now, of course. What has been done to them is irreversible. But even until the 1950s there were tribes of people in the Central Highlands of Annam who lived as their ancestors had a thousand years ago. They had no farms or industry. They had no calendar to tell the month or year. They gathered what they needed from the forest. History to them was remembered by what part of the jungle they had eaten when a great event took place."

"The Montagnards!" said Joseph. "You mean the Montagnards!"

"Yes," she said. "The mountain people. The ones whose forests were sprayed with Agent Orange, White and Blue. The colors of your flag, I think, if you see orange as a pale red."

"Your flag flies the same colors as ours, I believe, Nicole."

"Of course," she said. "Our nations are the same. The politics today are the politics of science and industry. Europe and America have formed a brotherhood of terror."

"Which you've vowed single-handedly to stop?"

"Which I and others have vowed to expose."

"By bombing labs?" He stared at her.

She lowered her eyes. "Malcolm was . . . a friend. I would not have hurt him."

156

"That doesn't answer the question, Nicole . . ."

She looked up. He could tell little from her eyes; they hid whatever secrets they might know behind a soft, brown veil. "The answer to your question, Mr Radkin, is that I am a coward."

"I'm sure you're not a coward, Nicole," he said.

The same eyes, so soft and gentle just moments before, now looked harsh. "That is something one can only determine for one's self, Mr Radkin," she said sharply.

"I suppose you're right," he agreed. He took another sip of whisky and then he asked, "What did you want from him, Nicole? Why did you come?"

She ran her finger around the rim of her glass. "I was sent by our committee . . ." she began.

"Your committee?"

"At the Conference of Concerned Scientists, we had divided up into action groups of interest. Some dealt with nuclear research, some with biological. I was especially interested in genetics."

"I thought you were an ethnologist," he said.

"Genetics, historically, has been the scientific rationale for genocide—a subject that interests most ethnologists, Mr Radkin. Eugenics, or the purification of a people through artificial selection, predates Hitler."

"Genetics also paved the way for abundant food supplies and cures for pretty bad diseases. It probably saved a lot of people, too, Nicole."

She closed her eyes for a moment. "The good that people do cannot be balanced against evil. The logical end of nuclear physics was the creation of the atom bomb to destroy large things that stand upon the earth in great explosions. The logical end of genetic engineering will be the creation of a microscopic device to destroy the tiniest of living things, the framework of our cells, in small invisible explosions. Of the two, the small and silent genetic bomb will cause more devastation than the loud and ugly atomic one."

"That's a pretty cynical view of the future."

"It's a realistic one, Mr Radkin. Look at our arsenal. We have the most murderous weapons imaginable. Could we possibly need more? Yet they are being created every day. If something more terrible, more lethal, and more secret could possibly be created, rest assured, it will be done."

"So your committee, the one you formed about genetics, was acting as a watchdog?"

"We tried to keep abreast of research programs that we deemed significant."

"And something in San Francisco attracted your eye?"

"We kept watch on certain key people. People who were well established in the field."

"Krohl was one, I suppose."

She nodded and took one of his cigarettes from the pack he had left on the table. He took out his lighter and lit it for her. "Yes, Krohl was one. Robin had been assigned to follow his research."

"What did she discover?" he asked.

She inhaled lightly and blew out the smoke. "Many questions. Few answers."

"But enough to make you want to continue your investigation."

"Yes." She puffed nervously on her cigarette again.

"And then one day you didn't hear from her. She had disappeared. You decided to come investigate yourself."

"We heard that she had made some discoveries through an informant at the highest of levels."

"Who was the informant?"

Nicole shrugged. "His name is unknown to me. I became worried for her safety and came to investigate."

"And that's why you contacted Malcolm."

"Yes. He was my link to both Robin and Krohl."

He stared at her through the hazy light. "Nicole, why didn't you just tell Malcolm about your concerns straight out? Robin was his sister after all. Why all the subterfuge?"

She drank her Martini and then looked down at the empty glass. "I knew Malcolm through Robin. She was very close to

158

him . . . perhaps too close. Their parents had died when she was a young girl. He took care of her, saw to her education; in short, he was more a father than a brother. Relations like that tend to be very confused."

"All relations between men and women, brother and sister, parent and child, tend to be confused, Nicole."

She showed the slightest of smiles. "Then, let us say that their relationship was particularly confusing. Malcolm had a difficult time seeing her as an independent woman. When she would present certain ideas to his attention, he tended to minimise their importance like many fathers do with their daughters."

"Or sons." Joseph put in.

"Perhaps . . . anyway, she had decided that she couldn't put her confidence in him without compromising her activities."

"She was afraid he'd blow the whistle on her?"

She shook her head. "No. She was just afraid he might have presented her with obstacles that would endanger others."

"So you approached him as a journalist. You just appeared one day out of the blue?"

"As I told you, I actually was writing an article for *Libération*. I had sent them a letter before I came. Unfortunately, the hospital was in crisis when I arrived."

"Malcolm was in the middle of his salmonella investigation, wasn't he?"

"Yes." Nicole fingered her cigarette. Her eyes looked distant again, as if pulling the event once more from the reaches of time. "He was quite . . . how shall I say . . . anxious when we first met."

"I'll bet he was!" said Joseph. "The crap was about to hit the ever loving fan, wasn't it? How did you get any time out of him at all?"

She shrugged. "He invited me to lunch."

"He took you to the Cherry Blossom, right? He introduced you to his friend, Johnny Lim."

"*Oui . . .*" She smiled. "A charming place. There is one like it where I have often gone in Paris. It is on Rue de la Boetie."

"What did you talk about? Did you really interview him, Nicole?"

"Yes, of course. I had done some research, you see. Malcolm had written an article for UNESCO about caring for the urban poor which I had read. He was quite surprised."

"I can imagine . . ." said Joseph, wondering, like most writers, whether anyone would ever admit to reading his stuff.

"There was also an article in *Time*."

"*Time* magazine had written about him?" Joseph found, to his great displeasure, that he was actually impressed.

"It was about the growth of alternative medical care. Malcolm was only briefly mentioned."

"Oh . . ."

"But he made small of his accomplishments," she said. "He was a modest man."

"What kind of questions did you ask him?" he said, more out of professional curiosity than anything else.

The smoke from their cigarettes formed a little cloud between them. "I asked him the obvious ones. Questions about funds."

"He must have been delighted with that," said Joseph sarcastically.

"In fact what he said was that funding was not his major problem."

"He said that?" asked Joseph with surprise. "I thought he was on the brink of being shut down!"

"He meant it in the larger sense. The problem he saw was the changing view of health and of disease. He said the rich saw health as a property they had a right to possess, like a fancy car or a country house. He said they saw disease as a consequence of being poor."

"Some people see disease as a divinely inspired form of population control," said Joseph. "Did you ask him about Krohl?"

She glanced back up at him. "Yes. Of course."

"How did he react?"

"He was disappointed. I think he suspected I was using him to get to Dr Krohl."

"But you were, Nicole, weren't you?"

She blinked and puffed nervously on her cigarette. "I suppose I was in the beginning . . . but that was before I knew him." She looked into his eyes. "Perhaps I am not a very good spy, Mr Radkin. Spies do not fall in love."

"Of course they do, Nicole," he said. "It's just that most spies never meet anyone worth loving, that's all."

"But he was very kind," Nicole continued. "He said that he would introduce me, if that was what I wished."

"And you set up an appointment?"

"Of course, that was difficult. At any other time, it would have been quite easy. But Malcolm was obsessed with his task. He had no time at all."

"So what did you do, Nicole?" This was part of the story he knew nothing about and he was anxious to hear her reply.

"I had information of a meeting at the university. It was a symposium on genetics and Dr Krohl was going to speak. I suggested Malcolm accompany me. It was in the evening, you see."

"Did he accept?"

"He said it would depend on his work. I was to phone him the next day at dinner-time."

"And, of course, you did," said Joseph.

"Yes." She let out a tiny laugh, remembering. "He had quite forgotten, you see. By then he had other things on his mind."

"By that time he had met with Dr Minh, hadn't he?"

"You know of Minh as well?" She looked at him with undisguised admiration. "You should be the spy, Mr Radkin. Not me."

"Are you offering me a job, Nicole?" he asked, pleased as punch to have his talents recognised at last. But then, suddenly recalling the mystery he had discovered, he asked. "Do you know about the buffalo?"

"The buffalo?" she said in a voice filled with absolute amazement. "But you couldn't have been there!"

161

"I wasn't," he said. "I was asking if you knew what it meant. Minh's son had told me that's where his father had gone. 'To visit the buffalo,' he said. Or perhaps, 'To visit Buffalo'—the city. It wasn't clear."

"It was the park," she said.

He looked at her curiously. "I don't understand."

"He was obsessed, you know, with finding the eggs, because he was convinced that they could prove the salmonella had been transmitted through Lim's birthday cake."

"So he went back to Dr Minh. Hoping he would lead him there."

"Yes. Minh took him to the park."

"The park?"

"That wonderful forest which takes up half your city."

"You mean Golden Gate Park," said Joseph.

"Of course. Malcolm told me how he followed Dr Minh through the forest that day, through vast fields of grass and heather and yucca plant and then through thickets wild and overgrown with thistles and prickly blackberry vines . . ."

"But where were they headed?" asked Joseph.

"To the bamboo," said Nicole. "Minh said he was taking him to the giant bamboo."

"This was in the night? How could they see?"

"Malcolm said the moon was bright. And Minh knew his way quite well. He described the scene to me, so I almost felt I was there. They walked for a long time. When they came to a small clearing among the bamboo stalks, they stopped. Minh squatted on the ground and told Malcolm they would rest.

"They waited a while and soon he heard a rustling through the leaves and a crackling of twigs. Then he heard soft murmurs, the sound of voices in the breeze. And through the stalks he claims he saw the glow of almond eyes . . ."

"What happened then?" asked Joseph.

Nicole shrugged. "I do not know . . ."

"He left you hanging?" asked Joseph in disbelief.

"It's very strange. Malcolm said he had a vision," Nicole

went on, "a recurring dream that had come to him ever since the war. Lately, it was happening more frequently."

"Did he describe this dream to you?"

She nodded. "It was always the same: a brilliant, red, ferocious sun rising over a field of rice; a water buffalo trudging in the yellow mud; in the distance, acrid curls of smoke."

"And?"

"That was all he said."

"You mean he had this dream right there in the middle of Golden Gate Park, in a field of bamboo, surrounded by a bunch of glowing almond eyes? The guy's got guts, I'll say that for him."

"Malcolm's condition was rare," Nicole continued, "but it was well known to doctors. I have asked about it and have found out that often these visions are associated with momentary blackouts that last for only a few seconds; they are so short that life goes on as normal, except for the little space of time which was lost to the conscious mind."

"So what happened that day in the park, Nicole?"

She made a movement with her lips—the kind of movement French people do which seems almost like a pout, but, in fact, is really a facial shrug. "Who can say? But one minute Minh was there, crouching by his side. The next minute he was gone . . ."

"And the almond eyes?"

"They had disappeared as well."

Chapter 12

Time had passed without their knowing. In this bar where businessmen made their deals over a glass of Canadian Club or Jack Daniels on the rocks, where high-class hookers plied their midnight trade and where other women's husbands and other men's wives found some momentary solace in each other's lugubrious company; here in this place of liquored dreams and alcoholic nightmares they sat and talked.

"What time do your meetings start?" asked Joseph. "What conference is this, by the way?"

"It's a convention of anthropologists," she said. "a terrible bore. They argue back and forth about the ruins of yesterday, yet so few of them can bear to think about the ruins of tomorrow."

"So why are you here?" asked Joseph.

"I was invited to present a paper."

"On what subject?"

"The tribal mind in the modern age," she said. And then she smiled. "Rather what we have been speaking of, is that not so, Mr Radkin?"

He found that without realising it he had been captivated. Maybe it was her brown eyes which seemed to speak so forcefully and yet were so gentle and, at times, even sad. And suddenly he understood how Malcolm Greene, a sensible doctor devoted to his work. might have ditched it all to fall in love with her.

"Perhaps we could get a bite to eat, Mr Radkin." Nicole suggested. "I haven't had much food today and now I feel quite famished." She tilted her head in a charming way, waiting for his response.

"OK," he replied, getting up, "but not in the Hilton. I didn't bring much money with me." He grinned. "Coming here was kind of a spur-of-the-moment thing."

"Then I have the privilege of taking a guest with me to

dinner. You see, Mr Radkin, academics who give papers at conferences rarely pay for meals."

"It's obvious that I'm in the wrong line of work," he said. His stomach agreed by sending forth a loud, gurgly growl.

They walked together back into the lobby and then took the corridor which led to the restaurant.

He glanced at her walking beside him. She was very beautiful, he thought. She seemed to glide as he tripped along, stumbling every once in a while over the loose bit of sole which had detached itself from the bottom of his shoe.

"Could I ask you a question?" he said, turning to her as they went.

"What would you like to know?" She looked at him sympathetically, without the mistrust that was present in her eyes before.

"Why did you decide to talk with me?"

"Perhaps I needed to talk with someone . . ."

"You haven't spoken of this with anyone till now?"

"Not about the personal things . . ." she said. Her face tightened again. "Sometimes, they say, you can tell things to a stranger that it would be impossible to tell people you know well."

"But how do you know you can trust me?" he asked. "I mean, you can trust me, but how did you decide that you could?"

"How do you know you can trust me, Mr Radkin?" she replied, before gliding into the dining room at the behest of the overgracious *maître d'*.

The restaurant was posh and pretentious, without the atmosphere of a decent dining hall. He felt uncomfortable being in a place like this, especially without a tie. But the last time he had worn a tie had been five years ago when he had applied for a job on the *Daily Blatter*. After the job was given to a young punk who had just graduated from the Columbia School of Unbiased Journalism (or the "Used Car School of Penmanship", as he liked to say) he had fashioned it into a noose in order to hang the managing editor in effigy.

Nicole, on the other hand, being French, appeared to be much more at ease.

The maître d' had led them to a corner table and, pulling out the chairs for each of them in turn, had sat them down. Then, handing them each a huge, unwieldy menu, he departed to seek a more affluent breed of clientele.

"Shall we have the buffet?" she asked, pointing to the elaborate pile of food heaped upon several longish tables.

"You sure you don't want to go out for a hamburger or something?" he asked her, hopefully, after glancing at the listings in the fancy printed sheet and then putting it down under his napkin like an unpaid bill with several months of accrued interest added on.

"What is this love affair you Americans have with ground meat on a bun?" she asked.

"The price," he replied. "When I was a kid there was this place called White Castle. You could get ten burgers for a buck. There was hardly any meat in them but they were loaded up with so much pepper and grease you couldn't tell the difference anyway. Man, they were really great!"

"It sounds disgusting!" said Nicole.

"Of course it seems disgusting to you! You're French! You eat things like frog legs and snails!" He said accusingly.

She laughed. "To tell the truth, my favorite lunch is a small salad and some cheese."

"That's why you're so thin, Nicole. I'll tell you what. Come visit us in San Francisco and Polly will fatten you up with a pasta sauce like you've never tasted in your entire life!"

"Polly is your wife?"

"She claims to be when it suits her. Right now it suits her."

"You do not get along?"

He shook his head. "We get along great. If she says po-tay-to, I say po-tah-to. If I say to-may-to, she says to-mah-to. It's the secret of our successful relationship."

166

"And you are going to have a baby? You said to me over the telephone . . ."

He stopped his cocky chatter and looked down at the table. He pressed his lips together and said, "That's what the doctors say." Then, glancing up at her, he said, "What do you think, Nicole?"

"I think it is not such a good time to be having babies," she said. And then she looked away. "Perhaps I will have the buffet. Will you join me?"

"Sure. If you're going to throw your money away, might as well do it up big, huh?"

They walked over to the buffet table. Each of them took a plate and made their way along the periphery, scooping in salads and meats and fruits and cheeses until there wasn't any room for more.

"What do you think they do with all the unused food at the end of the day?" asked Joseph as they brought their plates back to the table.

"Perhaps they feed it to the staff," Nicole suggested.

"Some places have slop trucks that come around and take the leftover stuff away. Then the guy who has the slop truck sells it to the farmers for their pigs."

"The pigs around here must eat very well," said Nicole, tasting her salads.

"Pigs before people. That's the motto of the western world, Nicole."

"But the pigs are chopped up after they have eaten," she replied.

"And after they are chopped up they are fed to other pigs," said Joseph. "Bigger pigs eat lesser pigs and so forth and so on until you reach the greatest pig of all."

"Who is that?" asked Nicole.

"The pig that I am after," said Joseph. "The porker who doesn't want the rest of us to live in peace."

She laughed. "Poor Joseph," she said. "I'm afraid you won't find your terrible pig."

167

"And why is that?" asked Joseph, holding a load of shrimp before his mouth.

"Because he doesn't exist. We like to think of him as some medieval dragon. And like brave knights, our mission is to slay the beast. But that is just a fable to protect us from the awful truth: there is no dragon. We have only ourselves to blame."

"Does that mean we have to cut off our own heads?" asked Joseph.

"It means we have to look elsewhere to find the source of our distress. If it were just a question of slaying the chief pig, our problems would have been solved long ago."

Joseph pondered her words and then replied, "You contradict yourself, Nicole. Before, back in the bar, you spoke with missionary zeal about the terrors that science has created in this world."

"I spoke before of a world gone mad, Joseph. I spoke of good people who do evil things; not of chief pigs whose death would set things right again."

"So if I find the source of this 'distress', as you say, what then? How do I proceed?"

"Then you become a teacher," she said.

"Like you?"

She shook her head. "No. Not like me . . ."

"Like Malcolm?"

"It was too complex even for a man like him."

He looked into her eyes. "Did you know that he was a morphine addict?" Joseph asked.

"Is that what they accused him of?" she asked. "They will say many things to discredit someone they despise."

"Who is 'they'? The chief pig or the good people who do evil things?"

"There are also evil people who do evil things," she said, her face showing signs of stress again. "But they are not all chief pigs. They are usually petty pigs who think they are chief pigs."

"What if we slay the petty pigs, Nicole?"

"There are too many petty pigs to slay. They breed like rabbits."

168

"Then I suppose we have to get rid of the rabbits," he said.

She smiled, a tired, unhappy smile. "Do you know what happened in Australia?" she asked.

"You mean besides the invention of the boomerang?"

"They once had too many snakes there. So they brought in the rabbits. The rabbits ate the snakes but then they had too many rabbits. And the rabbits ate the crops. So they brought in some scientists and one of them remembered how the Spanish slew the Aztecs when they conquered Mexico."

"With guns?" asked Joseph.

"With disease," replied Nicole.

"And that's how they killed the rabbits?" Joseph looked at her unbelievingly.

"They released a virus, similar to a strain of measles. Within a year the vast majority of the rabbits were dead."

"But how about the other animals?" asked Joseph. "How about the people?"

"They claimed the disease was specific to rabbits."

"But how did they know for sure?"

"They didn't. But in scientific terms, if you cannot see an effect, therefore it does not exist."

"Like tonsils, I suppose. If you can't see the use, then why not chop them out?"

"It is that arrogance of science, and our faith in its supremacy, which is killing off the smaller things: rabbits, snakes, and Montagnards."

Joseph glanced down at his plate. "I hope rabbit, snake or Montagnard wasn't on the menu today." And then, looking back up at her, he said, "Go on with your story, Nicole. What happened next?"

She finished her salad and wiped her lips, delicately, with the tip of the napkin. "The following day, Malcolm wrote up his report and presented it to Elias Hobbs at the hospital. Hobbs was skeptical, as you can imagine, especially since there were patients who hadn't eaten cake and had come down with salmonella.

"Malcolm told me that Hobbs was under pressure to present

the board with a final report in the next several days. But without any definite evidence, Malcolm could only present them with speculation. And there was something else as well. Malcolm said that Hobbs's attitude had changed. It was as if Hobbs was no longer in control . . ."

"So what you're saying is that Malcolm felt even more impelled to check out the duck eggs."

"And that meant finding Minh again . . ."

Joseph rubbed his chin. "How did you get back with Malcolm? I mean he certainly wouldn't have had time to go dancing, would he? What happened when you called him?"

"I didn't telephone him. He telephoned me."

"Why?"

"All the pressures on him had increased his concern about Robin. When he came home from work that day he decided to go into her room and search through her things. And that's when he found some medical records she had taken from the hospital. They had to do with rare forms of carcinomas in female reproductive organs . . ."

"And they were part of the university study directed by Krohl. Am I right?"

She nodded.

"But how did he link that to you, Nicole?"

"He also found a book I had given to Robin . . . inscribed with my name."

"You mean the book about the atomic bomb? But that was signed by Nadine Poiret, wasn't it?"

She smiled. "Malcolm was not stupid. The names are too similar to ignore. Besides, he found my picture on Robin's dresser."

"What did he say to you when he called?"

"Not much. He said he would pick me up that evening and take me to the symposium . . ."

"The one on genetic engineering that Krohl was to address?"

"Yes. At that time he didn't tell me of his suspicions. He let me believe that he was just being kind, that's all."

"But he had already begun to start piecing things together, I suppose. There was Robin's disappearance and the discovery of the records she had taken. There was Malcolm's feeling that things were strangely out of control in the hospital. And then there was you, the mysterious French Croi . . . I mean, lady, suddenly appearing under the pretense of doing an article on his clinic but, in fact, wanting to meet the very man whom Robin was clearly out to get."

"May I have one of your cigarettes?" she asked.

He took out his pack and gave one to her. "What happened when he picked you up?" Joseph asked, lighting her cigarette as she leaned close to get the flame.

"We went together to the university. The meeting was held at one of the very big lecture halls, but even so, it was quite difficult to get inside."

"The subject of genetics creates a lot of passion now," said Joseph. "Twenty years ago, when I was in school, it was something that only interested people who lived in monasteries."

"But it was more like a circus or a religious event than a meeting," said Nicole. "People had set up tables outside the hall, selling literature on the various paths to spiritual salvation. Inside, some were even waving placards with slogans like 'The Secret of Life Will Rest With God' and 'Don't Let Pandora's Box be Opened'."

"Sounds like the nuts were out in force for this one." said Joseph. "Did you see Krohl?"

"Yes. He was on the stage: a tall man, quite dignified, with fine white hair."

"I didn't think he was that old."

"He was in his late fifties, I believe."

"How was it arranged? Did he give a speech?"

"It was to be a symposium with various points of view. But feelings were so high, it was decided to have a question-and-answer session instead."

"What kind of questions were asked?"

"Basic ones, at first, such as why one would get involved in genetic engineering in the first place."

"What was Krohl's reply to that, Nicole?"

"He took the historical approach. The one that goes 'We have always sought the limits of our universe,' and 'From Copernicus and Galileo to Mendel, science has had to fight resistance to change.' Then he talked about how genetic engineering doesn't mean the random creation of new life but, rather, the improvement of the quality of the old. And that scientific breeding isn't a recent invention. He talked about how the ancient Egyptians knew their strains of wheat and processed them accordingly."

"But it didn't protect them against the locusts, did it?"

Nicole smiled. "You would have walked into his trap if you had asked a question like that. He would have said that only through genetic engineering can we finally construct a strain of wheat that would have survived the biblical plague. And who could be displeased with that?"

"Moses, I suppose," said Joseph.

Nicole laughed. "Malcolm told me Krohl once said it was that image of a vindictive God which pushed him into science!"

"So he could become a god himself?" asked Joseph.

"Someone stood up and asked that as well. He asked what Krohl thought of breeding a society full of supermen. Krohl replied that in order to breed a tribe of gods, one would have to develop a typology for a super race. And he wondered whether humanity would be a valued trait."

"Clever bugger!" said Joseph, showing signs of admiration.

"But there were some serious questions put to him by some women in the audience. One asked about the problem of checking amniotic fluid of embryos for congenital diseases. She asked whether we weren't on the road to plotting a genetic map of a 'perfect' child and, in fact, beginning a new eugenics program where mothers will be influenced to give birth only to children with certain so called 'positive' traits."

"And Krohl replied?"

"He thought the point was well made. He said that genetic counselling was a very serious business. He talked about the famous musician who had a congenital disease which caused

172

him a very painful death when he was forty. If that birth had been aborted, he said, the world would have been deprived of his magnificent artistry."

"A shrewd man, this Krohl," said Joseph. "Sounds to me like he had them eating out of his hand."

"He did," said Nicole. "Until . . ."

"Until what?"

"Until a man stood up and shouted for Krohl to explain about the Genesis Files . . ."

"What was his response?"

"Krohl seemed flustered. He tried to ignore the man and to go on to someone else. But the man persisted. He kept standing and shouting: 'Something happened in Vietnam, didn't it, Dr Krohl? Tell us about the Genesis Files!'"

"Did you know this man, Nicole?" asked Joseph.

She shook her head. "I never saw him before that day."

"And he had come to ask Krohl the same thing as you. Don't you find that strange?"

Staring at him with languid eyes, she said softly. "Yes. I find that very strange."

"What did he look like? Can you describe him, Nicole?"

"He was quite ordinary looking," she shrugged. "Your age, perhaps. Getting a little bald."

Joseph's hand went automatically to the top of his head, feeling for bare skin. "Did he have a strawberry mark up here?" he said, pointing to his forehead. "You know, like Gorbachev . . ."

"I wasn't close enough to see," she replied. "It was becoming very confusing and . . ." Her voice trailed off. She looked away.

"And what, Nicole?"

"I was becoming frightened. There were many policemen, both in uniform and dressed in ordinary clothes. When the man began to shout, they started to move forward. They were ugly, with leather faces and fat, like your football players are here. I felt it in the pit of my stomach. They were like the Gestapo . . ."

"Did they take him away?"

173

"The meeting became so disrupted, with people standing and shouting all around, that I could not see. We were seated near the back. I had to leave . . ." She glanced into his eyes and then looked down again. "As I said, I am not a courageous person."

"Courage doesn't always mean confronting the cops, Nicole," said Joseph. "What happened then?"

"I asked Malcolm to take me home."

"To your hotel?"

She looked into his eyes again. "No. To his house."

"I see . . ." Suddenly, he felt an obscene tingle run through his body.

"I didn't want to be alone."

"Of course. I understand."

"I think I would like some coffee," she said.

He signalled for the waiter and ordered coffee. Looking back at her, he saw her face had become slightly flushed. He took out his cigarettes and offered one to her. She took it and leaned toward him and he fumbled with his lighter. He fancied he could smell the scent of her perfume.

"How much do you want to hear?" she asked, looking boldly into his eyes.

"As much as you want to tell me," he replied. He lit a cigarette for himself as the waiter returned with their coffee. Then, stirring in two lumps of sugar, he settled back to listen.

"I knew he was attracted to me, of course. But he was very shy. When we were sitting next to one another at the meeting and our bodies would accidentally touch, at first he would move away. Later, he allowed himself to relax. By the end, our legs were pressed up against each other, in that hot stuffy auditorium. I could feel it. I'm sure he could, too. It's that moment when you know you'll eventually make love." She stirred her coffee and took a sip. Then she put her cup down again and looked into his eyes. "Do you know what I mean, Joseph?"

He blinked and then, nervously lowered his gaze. "I think so . . ."

"Anxiety often increases your desire. It's true with me . . ."

174

She inhaled some smoke and let it drift from her mouth, catching a tiny bit of tobacco with her tongue and then brushing it away.

"I know what you mean," said Joseph, rubbing the moist palm of his free hand against his trousers.

"Do you?" She smiled. "In a way, Malcolm was such an innocent. And yet, when we finally got to know each other, he told me stories of his experience with the whores in Vietnam that were quite amazing."

"He told you sex stories from the war?" Joseph asked in surprise.

"Just as I am telling you sex stories. But if you don't wish me to continue . . ."

"Go on," he said. And then he felt himself blush.

"It was a very hot night," she said. "Untypical of your foggy weather, Malcolm said. I asked for a cool drink. He went into the kitchen to open a beer. We were in the front room. I looked around at the books, the record collection . . ."

"Great jazz, not much literature. The good books are all in his bedroom." Joseph commented.

"Yes." She smiled, gently and looked away. "I walked down the hall. There was an open door to the left. I went inside the room. It was Robin's room—I could tell from the decor. I saw my book on her bed. I sat down to look at it. I turned to the inscription. Then I looked up. Malcolm was standing at the door. He said nothing. He walked towards me. Still he said nothing. He sat down by my side. I put my head on his shoulder. His hand was around my waist. I kissed his neck, tasting his sweat. Our lips met. Our tongues. He became passionate. His hands began to undress me. Very passionately. I tried to help. I understood his urgency. He laid me down on the bed. And then . . ." she looked into Joseph's eyes.

Joseph said nothing. He nervously puffed at his cigarette.

". . . then he began to cry."

"Cry?" Joseph felt a lump in his throat and tried to swallow it down.

"His face was on my breast. His tears were warm. He sobbed

175

like a baby. I smoothed his hair. I whispered that it was all
right for him to cry . . ."

Joseph lit another cigarette and stared at her.

"We lay there for a while. Then he got up. He apologised."
She let out a little laugh of irony. "Men always feel they have
to apologise . . ."

"That's all there was to it?" Joseph said with a trace of
disappointment in his voice.

"He was so sad. I told him we were both hungry and that I'd
make him a meal to cheer us up. He refused. He said that he
would cook for me: spaghetti carbonara. It's made with butter,
cream, parmesan cheese, eggs and bacon." She smiled. "Malcolm was a surprisingly good cook . . ."

"Most men are," said Joseph, somewhat defensively.

". . . but I'm afraid we didn't have much to eat."

"So I noticed. What happened, did you have a noodle fight?"

"I watched him cook. His hands were so agile—almost like
the hands of a dancer. His movements were so graceful, I was
quite amazed. I found myself growing excited. I came over to
him and pressed my body against his—playfully—hoping he'd
respond. He had just finished putting the spaghetti into a bowl
and had poured the sauce on top. He turned to me. 'Don't you
want to eat?' he asked. 'Of course,' I replied.

"He was carrying the bowl to the table. I circled around and
ducked underneath the bowl and came up between his arms.
He stopped. He laughed. I kissed him on the mouth and slowly
unbuttoned his shirt. I kissed his chest as each button opened,
one by one. Then I unbuckled his belt and knelt down on my
knees . . ." Her voice faded away.

Joseph wiped his forehead with his napkin. "Uh . . . what
happened then? I mean . . . go on . . . if you want to, that
is . . ."

She smiled. There was a strange light in her eyes. "He
dropped the bowl. The spaghetti carbonara started running all
over the floor. He fell to his knees, also, and then, suddenly,
we were passionately making love."

"In the sauce?" asked Joseph, wondering what it felt like.

176

"Yes. It was wonderful. It was the most passionate experience in my life. We rolled in it. Spaghetti and cream were in our hair, in our eyes, everywhere! We ripped and tore at each other's clothes until we were naked. And then, there on the floor, we made love over and over again."

"Over and over again?" Joseph asked, his voice trembling slightly. "Wasn't once enough?"

She shook her head. Tears welled up in her eyes.

He handed her his napkin to dry her tears.

"May I have another cigarette please?" she asked after dabbing the wetness away.

He gave her the pack and handed her the lighter as well.

"I think I have embarrassed you," she said, lighting up and taking in a deep breath of smoke.

He shook his head. "No . . . well, maybe a little, I suppose." Then he scratched the back of his neck. "I feel I should reciprocate and tell you one of my sexual adventures, but I can't really think of anything to compare with that spaghetti carbonara escapade—except, possibly, screwing Polly nine months pregnant and feeling as if I'm poking the baby in the head. But that's not the same thing, is it?"

"I didn't tell it to you for that reason." She put out her cigarette, extinguishing it in her plate.

"Why did you tell it to me, Nicole?"

"Because I needed to tell it to someone and you have chosen to be that person who fills this special role. And I wanted you to know that your journalistic observations cannot possibly touch another kind of truth—the physical and emotional bonds between people that aren't seen from artifacts or stains upon the floor."

"Journalism can tell a story, Nicole. But it's only one story among many. I know there are others. I also know you eventually got up from the floor, probably went and showered, and then had liqueur out on the verandah . . ."

"Drambuie and coffee," she said. "We should have ordered some ourselves."

"So it was Drambuie!" he exclaimed. Then, trying to set the

177

scene in his mind, he said, "What did you put on? I mean, I found fragments of your dress among the rubble . . ."

"Malcolm gave me one of Robin's dresses."

"You sat on the verandah, underneath the stars. It was a full moon that night. I checked it out in my almanac . . ."

"You are a very thorough voyeur, Joseph," she said.

"It's an obligation of the trade," he explained. "What did you talk about out there? Not different sauces to test, I presume . . ."

She gave him a look which meant that he was pushing it too far. "He asked me about Robin—how I met her, how we got to be friends."

"You told him everything?"

"I told him everything I told you. Then he asked me if I was a terrorist."

"And you said you hadn't the heart."

"Something to that effect, yes. Then he asked me if Robin was a terrorist."

"And you replied?"

"That I didn't know."

"Is that the truth?"

"Yes."

"Would you tell me if she was?"

She shook her head. "No."

He sighed. "That's just as well, I suppose."

"We spoke very little that night. It was one of those rare moments in time when you seem to be in a state of grace. And both of us knew it was just that, a brief moment. We never said anything about it, of course. But we didn't need to speak, we knew . . ."

"How did you know?" asked Joseph.

"Because so many events, beyond our control, had already been set in motion."

"So you drank your Drambuie and looked out at the stars and then what?"

"And then we went to bed and fell asleep in each other's arms. It was the most beautiful night of my life."

178

She looked at him. It seemed the evening stars were still there in her eyes. "Can we go?" she asked.

He felt his body tense. "Where to?"

"Perhaps we can take a walk. It has become too stuffy here for me." And saying that she motioned to the waiter to bring her the bill.

Chapter 13

They walked together down the deserted streets by the water-front. The harbour was quiet; the great ships at the quay sat like lonely giants in a salty bathtub brine.

A faint trace of sea mist was in the air, a cool refreshing breeze that reminded him of home.

There was a green near by with children's climbing structures. A promenade by the water's edge led the way. They strolled along without speaking till they reached a wooden bench. They sat down and Nicole continued her story: "That morning, as the sun came through Robin's curtains into her bedroom, we both felt the enormous wonder at finding ourselves still together . . . without fear, without naive commitment, with just an instinctual trust."

"So you spent the day together, is that what you're trying to say, Nicole?"

"Malcolm showed me your city: the little wooden houses painted pink and green and blue; the hills; the vistas; the glorious bay. We stopped at a charcuterie—a delicatessen, as you say—and bought sourdough bread and salads and cheese. We took it to the seashore—to a place something like this . . ." She pointed to the lapping waters near their feet and the piers which led to anchored rows of fishing boats.

"Aquatic park, most probably," said Joseph. "I often go there when I'm depressed. But it wasn't an ordinary day—the one you spent with Malcolm—was it, Nicole?" he said, glancing over at a young couple strolling down the promenade. The couple walked past them, hand in hand. They stopped for a moment to look out at the bay and then they walked on.

"No," she replied, "it wasn't an ordinary day . . ."

"Malcolm still had to find the eggs. So he took you to see Minh. Am I right?"

"It was in the evening. He took me with him to that desolate part of town where he said his Vietnamese friend still lived."

She smiled at the revived memory. "It was very strange to go there after such a lovely day. Any other time, I would have been unhappy to visit someone living in such a place. But that evening, in the full light of the moon, the jagged edges of those buildings were smoothed by a soft glow. The ruins could have been from Greece or Rome.

"We went to Dr Minh's house. A young man was there. His son. He told us Minh had left in quite a hurry just a while before we came. His father was very excited he said. He talked about a great event and mentioned something about buffaloes. Like you, I didn't understand the reference. But Malcolm knew where Minh had gone. He said there was a buffalo enclosure in your wonderful park."

"Of course!" Joseph slapped his forehead. "The wild buffalo enclosure! It's some acreage off the middle road. They're kept in a reservation just like our native Indians, living behind barbed wire." He shook his head. "I should have thought of it sooner—I've been there before."

"So have I," said Nicole, staring out into the distance.

"You have?"

"Yes. Twice. The first time was long ago. It was in a book . . ."

"What book was that?" asked Joseph.

She turned and looked at him. This time he could not avoid her eyes. "It was a book about the Montagnards of Vietnam," she replied.

The evening mist which swept in from the sea had begun to swirl around them. They were soon lost in haze. Their voices seemed disconnected from their bodies and cut off from time.

"We drove out to the park. It was as if we had come into a jungle for the evening fog was like the steam from a primeval forest.

"We travelled on and soon we came to a vast clearing of grassy fields surrounded by a tall barbed-wire fence. The clearing had let in the light. In the distance, in the confines of the fence, we could see the mighty buffaloes grazing under-

181

neath the moon. They were so proud! So magnificent! They were once everywhere, the lions of your west.

"We circled the enclosure until we found a jagged opening. Malcolm inspected it and said it had been newly cut since the wire hadn't rusted yet.

"We walked on and soon the grass turned into clay. And further on, the land turned into marsh. And then we saw the long, thin reeds with narrow, pointed, tender leaves that are eaten by the pandas in the forests of China."

"Bamboo!" said Joseph.

"Yes. We ventured on and soon we found ourselves deep in mud; first our shoes, then our ankles, then our knees were swallowed up.

"We climbed upon a rotted stump so we could see what lay beyond. The bamboo forest jutted out into the marshy swamp like a tiny peninsula. We decided to go back and then work our way around the marsh on firmer soil. Eventually we ended up in a small, dry clearing where we stopped to rest. There we sat down on a log and cleaned the mud from our shoes and legs.

"It was then I saw what appeared to be an encampment in a small thicket just a few feet away. We walked over and saw that hidden in the leaves were earthen jars and bowls. And, slightly beyond, there was another clearing with a small platform built out of cut bamboo. Around the platform were willow baskets filled with bags of hulled rice and small quantities of food. On the platform were primitive instruments like gongs and drums . . ."

"The Montagnards were there?" The sound of Joseph's voice was muffled in the mist.

"No. The encampment was deserted. But we could see it had been recently occupied. In the center of the platform was a ceremonial bowl. In it was a chicken; its throat was freshly cut. Another bowl was filled with blood, still warm and steamy."

"So they had completed some sort of ceremony . . ." said Joseph.

"No," said Nicole. "I knew from my reading that the ceremony had not yet begun . . ."

"How did you know that?"

"There were jars still filled with alcohol. They were meant for the holy men to drink."

"So they had gone off for some reason. Perhaps they were frightened away?" Joseph suggested.

'Or had gone to get something . . ." said Nicole.

"What happened then?"

"We began to explore. At the far side of the encampment, hidden in the trees, were rows of cages made of wire mesh, stacked one atop another."

"The ducks!" said Joseph.

"But they were empty. They were the cages for the ducks, however. We could tell that by the feathers."

"So the ducks had gone as well?"

"Not too far. We found them swimming in the marsh. The Montagnards did not keep their ducks in cages, but used them just to transport their game from one place to another."

"Well, then Malcolm found his ducks at last!" Joseph replied.

"It is not so easy to catch a duck if you are not used to its movements," said Nicole with a trace of amusement in her voice. "When Malcolm reached for them they flapped their wings leaving him dripping with muddy water.

"I couldn't help but laugh. His face was covered in mud! I tried to sneak up behind one and grab it by the tail. The duck flapped for all its might! Malcolm shouted for me to hold on. I closed my eyes and for a moment I thought I was going to be lifted in the air by the creature and flown away!"

"But you caught it!" said Joseph.

"No. I couldn't hold on. The duck finally struggled free leaving me with only a handful of its feathers."

"I think that salting its tail might have worked," said Joseph, trying to remember what he knew about catching birds.

"We finally found an old one that had just woken from its nap and was easier prey. It just put up a token fight and then went back to sleep. As Malcolm tucked the bird into his jacket, I happened to see that some ducks had built a nest behind the trees."

"And were there eggs?"

"There were indeed! We took the duck and the eggs and put it in a cage and then wired it shut."

"And then you got the hell out of there, lickity split, I hope!"

"There wasn't time," she said. "As soon as we set off to go, we heard a horrible sound. A wounded, bellowing cry, coming from the thicket just behind.

"We turned around. There was a violent movement deep in the bamboo and then an angry roar followed by some shouts. We ducked down behind the leaves, and then the bleating roar, which terrorised the night, became more violent still.

"We watched in fear. The branches from where the sound had come were crushed back as if it were being plowed down by a great iron machine. And then, through the moonlit night, we saw an incredible thing . . . it was a horrible sight: eyes of fire and snorting steam, hot white smoke, burning into the pale darkness. And hooves that kicked and thrashed, and a monstrous body, heaving in great blasts of terrified air.

"Behind this miserable, gigantic beast and on either side were shouting men who clung fast to the ropes that had caught the creature's horns. Some others were staking in huge pegs, deep into the ground. And when they finished their chore and the lines were tied, other ropes were thrown around the crazed and maddened animal. These cinched around his middle and were lashed tight. And then around his neck, another line, which bound his butting head while foam poured from its snout.

"Then, with a final roar, the beast gave in, as its neck line tightened cutting off its air. And falling to its mighty knees, it lay upon the ground: defeated. Prostrate now, it fought no more.

"The tiny men, dressed in loincloths and loose cotton shirts, wrapped bark around its horns, and passing it across its head, they twisted it around until the forehead was completely hidden by what might have been a halo or a crown. On either side of this were hung some bamboo leaves which cascaded to the ground.

184

"When this was done, the tribe, perhaps two dozen men and women and four or five young children, took their seats. On the stage were the elders and their shaman and one more . . ."

"One more? who was that?"

"A man decked out in bamboo leaves . . ."

"What was going on, Nicole? Could you tell?"

"Yes. I had read of it before. It all came back to me. It was a special ceremony to crown a king . . ."

"A king? In Golden Gate Park?"

"The shaman, who wore a painted mask, took the shoes off the man bedecked with garlands and washed his feet. Then, as some tribesmen took up the drum and gongs, the masked one began his chant and a bowl of rice was passed around. After that some jars were filled with alcohol.

"The man in the mask descended from the stage. He carried in his hand a giant sabre. Along with him came another who brought along the bowl of chicken blood. The man in the mask went first and anointed the pole to which the buffalo was tethered with the blood. He chanted an incantation. Then he stood before the tethered buffalo and passed blood over the head of the humbled creature, anointing its brow. He chanted another incantation. And with that he took his mighty sabre and with a sure, swift blow, severed off the creature's rear hooves, forcing it to fall upon its knees. He chanted a third time. Angered by the pain, the buffalo regained its fury and, lurching forward, it tried to kick. It staggered upright and then fell again on to its bloody stumps.

"Holding the sabre over his head, point down, the masked man drove it with all his might into the side of the buffalo. The force behind the blade sunk it deep, piercing through the entrails. Blood gushed. It splattered the man, the executioner, the priest, soaking his shirt and loincloth. The animal let out a bleating scream, almost a cry, pulling frantically one last time at its tethers. It whimpered and, with a final gust of hot breath in the chill of the night, it fell to the ground.

"It lay there for a while, its muscles jerking in life's last tremble, as the masked man said a final prayer. Then, taking up his sabre once again, he cut off the beast's testicles and placed them in a bamboo tube . . ."

Joseph took a deep breath. "Was it over, I hope?" he asked.

"Yes. The masked man took the hallowed wrapping from off the animal's head and brought it to the stage. The man to be crowned rose to his feet. The garlands were removed. He did not look like the others. He wore a beard and glasses."

"Beard and glasses?" asked Joseph.

"The crown was placed upon his head. The bamboo tube containing the testicles of the slaughtered buffalo was put into his hands . . ."

"Did you say beard and glasses?" Joseph asked again.

"You're right," said Nicole. "The man who was being crowned was Dr Minh . . ."

Transported to this primeval forest of the mind, Joseph could hardly let it rest. The story was unfinished. Minh, a refugee from Vietnam, had been crowned king of twenty-four Montagnards plus kids after a gory buffalo sacrifice in the middle of his favourite park. He wasn't going to leave it there.

"What happened then?" he asked.

"We took our cage and left, withdrawing quietly into the thicket of bamboo while the celebration began. We wound back around the marsh and then came again to the grassy fields where the buffaloes still grazed. We found our hole and squeezed back out. Before we departed I turned around. Underneath the moon I saw a silhouette: a lone bull, like an ancient mastodon, let out a call, its head lifted up toward the sky."

"So Malcolm had his eggs to test . . ." said Joseph.

"Yes," she sighed. "Dear, sweet Malcolm had his precious eggs."

"What then? You took them to the lab?"

The moisture of the night made her eyes seem damp. "We never got that far," she said.

"Why not?" he asked. "You tripped and fell?"

"We went back up the access road to get his car. The moon

had gone behind a cloud. It was dark and difficult to see. Then, around a bend, we saw them. Like a hornets' nest on fire, they lit the air in a harsh, contorted blaze."

"What?" he asked, confused.

"Red lights. Bright red lights, flashing, turning round and round in circles. And then, all at once, a blinding searchlight, brilliant white, froze us in its glare."

"The cops! What the hell were they doing there, Nicole?"

"I don't know. We thought perhaps they had made some mistake. But then a man stepped forward. He called Malcolm by name."

"He knew him?"

"Yes. 'Well, Dr Greene,' he said, 'out for a little midnight stroll?' "

"What did he look like, this man?"

She shrugged. "We could only see his shadow."

"What happened then?" he asked.

"There were many men whose shadow I could see. They were in the bushes and the trees."

"Surrounding the enclosure, I presume."

"Yes. They were waiting."

"For the Montagnards?"

"Who else would they be waiting for?"

"They took you away?"

A cold breeze blew in from the west. It brought with it a thin salt spray. "They grabbed us, these men without faces, and put Malcolm in a car . . ."

He pulled up the lapels of his jacket to ward off the chill. "And you?"

"I was taken, too. In a different car."

He looked out into the bay. In the distance a lighthouse sent its searching beam. A foghorn sounded its hoarse cry . . . "And that was the last you saw of him."

"He called to me. 'Don't worry, Nicole! I'll meet you . . .' "

"Where?"

"He didn't say. Or, perhaps, I didn't hear."

"They drove you straight to your hotel?"

187

"To get my things."

"And then they escorted you to the airport?"

"Yes. We waited for the first direct flight to Paris. They put me aboard."

"They didn't give you an excuse? No hearing? No chance to speak?"

She shook her head. "They had some documents that they showed to the airport people."

"Deportation orders, I guess."

"Probably."

He looked at her. The spray had made her wet. Her hair was matted to her face. Water trickled down her forehead and her cheeks.

"You tried to call from Paris?"

"Every hour."

"No one responded?"

She shook her head.

"Two days later he was dead."

"Yes . . ."

"You don't know what happened?"

"No."

He took her hand. It was cold and wet and soft. "I'm sorry, Nicole . . ."

She lifted his hand to her cheek. "I'm still very afraid," she said. "In the end, I was more afraid for myself than I was for him."

He put his arm around her and felt her trembling body.

"Would you sit here with me for a while?" she asked.

"Yes," he said. "As long as you want."

They sat together, silently. He took off his jacket and wrapped it around the two of them. They said nothing, but listened to the sound of their beating hearts.

Nicole accompanied him on the taxi ride back to the airport that night. It wasn't till they reached their destination that Joseph said, "Nicole, I want you to tell me something."

"If I can," she replied.

188

"I need to know about the Genesis Files . . ."

She looked away. And then she said, "In 1968 something happened in Vietnam, Joseph. Something very terrible. It started with the defoliation program . . ."

"The dumping of Agent Orange to expose the Ho Chi Minh trail?"

"Yes. The massive use of Agent Orange herbicide killed thousands upon thousands of acres of plants and vegetation. In doing so it destroyed an ecosystem that was millions of years in the making. It caused the basis for soil erosion and flooding that swept away much of the topsoil in the South."

"I know," he said. "I read some of the reports. Not only plants were affected but also animals which were suddenly denied their food and shelter."

"And fish, and fowl, and all living things that breed upon this earth," she said. "No one escaped unscathed . . ."

"But that's old news, Nicole. That information's been around for a while."

She nodded. "The Genesis Files have to do with a project attempted by some well-meaning scientists who were horrified by what had been done and tried to convince the miltary to limit the damage."

"I don't understand," he said. "You can't undo that kind of thing, can you?"

"The project was led by a man, a genetic engineer . . ."

"Krohl?" he asked.

She nodded. "Krohl's team had been working to create a viral agent which would act as a stimulus for procreation. The idea, as I understand it, was that these viral agents had a genetic code which would help release certain enzymes and other substances from the soil, causing in years what perhaps it would take centuries for nature to accomplish . . ."

"Sort of a super-fertilisation process, huh?"

"You could call it that."

Joseph shook his head in wonder. "Are you trying to say that the military was out to destroy all the flora and fauna in Vietnam and regrow them at the same time?"

"Isn't that the essence of American liberalism?" she asked. "Creation and destruction are part of the same process; your government wanted to destroy a country and save it simultaneously."

"But, Nicole, there aren't any new forests that grew in Vietnam. The bomb craters still have stagnant pools of putrid water; the land still lies fallow; the crops still don't grow. What happened?"

"The scientists convinced the military to allow them to experiment on a little patch of land—a tiny section of the forests that had been defoliated. The problem was that Agent Orange had a very toxic impurity connected with it called dioxin. Dioxin, it turned out, was a mutagen. Do you know what that is?"

"I think it's a chemical that makes things mutate, right?"

"Yes. It's so toxic that just a microscopic drop can cause a woman to abort or worse . . ."

"Or worse?"

"It can cause malformation of the uterus, it can react with the gestation process causing something known as molar pregnancies."

"What's that?" he asked, in spite of himself.

"That's where the ovulation inside a woman goes crazy and instead of a baby growing in her womb, there's something else—a living mass, a mole."

There was a throbbing in his head. He felt the pain. "Nicole, are you saying that the genesis virus reacted with the dioxin and began a process of mutation?"

"Yes. According to the file, the virus was disseminated from the very same planes that dropped the Agent Orange."

"And instead of helping things to grow, it caused things to abort or malform?"

"Yes. And in that part of the forest lived a small and unknown tribe—a tribe of Montagnards who were lifted from their world and brought to San Francisco after the war."

"And nothing was said about this?"

"Do you find that surprising, Joseph? For every military

190

secret that has been exposed, there are fifty or a hundred that haven't. Maybe we'll find them all out someday. And if we do, who can say what terrors lie in store?"

"But how does that relate to what happened in Krohl's lab? Why was Malcolm killed? Why, indeed, was Krohl?"

She took his hand into her own. "Listen to me, Joseph. There was a time when I would have given my life to find that out. But whatever happened in that lab is now beyond our control. Take my advice. Forget it. If you want to help, begin to work with us in other ways. We can use you, my friend. We can use anyone who can write or speak . . ."

He looked at her, pleadingly. "But, I need to know what happened there. It's very important to me."

She brushed a tear from her eye. "Joseph, I know it's important to you. I truly wish I could help."

The taxi reached the airport departure ramp and drove up to the curb. Joseph turned to her and smiled. "Goodbye, Nicole."

"Goodbye, Joseph."

He took her in his arms and hugged her tight. And for a moment he wished he could stay.

Then he opened the door and climbed out.

"Perhaps we'll meet again," he said to her through the open window.

"Perhaps," she said. And then the taxi drove away.

He caught the morning flight back to San Francisco. On the plane trip home, he took out his notebook and wrote: "A man-made virus is going around which deforms babies. My wife is just about to have a kid . . ."

Chapter 14

She was sitting in the kitchen poised over a cup of herbal brew when he walked in. She looked up. "Joseph! You startled me!" she said, nearly spilling the tea over the book she was reading.

He sat down beside her and leaned forward. He kissed her mouth and her cheeks and smoothed her hair with his hand.

"It's nice to have you home again," she sighed.

He put his hand on her belly. "How's everything down below?" he asked in a gentle voice that seemed strange even to him.

"Like a volcano ready to erupt," she said. "How was your trip?"

"Eventful . . ." He gazed into her face. She looked so weary, but with a beautiful glow of child, he thought. "How long was I gone?"

"About twenty-four hours," she said, glancing over at the clock on the wall.

"Is that all?"

She nodded. "You look different somehow, Joseph," she said, studying his face. "I can't exactly say what it is, but you do look different . . ."

"I didn't get much sleep," he replied, rubbing his eyes.

"That's not it. I've seen you sleepy before." She took his hand and drew it to her cheek. "I needed you, Joseph. In the middle of the night I was sure I had started to go into labor. Suddenly I realised I was out of control. I was frightened. There was no one I could call. I needed you so much."

He felt the guilt well up inside him. "I'm sorry, Polly. I know I shouldn't have left you like that . . ."

"I said you could go," she said, caressing his hand and looking up at him. "What did you find out?"

He shut his eyes and saw Nicole. He opened them again. Polly's face was filled with expectation.

"Something terrible happened in Vietnam . . ." he began. And then his voice trailed off.

"Something terrible did happen in Vietnam," Polly agreed. "but you didn't have to fly to Vancouver to find that out." She tried to make out the curious expression on his face. "Did she tell you about the Genesis Files?"

He nodded and repeated what Nicole had told him about Krohl and the mutant virus.

Polly kept her eyes riveted on his face. "What is it supposed to do to us . . . this virus?"

He shrugged his shoulders and looked away. "Give us cancer, I think . . ."

"How is it passed on?"

"I don't know," he replied. And then he looked at her and tried to smile.

"Did she know why the lab explosion happened?"

"No." He shook his head.

"Or what research was going on there?"

He shook his head again and then looked at her helplessly. "Polly, what are we going to do?"

She put her hand on her belly and kept it there. "Joseph, I want to have my baby. It's time."

"I know it is, Polly."

"I can feel it knocking at the door. It's ready. So am I."

"I'm ready, too," he said.

"It's one of those never-ending stories, Joseph. You understand that now."

He nodded. "Yes. It's like seeing something in a mirror and finding out it's just the reflection of a reflection. The more answers I find, the more questions I have to ask."

She hugged him. "This baby is too important to us, Joseph. It's our future that counts, not the past."

He kissed her tenderly on her neck. "I love you, Polly," he said softly.

"And I love you, Joseph."

"Do you mind if I lie down for a while? I haven't had a wink

193

of sleep," he whispered in her ear. "And I want to be alert for our special delivery."

"Call your mother first," she whispered back. "She's mad as hell. Thinks you don't give a damn about her anymore."

He pulled away. "Jesus Christ!" he said. "I forgot all about her!"

"That's what she said, too."

"Well, what did you tell her, Polly? You didn't say I went to Vancouver, did you?"

"Of course not! I might be pregnant but I'm not crazy!"

"So what did you tell her?"

"I said you were sick."

"What did she say?"

"She said even sick people can pick up the telephone."

"God, she's right! What did you say to that?"

Polly smiled. "I told her you had laryngitis."

He grinned and kissed her on the lips. "Polly old girl you've got a great future in store for you in the newspaper business if you want to continue your career after motherhood."

"Give her a call, Joseph. Tell her we'll stop by to see her this evening. One of the people from my office dropped off a bottle of champagne last night to launch the kid. We'll bring it to her. That'll cheer her up."

He phoned his mother and then went to bed. He fell asleep at once.

Some hours later he woke with a start. He bolted upright and rubbed his eyes. He was covered in a cold sweat.

Dragging himself out of bed, he stumbled into the living room. Polly was there, on the floor, doing her breathing exercises. Her face showed the strain.

"What are you doing down there?" he asked, still groggy from sleep.

She held up a finger for him to wait while she did her dog-like pants. She looked at her watch and then noted the time. "They're coming every ten minutes now," she said.

Suddenly, he was awake and beginning to panic. "Does that mean it's about to happen?"

"It means it's probably getting near the time."

"Well pack your stuff!" he said. His voice was trembling.

"It's been packed for two weeks now," she said.

He rubbed his head, "What time is it?" he asked.

"It's after eight," she replied, looking at her watch.

"After eight? At night?"

She smiled and nodded.

"Why didn't you wake me up?"

"I wanted you to get your sleep. You might not have a chance again for several years."

He felt the taste of yesterday's cigarettes in his mouth and said, "Let me brush my teeth and throw some water on my face. Should we take the Vespa or do you want to call a cab?"

"Might as well go in style," she said, going to the phone.

He went into the bathroom and turned on the taps. He put his face into the sink and let the water run until he felt the world start to come back into focus. Then he took a towel and rubbed until the blood began to circulate again.

"Joseph!" he heard her call. "Guess what?"

"What?" he replied.

"Yellow's out on strike! The other taxi companies aren't coming out for calls!"

"Why not?"

"Too many people on the streets. Why waste the gas?"

"I guess you'll go in style then," he replied. "I'll just put on my shirt."

"No hurry," she said. "The contractions have stopped."

He turned abruptly: "What?"

"They went away."

"Come on, Polly!" he said. "I thought you were all ready to go!"

"I've been all ready to go for weeks, Joseph!" she said with some annoyance.

"Well what does this mean? Are you in labor or not?"

"It means I'm not in labor yet. But I may be soon."

195

"Can't you be more definite than that?" he asked. Walking out of the bedroom and meeting her in the hall.

She put one hand on what used to be her hip and made a defiant stance. With her other hand she pointed to her belly. "I'd be happy to let you carry on from here if you think you can do any better."

He sighed. "OK, forget it. I was just all psyched up, that's all."

"I've been psyched up for nine months," she replied. "Anyway, we're still going to the hospital to visit your mom, remember?"

"Right," he said. And then he said, "Maybe you ought to take your bag."

"Are you kidding? I'm not going anywhere without my toothbrush—not until the kid makes up its mind!"

He chuckled. "OK, Polly. I'll go start up the Vespa."

"Fine," she said, ducking through the bedroom door. "I'll grab my case."

"And don't forget the champagne!" he called out to her as he opened the door.

It was dark outside. The street lamps had been lit, but the San Francisco fog had already drifted in. The moistness of the haze always made it difficult climbing down the stairs and he told himself to remember to hold Polly extra tight.

The Vespa was parked in front of the garage. He took out his keys. As he reached down to unlock the chain he felt a queasy sensation in his stomach.

Maybe it was nerves, he thought. But he fancied he saw a shadow through the haze.

He straightened up. And, as he did, he sensed that someone was coming toward him from behind. Instinctively he tried to turn. Then, suddenly, he felt a hand around his neck and the cold metal of a knife.

"Fucking hell!' he shouted. "I don't have any money!"

"Shut up!" hissed a voice. "You Radkin?"

"Who wants to know?" asked Joseph. He didn't think the

196

answer was what the guy had wanted, but he always tried to hedge his bets.

The man pressed the knife blade flush against his throat. "Keep your voice down and move it!" he ordered.

"Move it where?" asked Joseph, hoping someone big would come along.

"Up the stairs, wise ass, and be quick!"

"The stairs are wet and slippery," said Joseph. "Couldn't we just chat down here?"

"I could cut your throat down here, if that's what you want." The flat of the blade pressed harder to his neck.

"No," said Joseph. "That's not what I want." And he moved awkwardly toward the stairs, with the man's hand still around his neck and the knife at his throat.

"You a cop?" asked the man as he pushed Joseph painfully from one step to another.

They had reached the top stair and were standing by the door. Joseph tried talking fast. "You got your wires crossed, buddy. I'm not a cop, I'm a reporter!"

"All reporters are cops, as far as I'm concerned," the man said. "Open the goddamned door!"

"I don't have a key," Joseph lied.

"Hey, don't try to mess with my head!" the man shouted hoarsely. His tone made Joseph understand he didn't want to joke around. "I saw you take some keys when you were unlocking your bike!" The flat of the knife dug deeper into Joseph's throat.

"Listen," Joseph rasped, barely able to breathe, "my wife's in there. She's pregnant and nine months overdue. If she sees me like this she'll freak out and go into labor right on the floor and we'll have to deliver the kid ourselves. Why don't we settle this out here, OK?"

"I want to know how come you been askin' questions about some fucked-up vet?" the man hissed. 'How'd you know I wasn't . . ."

He didn't have time to finish the sentence as Polly opened up the door and smashed the champagne bottle over his head.

197

The man dropped his knife and crumpled to his knees. Blood began to ooze from the gash in his head. He put a hand to the wound and looked at the blood and then held it up to Polly. "Jesus Christ, lady, see what you done!" He stared up at her with wild eyes.

Polly looked horrified. She glanced from the bloody vagrant on the steps to Joseph, who was staring down at the man. "Do you know this guy?" she asked.

"Yeah," said Joseph, "I think I do. Get the first-aid kit, Polly. I'll help him inside."

"Help him inside?" asked Polly, throwing him one of those "You must be crazy!" looks. "Why can't we just fix him up out here?"

"Because I think he has something to say to us, Polly," Joseph replied, brushing away some bits of broken glass and helping the man to his feet.

"Watch out for that leg," said the man, pointing to the one on the right, "it don't work too well."

"I thought Malcolm fixed it up for you," said Joseph, helping the man inside the door.

Polly met them in the hallway. "Take him in the kitchen, I guess. I'll set up a chair next to the sink."

Blood was still oozing from the wound as Joseph helped him down the hall. Polly took a dressing from the pack and handed it to him as they walked. "Here," she said, "press this up against your cut!"

The man let out a hoarse laugh. "Don't worry, lady, I won't muss up your floor!"

"It's not the floor I'm worried about," said Polly. "I just don't want you to bleed to death in my kitchen." Then, in a reprimanding tone of voice, she said, "People like you shouldn't play around with knives! You could have killed him, you know. And I made it absolutely clear that I'm not raising the baby alone!"

"I told you she'd be upset," said Joseph as he sat the man down in a chair that Polly had brought over to the kitchen sink.

"I wasn't tryin' to kill him, I just wanted to scare him so he'd

198

stop askin' questions . . ." the man whined. Polly began to dab his forehead with some hot soapy water. "Hey, lady, that hurts!"

"You want some morphine to ease the pain?" asked Joseph.

The man stared at Joseph and crinkled his brow.

"Who is this guy, Joseph?" Polly stared at the two of them while she opened up the bottle of disinfectant.

"This is Charlie," said Joseph, studying the man's grizzly face.

"You mean Charlie-the-Weirdo? I thought you said he was dead?"

"I guess that's what he wanted us to believe. Right Charlie?"

Charlie gave Joseph a nasty look. "Listen, man," he said, "I had this all set up fine till you came around askin' a lot of questions!" And then, turning his head abruptly as Polly rubbed the disinfectant in, he shouted, "Hey, shit! That stuff stings!"

Polly gave him a slap. "Don't be a baby! Keep still!"

"What happened Charlie? Why'd you want to disappear?"

Charlie had a mean smile on his face. "I ain't sayin' nothin'!"

Polly took the soapy rag and washed the other side of Charlie's head, exploring underneath the dirt for bruises. "Criminy! Don't you ever wash?" she asked him.

"The city don't provide no bathtub on the streets, lady," said Charlie.

"Stop calling me lady!" Polly ordered.

"What's with her?" he asked, looking questioningly at Joseph.

"She's thinking about all those midnight feedings she'd have to do alone if your hand had slipped going up the stairs," said Joseph. Then, gazing hard into Charlie's ugly face, he asked, "What happened between you and Malcolm Greene?"

Charlie gritted his teeth as Polly poured on some more disinfectant alcohol. He stared back at Joseph and said nothing.

"You were there the night before he was killed, weren't you, Charlie?"

"I didn't have nothin' to do with that!" said Charlie.

"I know you didn't. I just want to know what happened there that night."

"Are you a dealer?" asked Polly, applying a gauze bandage to his wound. "If you are, I don't want you in my house!"

"He's not a dealer, Polly. He's a user. That's why he went to see Malcolm that night, right Charlie? You needed some more stuff, didn't you?"

"You mean Malcolm really was a dealer?" asked Polly with surprise. "I don't believe it!"

"He was a dealer," said Joseph, continuing to study Charlie's face. "But only to Charlie . . ."

"Only to him?" asked Polly. "How come?"

"How come, Charlie? What did you have over him?" asked Joseph.

"So that's it!" said Polly. "Blackmail!"

"Blackmail, shit!" said Charlie, spitting out the words like poison.

"But something happened," Joseph said. "Something that must have scared the hell out of you. Something that made you try to pull this stupid stunt."

"Listen, man!" said Charlie, a sudden look of fear now in his eyes. "They're after me 'cause of what I saw! I didn't do nothin'! I'm just a dumb fuck ex-GI who ain't got beans! So I use some stuff now and then. Who doesn't? That's no call to bump me off!"

"What did you see?" asked Polly.

"I'll tell you what he saw," said Joseph. "He saw them take the Montagnards . . . the ones who used to rummage through the trash late at night . . ."

There was a terrified look in Charlie's eyes, the echo of a nightmare he had dreamed. He shook his head. "I wasn't gonna tell anyone, mister! I swear!"

"You told Sandy Grey from the veterans' organisation, didn't you?"

"She was the only one!" he said, still shaking his head.

"You convinced her to help you, right?"

Charlie didn't speak.

"What happened, Charlie? Did you find another bum? An ex-GI who OD'd on the streets?"

Charlie's face looked blank, used up, like an auto out of gasoline.

"He probably didn't even look much like you. But who would care? One dead street-bum is just like another, am I right? I mean who's going to care if you change names . . ."

"Joseph, you're going too far again," Polly warned.

Charlie shook his head. "He ain't goin' too far. He's right on course. No one cares. They didn't even care that he didn't have a phony leg or that he only lost half his rotten teeth. They just put him in the wagon like a load of trash. Sandy identified him as me. That's all they wanted. Just a name. Then they probably tossed him in a ditch."

"Why'd she do it, Charlie?" Polly asked. "She could have gotten in a lot of trouble."

Charlie shrugged his skinny shoulders. There was a rattle in his voice. "I don't know why she done it . . ."

"Maybe she believed you, Charlie," said Joseph.

"Nobody believes a guy like me," said Charlie.

"I believe you," Joseph said. "I think you're right. I think they were sweeping the Montagnards off the streets. You happened to be in the wrong place at the wrong time, that's all . . ."

"I'm always in the wrong place at the wrong time," said Charlie. "Man, that's the story of my life!"

"Do you want some coffee, Charlie?" asked Polly, looking at him a little more sympathetically now.

"You got a beer?" he asked her, hopefully.

"I'll see," she said, going over to the fridge.

"What happened that night you went to see him, Charlie? The night before he got killed?"

Polly brought him an open can of beer. He took it gratefully, put it to his mouth and guzzled it down. Then he wiped his mouth with his sleeve and said, "I had the shakes pretty bad that day. I was really scared, man! Really scared!"

"So you went to his house, hoping to score . . ."

"Yeah. He didn't like me coming there. But I was really desperate that night."

"You knocked on his door," Joseph prompted. "How did he look when he answered?"

"Spaced, man. Fuckin' spaced . . ."

"On drugs?"

Charlie nodded. Then he looked at Polly. "You got another beer?"

"You came in," Joseph continued. "You asked him for some morphine . . ."

"I was hopin' he could fix me up," said Charlie.

"What did he say?" asked Joseph.

Polly brought him his second beer. He drank it slower this time. "He was blathering, man. I couldn't make heads or tails out of it. The man was too far gone . . ."

"Try to remember," said Polly, sitting down next to them. "Try to remember anything he said."

Charlie shook his head. "It was too weird, too weird . . ."

"Just tell us anything," Joseph said.

"He kept saying that they took him away or them away or her away . . . somebody away . . ."

"What else?" asked Joseph. "Did he say anything about experiments at a lab?"

Charlie made some creases in his brow. "He went on about some experimental animals . . . some strange kind of experimental animals . . . 'Evil!' He kept calling them 'evil!'"

"Experimental animals? For what?" asked Polly.

Charlie shrugged. "You got me. I get hallucinations too. Don't try askin' me about them."

"Try to think," Joseph pleaded. "Try to remember."

He strained his eyes as if he were trying to see something far away. "He kept shouting about the bumbuck. He kept laughing and shouting: 'You want to know where? It's in the bumbuck!'"

"What the hell's a 'bumbuck'?" asked Joseph, looking at Polly.

Polly shook her head.

"I kept askin' him for the stuff," said Charlie. "He grabbed me by the neck and kept shakin' me and yellin' 'I got it all

202

here! I got it all here! For all the world to see! But they can't get it, 'cause I hid it in the bumbuck!'"

"What?" asked Joseph.

"The stuff. I thought he meant the stuff. But after I heard about the accident, I went back to look for it. There wasn't any stuff there, man! Unless someone took it!"

"Did you look in his bedside drawer?" asked Joseph.

"I don't know, man. I tore the house apart."

Joseph looked over at Polly. "Maybe the cops weren't there at all. Maybe it was him," he said, pointing at their confused, scroungy-looking guest.

"You went there too?" asked Charlie.

"Can't you remember anything else?" asked Joseph, avoiding his question. "Just a tiny, little thing more?"

"The man went back into his room and fell asleep," said Charlie. "He was too stoned to talk to me."

"What room?" asked Joseph. "What room did he go into?"

"A room with a bed . . ."

"Was it off to the left or off to the right as he went down the hall?"

"Man, I was so dry I could hardly find my nose let alone tell my right from my left."

"Don't push him too hard," Polly advised.

"Thanks," said Charlie, looking at her and giving her a toothless grin.

"Charlie," said Joseph in a quieter voice. "What happened between you and Malcolm in Vietnam?"

He looked down. His face was serious now. "Don't ask me about that," he said.

Polly took his dirty calloused hand in hers and said, "Charlie, tell us. Don't be afraid. We're your friends."

He looked up at her and she smiled at him encouragingly.

Charlie was quiet. He stared at the floor. Joseph was about to say something to spur him on, but Polly looked at him and put her finger to her lips.

They waited. And finally Charlie spoke:

"That was nearly twenty years ago. I was young then. Man,

203

I had the world at my feet . . . that's when I had two real feet. I was a kid from Baltimore just out of school. Had a job in a grocery store, not a great job—a good job, though. But I knew some punks who wanted to knock the joint off. They made me give 'em the keys. Anyway, they got caught and they squealed. I went before this judge. He says to me, 'Two years in prison or two years in 'Nam. You got your choice.' I said to him, 'Two years in 'Nam don't sound so bad! Shit, why not make it three?'

"So there I am in 'Nam. A kid from Baltimore who never seen ten real trees next door to each other let alone a jungle. I get attached to this medical unit, though, 'cause they trained me at Fort Sam to give shots. Anyway, one day I meet this doc who says he needs an aide. He asks me if I want to come along with him. I say 'Sure, where to, man?' He says, 'We got to check out all the whores.' Man, my eyes light up. I say, 'Fuckin' hell! That's the job for me!'

"So, for the next year, me and the doc do our rounds from Saigon to Quan Tri, checking that the whores got all their shots and tracin' down the guys with sloppy pricks . . ." He shook his head and smiled sadly. "Man, what a job!"

"I guess you saw it all," said Joseph.

"Yeah, I saw too much," said Charlie, staring back down at the ground. "I saw these kids come back from combat, still shaking at the sight of the headless bodies and rotting flesh, all lookin' for a hole to put their peter in, to hide ten minutes in a cunt. That's what I saw. I saw 'em drink and vomit in these women's faces and then they'd rub it in . . . and all these broads done to them was smile . . . scared kids who wanted to be men. You know what a 'double veteran' means?" he asked.

"No," said Joseph.

"Someone who fucks a whore and slits her throat . . ."

Polly gasped. "You can't mean that!"

He looked at her and said, "It happened, ma'am. But there were others, too. The ones who fell in love . . . or thought they did."

"Yeah," said Joseph, "I bet there were a lot of those."

"A lot of kids are there in 'Nam. A lot of kids from whores

bought by some GI. A lot of babies. They must be twenty years old by now." He shook his head. "Maybe I got a few myself. Maybe . . ." He looked at Polly's swollen belly and then down at the floor again.

"So you and Malcolm inspected the whores," Joseph said. "Then something happened. What was it, Charlie?"

"The doc, he had someone, too. A woman he liked to go and see. She was smart . . . educated, I mean. She came from a family who had worked with the Frenchies in their civil service. Doc told me they were well off with the French, but after Dien Bien Phu they lost it all, I guess. Anyway, they were killed off in the war and she was left with nothin'."

"So she became a whore?" asked Polly.

"Not a whore exactly. She was more a hostess at this place. She had class. The doc, he liked to talk to her in French. He'd visit her whenever we went by. They'd go off into her room. I'd joke with him about it, but he said that all they did was talk . . ." His voice trailed off and he began to rub his missing leg.

"Go on," said Joseph. "Tell us what happened."

"That day . . ." His voice was softer now, perhaps because of painful dreams. "That day we came she wasn't there . . ." He stopped again and looked at Joseph. "It wasn't the day we usually come."

"What?" asked Joseph.

"It wasn't the day we usually come," he repeated. "She wasn't there. The place was packed with young kids, hot off the plane, still virgins, wet behind the ears, waiting for their first lay . . . He asked for her. She wasn't there . . ."

"You said that before," said Joseph.

"Then she comes in. We're standing by the bar. She's carrying a basket in her arms . . ."

"What kind of basket?" asked Joseph.

"A bamboo basket. The kind the Viets use to carry eggs . . ."

"A bamboo basket full of eggs?"

"I don't know. It's covered with a piece of cloth. Now she sees us. Her face turns white. Doc, he can tell that something's

205

wrong. He walks over to her. She screams something at him and then pushes him away. I go up to see what's going on. I go up to see what's going on . . ." Charlie looked at them helplessly.

Polly took his hand again. "Go on, Charlie. Tell us."

"She yells something at me, too. I can't understand. The cloth comes off the basket, somehow. I see them . . . I know what they are . . ."

"The eggs?"

"The eggs . . ." He laughed nervously. "The eggs . . ."

"Go on," said Polly. "Go on."

"The eggs . . . they fell . . . the one she was holding in her hand, the one without a pin . . . they dropped . . . I kicked at them . . . I kicked at them . . ."

Joseph looked at Polly and signaled with his eyes.

"That's OK, Charlie. You don't have to say any more," he told him. "I understand."

"They were rolling toward the kids . . . The doc, he sees . . . he pulls at her . . . she pushes him away . . . then . . . too late . . . all I see is red . . . the ground heaves up . . . red . . . I hear nothing . . . then I see pieces of flesh splattered everywhere . . . I feel nothing . . . except the leg that isn't there . . ."

"The woman?" asked Joseph. "Malcolm's friend?"

"Nothing left of her. Nothing left of her at all . . ." He shook his head back and forth. "I feel nothing . . . I hear nothing . . . then I feel the pain . . . I feel the pain . . . I shout, 'Help me, doc! Help me, doc! Give me something! I need something! I can't stand the pain! It hurts too much to breathe! Kill me, doc! Kill me, doc! I can't stand the pain!' "

"You don't have to say any more," Joseph repeated. "I understand everything now."

"The doc's alive. I keep calling to him. 'Help me, doc!' I shout. 'Help me!' He screams to me, 'I can't give you any more! I've given you too many now!' I shout, 'It's starting to hurt again! I can't stand the pain!' I say, 'Shoot me up or kill me, doc, I don't care!' "

206

Charlie had begun to tremble. His limbs began to shake. Even the one made out of metal.

Polly tried to soothe him. "That's OK, Charlie. It happened a long time ago. Twenty years ago. It's all over now."

But Charlie's limbs continued to shake.

"What should we do, Joseph?" Polly asked, realising now that they had set in motion something that they couldn't stop.

"Pour him a whisky," Joseph said; "I'll be right back."

She poured him a whisky and he drank it down. Then she poured him another.

Joseph returned carrying a plastic bag. He handed it to Charlie.

"What's this?" he asked, looking into Joseph's eyes.

"Something you need and I don't," said Joseph. "It's part of Malcolm's will. You can't use it here."

"But you can rest here for a while," said Polly.

"No, ma'am," he said, dropping the plastic bag into his pocket and struggling to his feet. "I think I'd like to go now."

"Whatever you want, Charlie," she said, giving him a hand to help him up.

They saw him to the door. "Next time," said Joseph, "Don't bring your knife, Charlie. OK?"

Charlie shook his head. "There won't be no next time, man. I'm goin' away."

"I won't ask you where," said Joseph, opening up the door.

"I won't tell you neither,' said Charlie, hobbling down the stairs.

"Watch out," Joseph called after him, "they're slippery when wet."

"I thought I told you to get rid of that stuff!" she said when they were back inside. She was tapping her foot, waiting for his response.

"I did," he said. "I gave them to Charlie."

"I know you gave them to Charlie. But that means those morphine syringes were here all the time!"

"But I was trying to figure out the proper way to dispose of them!" he replied. Then, changing the subject, he said, "What do you think all that gibberish that Malcolm spouted to Charlie was about?"

"I don't know," she said, "but whatever was hidden was probably there all the time. You just didn't know where to look, Joseph."

"I know," he said. "Maybe the cops have already been there. It's probably gone by now." He looked at her hopefully.

"Well, we'll never know, will we?" she said firmly.

"I guess not," he replied. "Unless . . ."

"Unless nothing!" she said, picking up her case.

"Polly," he said, "I could be there and back in three shakes of a lamb's tail!"

"Not on your life!" she said. 'We're going to the hospital!"

"It could be real important, Polly!"

"More important than our kid?"

"No."

"Then give it up, Joseph," she pleaded. "Concentrate on what I want for a change!"

"We both want the same thing, Polly."

"I want to have my baby!"

"I want to have our baby, too."

"Then let's go," she said.

"It's just that if I could spend five minutes looking for it very quickly, then I could be at the hospital before you even got undressed!"

"You don't even know what it is that you're looking for!" she shouted.

"Yes I do. I'm looking for something about Krohl's research."

Polly rubbed her weary eyes. "Where would you look?"

"In the places I didn't look before."

"You'll be there forever," she said.

"No. Five minutes at the most. I promise. Cross my heart and hope to die."

"I don't want you to die!"

"I won't die."

She glared at him. "Joseph, if you're going there then I'm going with you!"

He shook his head. "That's ridiculous, Polly . . ."

"No it isn't. I'm not letting you out of my sight until this baby is born!"

"But Polly . . ."

"Don't 'But Polly' me, Joseph! I made up my mind. Besides, I know where to look and you don't."

He narrowed his eyes. "How do you know where to look? Did Charlie say something to you he didn't tell me?"

"No. It's just that I know what 'bumbuck' means."

"You do?"

"Yes. It's the book you found there. The one about the atomic bomb."

"You think 'bumbuck' means 'bomb book?'"

"Yes."

"But we have the bomb book. Nothing's hidden in there, Polly."

"I know nothing's hidden in there, Joseph, the great detective. But you didn't read it like I did."

"So?"

"So, there's a passage in it that's all marked up. It's all about hiding things."

"What do you mean?" He looked at her, suspiciously.

"I mean, the secret of whatever it is that's hidden in Malcolm's house is in the bumbuck . . . I mean the bomb book."

"Well, give it to me then!" he ordered.

She shook her head. "No."

He sighed. "It's crazy Polly. What if you go into labor?"

"Then you will take me to the hospital immediately!"

"On the Vespa?"

"No. While you were outside, supposedly starting it, your mother called. That's what I was going to shout down to you when I opened the door."

"What did she want?"

"She wanted to tell us that she was sending Morris over to give us a lift."

"What?" He looked at her with wild eyes.

The doorbell rang.

Polly smiled. "I think that must be him now."

Chapter 15

"Listen, Morris," he shouted as the tiny MG swerved around the bend, "I've got precious cargo on my lap!"

"Am I driving too fast?" he asked as he down-shifted in fourth gear. "Just tell me if I'm driving too fast."

"You're driving too fast!" said Polly, trying to distribute her weight so that the baby wouldn't be crushed up against the dashboard. "It's dangerous in this fog, Morris."

"I think the visiting hours end at ten," Morris said. "Your mother insisted we get there by nine-thirty."

"A few minutes one way or another isn't going to matter," said Polly, holding tightly to a bar on the door.

"But you want me to stop . . . where is it again?"

"Turn right here," Joseph directed. "It's the third house on the left."

Morris pulled the MG over to the side of the road and came to a stop. He looked at his watch. "It's after nine already," he said. "You know your mother, Joseph. I don't have to tell you."

"That's right," he said, trying to pry Polly from his lap and out the tiny door, "you don't have to tell me."

"We'll just be five minutes at the most," Polly said to him.

"I'll wait here," said Morris. "Maybe you can give Rachel a quick call from your friend's house and tell her we're on our way."

"Right," said Joseph. "Just stay in the car."

They walked across the street. Up here on the heights, the fog had just arrived, working its way ever forward from the bay. It gave the homes an eerie look, as if some protoplasmic seepage was taking place.

"It's so dark!" Polly whispered as Joseph pointed out the house.

"There's nobody home to turn on the lights," said Joseph.

211

"I'll go around the side and climb in. You wait for me on the porch."

"Joseph . . ." She grabbed his hand.

"I know," he said: "'be careful, I don't want to raise Spinach all alone.'"

It was a curious feeling, he thought as he lowered himself inside through the open window, to know your way around a strange dwelling. Especially when you were uninvited and the occupant was dead.

The study, it seemed, was as he left it. The desk still showing signs of his last visit; the glass from the picture frame still scattered on the floor.

He went through the study and then left, down the hall to the front room. He opened the door and let Polly inside. "I don't want to turn on the light in here. It might look too suspicious."

"You mean having a pregnant woman about to burst standing alone on a front porch and a seedy guy climbing in through the side window doesn't?"

"As long as you don't turn on the lights," he replied. "People are used to seeing strange things in the dark."

"OK, Inspector Clochard, how are we going to see what we're looking for?"

"If we close the curtains and the shades we'll be all right," he said, leading her through the hall to Robin's room.

"That's like saying if you dig your head deep enough in sand, no one will notice you."

"It's true," he replied. "People might see you, but they won't notice you. Try it sometime."

"I am," she said. "Right now."

Somehow, he felt perfectly at home. He even thought of offering her a drink. But then he remembered there wasn't any beer in the fridge. Besides, he hadn't cleaned up the kitchen all too well and he was a bit embarrassed at taking her inside.

He had her wait while he closed the drapes in Robin's room and then turned on a lamp. "Come in," he said to her. "Don't be shy."

212

"Looks like someone was having a jolly good time here," she said, looking around at the messy bed and the strewn lingerie.

"You should know the secrets this room holds," he said.

"That's what we're here to find out, I guess," she replied, letting her weight down on a corner of the bed.

The soft light of the bedside lamp bathed the room in a glow that gave objects there a peculiar dimension, like a drawing with too much shading penciled in.

"It all happened here," said Joseph, slowly surveying the scene; letting his eyes drift over the books in Robin's shelves that traced her intellectual history from scientist to supposed saboteur, the bed, in which not only she had slept but also Malcolm and Nicole, and then the wardrobe where Gasser had discovered him that day. "All the central characters of our story came together in this very room."

"Connected by a thread," said Polly, "a strand of an idea that somehow relates to another story from forty years ago."

"The 'bumbuck' . . ." Joseph held out his hand. "Give it to me, Polly."

She reached into her purse and pulled it out. "You should have read it, Joseph."

He grimaced as he took it from her. "I didn't have the time, Polly. Anyway, you're the family intellectual." He flipped through the pages and then glanced back at her. "Where am I supposed to look?"

"I noticed there was a section that was all smudged up," she said. "It occurred to me that when I read a book and find a passage that I really like or that I want to study it often gets like that."

"So what's it all about?" he asked impatiently.

She took the book back from him and turned to the section she had read and read again. "It's about the first beginnings of the Manhattan project, Joseph, when the most enormous scientific organisation the world had ever known was secretly being put together to construct all the bits and pieces of what they euphemistically referred to as 'the device'. One enormous puzzle was divided up into a bunch of smaller puzzles: tiny questions that, in themselves, were of little importance, but put together made the workings of the first atomic bomb. What this section talks about is how these scientists got involved in their tiny projects, like figuring out special lenses for refraction, or purifying certain kinds of ore, and became totally engrossed in their work without giving any thought to how all their small discoveries would soon be used to destroy two cities on an island in another part of the world."

"But what does all this have to do with Malcolm's secret hiding place?"

"It's all in here," she said, pointing to the page. "It's even underlined. You see, when this work was first divided up, they had many sites that were scattered all across the country. Since twenty years' of work was being compressed into three or four, at first they didn't have proper facilities and they began by setting up shop anywhere they could: in unused garages; vacant storerooms; even a college kitchen."

"They made the workings for the bomb in old garages and kitchens?" he asked, mulling over this notion of an atomic bathtub-stew.

She nodded. "Part of it at any rate. But here's the thing: these scientists, many of them, had never worked on a secret project before. They were like most research professors you might know—their heads always in the clouds. The section that's underlined by someone, Joseph, is a quote from one of these men who told how every day he would take the notes from that day's work and hide them."

"Hide them? They didn't have a safe?"

"A safe? These guys didn't even have a proper lab!"

"So where did he hide them, Polly? Don't keep me in suspense!"

"Right there!" she said, pointing to Robin's bed.

"Where?"

She read the passage that was underlined. "'They told me to take special care not to let my notebook out of my sight. What was I supposed to do?'"

"What was he supposed to do, Polly?"

" 'I wanted to keep them with me all the time. So every night I stuffed them in the lining of my pillow. That way they'd be underneath my head!' "

"You're kidding! You mean the secret of the atomic bomb was stuffed in the lining of some old fart's pillow?"

"Yes. But they were probably meaningless to anyone who couldn't put them all together anyway."

They stared at the four pillows piled two and two on Robin's bed. "So you think it's in one of them, is that it Polly?"

"It's worth a look," she said.

He leaned over, grabbed two pillows, threw her one and took one himself and prodded it with his hand. "Not in here," he said, throwing it back.

"Nor in this," she said. "Toss me another!"

He threw her the third pillow and took the fourth. "Any luck?" he asked.

"No," she replied, disappointedly. "Are you sure you didn't give me this one before?"

He threw his down. "I'm not stupid, Polly!"

"Isn't there another bedroom?" she asked.

"Yes, but I think it's hidden here," he said.

"Try the pillows in the other bedroom," she suggested.

"Look," said Joseph, "maybe it's a good clue, maybe it's not. But whoever hid whatever's hidden—if, in fact, there is something hidden—might have taken the substance of the idea without following it to the letter."

"You mean, maybe they thought it was a good idea to sleep on it without putting it in their pillow?"

"How would you like to put your head on a pile of notes every night, especially if they're what I think they are."

"What do you think they are?" she asked.

"Get up, Polly," he ordered, ignoring her question. "Let's take off the sheets."

She helped him take off the covers and the sheets and then feel around the mattress. They found no sign of patches or of tears.

"Shall we turn it over?" he asked.

215

"No," she replied, her face suddenly tensing up. "Help me put the sheets back on."

"Why?" he asked. "Nobody's going to know the difference, Polly. You should see the rest of the house!"

She spread the sheets back on the bed herself, and then her body suddenly stiffened.

"What's wrong, Polly?" he asked. "What happened?"

"Just a contraction," she said. And then she pointed. "Joseph, look over there!"

"Where?"

She pointed toward the dressing table. On the chair set before it was a very large, fluffy, pink throw pillow. He walked over and picked it up.

"Do you feel anything?" she asked.

"Yes, but it might be the kind of material used for the stuffing." He turned it over in his hands. "There seems to be some stitching missing, though . . ." He stuck his hand through the seam and felt around.

"Polly!" he shouted. "There are some papers in here!" He pulled them out. "They're files." His hands trembled as he opened the first and read the words. "Polly! The Genesis Files! We found them, Polly! And, wait, there's some other stuff inside! Some medical records! And an envelope!"

He turned around, excitedly. She was lying on the bed, doing her deep-breathing exercises.

"Polly are you all right? Listen, let's just see what's in the envelope and we can go, OK?"

He opened up the envelope and pulled out some film. "It looks like a contact sheet of photographic prints from a very small camera. Probably the kind of camera that spies use, what do you think?" He held the contact sheet up to try to determine what the series was about.

Polly's breathing had gotten louder and more intense as Joseph kept talking: "The first one's an exterior of the hospital. That's easy to see. The next one's of the old building that adjoins the incineration room where they burn the trash. I remember it because I had asked about the smoky chimney

216

once. It reminded me of a picture I had seen of Auschwitz. The next one's of the inside of a lab. It's a long shot. It just looks like an ordinary lab to me with microscopes and instruments and large worktables. The next one's of the lab again, but a different angle. You can see a glass wall in the background. The next one is hard to make out. It's the glass wall. It looks like a glass cage in a zoo. You can barely make something out behind it. It looks like trees or something. The next shot is of the glass wall, again. It seems like there are some animals under the trees. It must be the laboratory animals. The next is closer. It's focused on one of the animals . . . an ape or something. Then next . . ."

Suddenly, he stopped. He looked at her. "Polly, these aren't animals behind that glass partition. They're people . . ."

He looked back at the sheet of tiny photos. He tried to speak. He couldn't recognise his voice. It was the voice of someone who had been stunned—the voice of someone reporting a great disaster: "The next shot's a woman, Polly. An old, skinny, shrivel-faced woman, with wooden plugs in her earlobes. She's naked, Polly. Her face is pressed up against the glass. She's staring out at whatever's taking the photo. Her eyes are dark. They're black as coal . . ."

He turned to her again. "Polly, she's staring out at me!" There were tears in his eyes. "I know her. She's one of the Montagnards!"

Her face was full of emotion. "Joseph, I have to tell you something . . ."

"Yes." He touched her hand. "I know."

"No, you don't. Listen to me. My waters, they've burst."

"What do you mean?" He couldn't understand what that had to do with the Montagnards.

"My waters, Joseph. The sack that protects our child. It's broken. It means I'm going into labor."

He felt a wave of panic well up in him. "OK, Polly," he shouted in an excited voice, "stay calm! I'll carry you out and we'll be at the hospital in no time."

"You don't understand, Joseph," she said. "I can't go in

217

Morris's car. Once the waters break there's no protection. You'll have to call an ambulance."

"But I don't know whether Malcolm's telephone is still connected!" he yelled.

"Don't panic, Joseph," she said calmly. "We still have plenty of time. Check the telephone. If it works, call the ambulance. If it's not connected, then go outside and tell Morris to find a telephone and call the ambulance."

"Where's the telephone in here?" he shouted, getting up and running into the hall. "Don't go anywhere, Polly! I'll be right back!"

Just then the doorbell rang.

"Maybe it's the ambulance!"

"You haven't phoned them yet!" Polly called out from the bedroom between contractions.

"Christ! Maybe it's the police! You're going to give birth in prison, Polly, and it's all my fault!"

"Calm down, Joseph," she pleaded. "I need you to have a cool head now."

"That's OK, Polly, I run better when I'm hot!" he said with some bravado as he lifted a corner of curtain at the front window and peaked out. And then he groaned.

He went over to the door and opened it. Morris stood there, hat in hand. "I'm sorry to disturb you, Joseph," he began, "but . . ."

"Listen to me, Morris," Joseph said, cutting him off short, "Polly's gone into labor!"

"Into labor?" Morris looked confused. "Then maybe we should go . . ."

"That's the problem. We can't put her in your car. She said her waters broke and she can't drive all scrunched up like that!"

"Perhaps if we lay her across the seat . . ." Morris suggested.

"There isn't room," said Joseph impatiently. "I'll have to call an ambulance!"

"Yes," Morris agreed, "that's probably the best thing." He poked his head inside the door. "Should I come in?"

Joseph sighed nervously. "I guess so . . . maybe you can help me find the phone."

"The phone?" asked Morris, coming inside and closing the door. "But why don't you ask your friend?"

"My friend?" Joseph stared impatiently at the old man standing in the darkened room.

"Your friend—the person you've come to visit. He must know where he keeps his telephone, doesn't he?"

"He had to go!" Joseph snapped.

"Go? But I didn't see anyone leave . . ."

"He went out the back!" shouted Joseph. "Now help me find the phone, damn it!"

"Perhaps if you turned on the lights?" Morris suggested timidly.

"I don't know where the goddamned light switch is!" Joseph yelled in a voice that was moving up the harmonic scale in an ever increasing crescendo.

"It's right here by the door," said Morris, reaching over and flicking it on. "And there's the phone on the telephone table." He pointed to a red phone sitting within biting distance on a mosaic table. "Would you like me to call?" he asked.

"No!" shouted Joseph, going over and picking up the receiver. And then furiously hitting the disconnect button several times he slammed it down again. He stared at Morris. His eyes were growing wild. "It's not working!" he shouted.

"Not working?" said Morris.

"Yes, you old fool! Can't you understand English? It's been shut off!"

"Maybe your friend didn't pay his bill."

"Of course he didn't pay his bill, you . . .!"

"Joseph!" Polly yelled from the other room. "Ask Morris to go next door and call from there!"

Joseph grabbed the old man by his arm and headed him out through the door. "Call for an ambulance! Tell them to fucking hurry! Tell them a woman's life is at stake!"

"Where should I tell them to come?" asked Morris.

"Here, you nitwit! Where else would you tell them to come?"

"But what's the address?"

"The address? How the hell should I know?"

"Look at the number on the door!" Polly shouted from the bedroom.

"You see a number?" asked Joseph going out on to the porch and inspecting the outside wall.

"No," said Morris. "Maybe in your address book?" He looked at Joseph and raised his eyebrows.

"My address book?" Joseph stared back angrily. And then he remembered that he did have Malcolm's address written in there. He pulled his black book from his pocket and paged through with moist, nervous fingers. "Where the fuck did I file it under? Greene? Malcolm? Doctor?"

"Sometimes I just write listings in the back when I haven't time to . . ." Morris said in a suggestive way.

Joseph flipped to the back. "Yeah! Here it is! 14 Perne." He glared at Morris. "P-e-r-n-e! Got it?"

"P-e-r-n-e," Morris spelled it out. "Number fourteen. I'll be right back."

"And tell them that if they're not here in five minutes, I'll write such a scathing article about the ambulance service that they'll wish they had run away with the circus instead!"

"All right, I'll tell them that," said Morris, walking quickly down the sidewalk toward a neighbouring house.

"And if anyone asks you, tell them that we've just moved in!" Joseph shouted after him. "Got it?"

Morris stopped and turned around. "You just moved in? But what about your house?"

"So we've got two! All right?"

Morris shrugged and hurried on. "All right. But your mother will be very surprised."

Polly's face was in a sweat. She sent him for a towel. He brought back a warm bowl of water and a cloth and began to sponge her down.

He could sense the change. Unlike before, when she could easily breathe through her contractions, now she was fighting for control. They were coming on like waves rolling in from the sea. The swell increased with each succeeding group; each one bigger, more intense than the one that came previously. Between the waves were moments of calm, of serenity, when she could smile. He kissed her lips, so dry, so hot. "I'll bring you water," he said.

She shook her head. "Don't leave, Joseph . . ."

"Just for a glass of water," he said. "I'll be right back."

She squeezed his hand. "Not even for that. Just stay . . ."

He stayed and felt the next wave hit. Her body tensed and then, like a swimmer out at sea, she rode it through again.

"You're doing fine," he said. "They'll be here soon. You're doing fine."

"It's harder each time . . ." she said. Her eyes were fearful of what was yet to come. "I keep thinking I'll be swept up and then I can't help it any more."

"You're in control," he said. "I'm here. They're coming soon."

The doorbell rang. She squeezed his hand.

"It's them!" he said. "It's your ambulance!"

"Joseph!" she whispered. "Don't go!"

"I must. I have to let them in!"

"Wait!"

She was breathing hard, Trying to stay above the water. He held her hand and saw her through.

It passed. She looked into his eyes. "Go fast!" she pleaded. "Then come back! I don't want to be alone!"

He ran to the door. It was Morris. "I called!" he said. "They're coming!"

"How soon?" he shouted.

"I told them what was going on. They said they'd send a paramedic team."

Just then Polly screamed. "Joseph! Please!"

"I have to go!" He ran back to the bedroom. Polly's legs were drawn up to her belly. She was clutching the sheets. "Joseph! I can't stand the pain!"

He knelt down again. "Breathe!" he whispered, grabbing her hand. "Breathe through it, Polly! Breathe!"

She was lost in the ocean, struggling to survive. She had slipped under and was gasping for air.

"Stay on top!" he whispered. "You can do it, Polly! Stay on top!"

"Undo her clothes," said a voice. "She needs more room to breathe."

Joseph turned quickly. "What?" he glared.

"Undo her clothes!" Morris ordered.

He loosened up her blouse.

"Her skirt . . ." Morris pointed. "Take it off. I'll undo her shoes."

The next wave had come. Morris stopped. "Help her through," he said. "We'll wait until these contractions have completed."

He held her hand. She squeezed so tight she cut off the circulation of his blood. His fingers had turned white. He felt her pain, her agonising pain, and wept.

"Don't cry," said Morris. "There's too much for us to do. Now's not the time to think of yourself, Joseph. Slip off her skirt, her hose, her underwear! Take off everything!" Morris said.

"They'll be here soon," Joseph intoned, still clutching her hand.

"We have to get ready!" said Morris. "Just in case . . ."

"In case of what?" asked Joseph, not daring to believe.

"In case we have to do it ourselves."

"But we can't!" Joseph whispered. "We can't! We don't know how!"

"We might not have any choice," said Morris. "Help me hunch up her legs. I want to see something."

The bed was wet as were her clothes which they had taken off. The sheets were soaked with her waters, her plug of blood, and the sweat from her heated limbs.

He helped lift her legs. "You know about these things, Morris?" asked Joseph hesitantly.

"I was a medic once," he said.

"A medic? When?"

"During the war . . ."

"Which war was that? Korea? World War II?"

"The one before. The Spanish Civil War. See her through the next contractions," he said. "I want to wash up before I examine her."

Her eyes had changed. They were larger. They no longer saw his world. Her breathing now was choppy, labored, suffering.

Morris had returned. "Spread her legs," he said and then he looked. "She's dilated . . ." he said. "I can't tell how much."

Joseph looked at the old man. He seemed so different from before. So confident, so much in control. "Morris," he said, "have you ever delivered a baby before?"

He shook his head. "No, but I've assisted several times. Once in Spain. Some women were caught behind the lines. One of them gave birth. We were the only medical team around—me, I knew nothing, just how to clean and bandage wounds, and a pharmacist from Madrid. An old woman there made the delivery. All we did was make her wash her hands. The second time was forty years ago. My wife gave birth at home. I helped the doctor with his gear."

"So you don't really know how either . . ." Joseph said nervously.

Morris smiled. And put a gentle hand on Joseph's shoulder. "It happens on its own, my friend. I've been through the experience. It's not something you easily forget."

He looked at Polly. Beads of sweat had formed on her forehead and were running down her face. Her eyes were growing more disoriented. Her movements were jerky. Joseph fell to his knees again. "Breathe, Polly!"

"I feel . . . I feel . . ." she gasped.

He squeezed her hands. "What? Polly, tell me! What?"

"I feel like I can't do it anymore. Oh, Joseph! I need something for the pain!"

223

"But I don't have anything to give you, Polly!" he said softly. "You'll have to be brave!"

She cried: "Joseph! Here it comes again!"

"Breathe, Polly!' He began rubbing her stomach gently, in circular movements. He could feel the iron grip of her uterine muscles seizing up inside of her. "Breathe, Polly!"

"I can't!" she shouted. "I'm losing control!"

"What can I do, Polly? What more can I do?"

"Give me something for the pain!" she yelled. "Give me something! Give me anything! Morphine! Give me morphine!"

He turned to Morris. "What can I do?" he pleaded. "I can't bear to see her like this!"

Morris bent down on his old bones and took a chain from around his neck. On the end of the chain dangled a bullet. "Polly, dearest, listen to me . . ."

"Help me, Morris!" she gasped. Her face was red and dripping with sweat. "Please, give me something for the pain!"

"Listen to me, Polly. Do you see this bullet?"

"It hurts so much, Morris . . ." she sobbed.

He put his hand on her cheek and stroked her hair as Joseph coached her to breathe.

"When I was fighting in Spain I was shot with this bullet," he said to her. "It came from Franco's gun and lodged itself into my neck. We didn't have any drugs, Polly. No morphine. But they had to take it out or I would die. So someone took a knife and cut into me. And it hurt so much I thought I was going to die. But I didn't die, Polly. I didn't die."

"I want to die!" Polly shouted. "I don't want to have a baby! I want to die now!"

"No, you don't want to die, Polly," he said softly. "You want to have your baby. And soon you're going to have a beautiful, beautiful baby."

The next wave of contractions came and Polly tried to breathe through them again. "I can't do it anymore!" she shouted. "I need something for the pain! Please!" she pleaded. "Help me!"

224

"Go to the kitchen," said Morris to Joseph; "get some honey. If there's no honey, bring back some sugar."

He found some honey and brought it back. Morris took the jar and stuck his boney finger in. Then he painted it on Polly's mouth. "Lick your lips, sweetheart," he said. "I put some strengthening medicine on."

"I want to . . ." she began, and then licked her lips as the next gigantic wave hit her again. "I want to . . ." Her eyes were glazed. "Joseph, I want to push!"

"Tell her she can't push yet, Joseph," said Morris, checking her dilation. "If she pushes now, she'll tear herself and perhaps even injure the baby."

Joseph put his hands on her stomach again and gently rubbed in a circular motion. "You can't push yet, Polly. Not now. I'll breathe with you when it comes again. Remember to pant. Instead of pushing, pant!"

"I'm going to search for some equipment," said Morris. "I need a table, bowls, hot water and clean towels."

"The kitchen is down the hall," Joseph said.

Morris left. Joseph saw Polly through some more contractions, but he could tell she was becoming less and less responsive to his pleas to breathe, to ride the waves, and to pant when she felt the need to push.

"I can't wait any longer," she shouted. And then she spread her legs and pushed.

Joseph looked at her, horrified. "Polly, please! Polly, stop! Don't push! Pant! Don't push!"

She pushed. Her face was red as blood. "I have to push!" Between her legs an opening grew larger.

"Morris!" he shouted. "Come quick!"

She pushed again and again. The opening grew bigger still. A furry thing appeared, like a hairy stopper for a tap.

"Morris!" He watched, transfixed and catatonic, as the hairy stopper worked its way on out, exposing first a forehead, then a brow, two eyes and then a flattened nose."

"Oh, Joseph, help! Our baby's coming out!"

225

He grabbed the head. "Push! Polly, push with all your might!"

Her voice, euphoric now, called out: "I'm pushing! Can you see it? Joseph, can you see?"

Morris was beside him, setting up the table. "Work the head gently, boy. Now grab the shoulders. That's the way. Don't pull. She's doing fine. Let her push it out herself . . ."

The doorbell rang.

"They're here," said Morris. "I'll go and let them in!"

Through blood and mucus it came twisting out. A tiny explorer, landing in his hands, on to planet earth. He felt the moment deeply. More deeply than anything before. It was the recreation of the world. It held a force more awesome than the universe. It was his child.

One of them took it from him while another cut the cord.

"Is it alive?" asked Joseph. "Is it all right?"

"She looks fine to me!" said one of the paramedics, a young woman, who gave it a slap to clear its lungs.

He turned. "Oh, Polly!" he cried. "It's a girl. Our Spinach is a girl!"

But Polly didn't hear. She was still in heated work.

The other paramedic bent down to check. "There's something wrong here . . ." he said.

"Wrong?" Joseph felt his heart begin to pound. "What's wrong? Tell me, what's wrong?"

The paramedic didn't answer.

Joseph knelt down by Polly's side. Her head was hot. The sweat dripped from her brow. Her face was agonised.

She pushed.

Chapter 16

He held out the tabloid like a star-spangled banner. The grin on his face told all. He ran his index finger under the blazing front-page headline as he read it to her:

"REPORTER DISCOVERS SECRET OF EXPLODING LAB! HOSPITAL CLOSURE CAUSED BY ESCAPE OF DEADLY VIRUS! LETHAL MAN-MADE BUG BROUGHT HOME FROM VIETNAM!"

"Pretty heavy stuff," she said, looking up from the easy chair and then down again at the tiny mouth sucking eagerly at her breast.

"And dig this!" he continued, pointing underneath to the byline. "My name is in ten-point type!"

"Great," she said, prying the little one off her nipple. "You better hand me the other before I run out of juice."

Joseph put down the paper and gingerly lifted the impatient infant from the bassinet. "You don't seem to appreciate the significance of a ten-point by-line, Polly," he said, holding the baby out to her. "Which one is this, Abe or Tanya?"

"I've got Abe. You've got Tanya," she replied, making the exchange. "I think I could have appreciated the ten-point by-line better if someone else's name was there as well . . ."

"Jezus, Polly! I gave you credit! Didn't you see that little sidebar at the end of the article?" he asked, putting the full one down on its blanket and peeking underneath its diaper. "By the way, how did you know you had Abe?"

"He's cute as a button, Joseph, and I love him dearly; but just like you, he eats like a pig, and doesn't want to leave anything for his sister."

"I think he's repented, Polly . . ."

"Fat chance."

"He's given up his most cherished possession," said Joseph, pointing to the diaper.

Polly felt the downside of the one at her breast. "Oh . . ."

"Don't worry," he said, "I can't ever tell them apart either."

"I put an 'X' on Tanya's earlobe to help identify her but it must have come off in the bath."

Joseph let out a chuckle and then looked at her more seriously. "You're not really upset about the by-line, are you?"

She shook her head. "Of course not, Joseph. It's your career not mine."

He smiled. "Thanks, Pol. I couldn't have done it without you. But I think things are really going to start happening now. In this business all you need is one big break. I mean look at Woodward and Bernstein. They were just a couple of hacks until they broke the Watergate story. Now they write pretty much what they damn please and no two-bit editor dares to touch it."

"That's not what I remember about Watergate . . ." said Polly putting Abe over her shoulder and gently patting out a burp.

"What do you remember then?"

"I remember that nobody really cared when it happened. Everyone just sort of shrugged their shoulders 'cause they knew things like that go on all the time. And Nixon was elected right after it happened. You can't forget that, Joseph. The facts were there all the time. It only became a big story because they needed an excuse for Nixon to go, not because of Woodward and Bernstein."

Joseph reached into his pocket and pulled out a check. He winked. "Well, then there's always this. Five hundred smackers . . ." He gave the check a kiss. "I didn't think Lamont even knew how to count higher than twenty-nine!"

"A word to the wise . . ." Polly began as she stood up from the chair and walked toward the nursery, formerly Joseph's study.

Joseph lifted the bassinet and followed her in. "Yes, exalted one?"

"Cash that thing before it turns into rubber!"

"First thing tomorrow, chief. I might be stupid but I'm not crazy!"

She tucked the babies into their tiny beds and then turned to him. Her eyes were full of love. "I don't think you're either stupid or crazy, Joseph. I admire you for what you did. Despite Lamont and his ludicrous headlines, it's an important story. We still don't know what really happened in that lab or what happened to the Montagnards or even whether a virus is actually being spread which deforms infants in their mother's womb . . ." She looked down at her sleeping babies. "Ours are safe, thank God."

He took her hand. "Maybe we're lucky, Pol."

"Maybe so. But the real power of your story is the exposé of technology gone mad. And the link you made with the nurses' strike and the closure of the People's Medical Clinic."

"You want some coffee?" he asked.

"Wouldn't mind," she replied.

They walked back through the living room and into the kitchen. Joseph put the kettle on.

"With all that technology you'd think they could have predicted we'd have twins," he said as he measured out the coffee into the filter apparatus.

"I kept asking that question myself. They said it was impossible." Polly sat down at the table and stared over at him.

"They always say it's impossible until it turns out to be true."

"Then they try to pretend they knew it all the time." Polly mimicked the doctor's voice: "Oh, did we forget to tell you?"

"One of them tried to convince me that Abe was hiding behind Tanya's back so of course they couldn't find him!"

"Anyway," said Polly, "the impossible happened and we have two instead of one."

Joseph shook his head as he poured the boiling water into the coffee cone. "Morris and I talked about it for hours after the birth. He's really a terrific guy, you know. Maybe I'll do a story sometime about his adventures in Spain."

"You always liked him, didn't you Joseph?" said Polly, taking the mug of hot brew that he set before her.

"Yeah . . ." He sat down beside her and stirred in a spoonful of sugar.

"I'm really astonished at your ability to judge someone's character from the word go."

"It's a talent, Polly. It's inbred. It isn't anything you can acquire."

"I suppose not," she said.

He took a drink and then stared over at the far wall. "You know, the full impact of the mutant virus won't be felt for many years."

"Civilisation is always living with plagues and epidemics," she replied.

"But this one would be so terrifying if it really spreads."

Polly's face tightened. "I worry about Tanya . . ."

"The seeds we sow . . ." Joseph began, off on his own train of thought and not picking up on her reference.

"Men playing God!" she replied. Her words were angry and abrupt.

"Their favorite game. But even God doesn't throw herbicide on forests and then offer to clean up the mess by letting a virus do the dirty work."

"To be mutated by an impurity in the poison! Imagine! An impurity in the poison! We can't even make pure poisons anymore!"

"And then to spray it on an isolated tribe who had lived in those forests for thousands of years."

"And cart them away in the dead of night, bringing them to San Francisco."

"To dump them in the Tenderloin."

"Where they ended up in an experimental lab!" Polly narrowed her eyes and stared at him. "Who blew the whistle, Joseph? Who took the photos? How did Malcolm get them?"

Joseph shook his head. "I don't know."

"And who planted the bomb that killed Malcolm and Krohl?"

"I don't know."

She kept her eyes fixed on his face. "Joseph . . ."

"Yes?" He knew what she was going to say.

"Perhaps the story isn't over yet."

He smiled weakly, pulled the check out of his pocket and waved it in the air. "I've got five hundred simolies that says it is, Pol!"

It was hard to hear the ringing through the sound of screaming babies. Joseph reached for a safety pin and shouted, "Is that the telephone?"

"I thought you were going to answer it! I've got Tanya on my tit!" Polly shouted back from the other room.

"Abe just took a poop! I'm in the middle of changing him! Can't you answer it? It might be my agent asking me to appear on the *Today* show!"

Polly groaned. "Good God! Sometimes I wish I'd never married a celebrity!"

A moment later she appeared at the changing table. Tanya was still clinging to her breast for dear life. "It's for you, of course," she said.

"Who?"

"Your sweetheart editor, I think."

Joseph gave a final wipe and, wrinkling his nose, tossed the soiled nappy into the plastic can. "Probably wants to offer me a half-interest in his paper," said Joseph, placing Abe in Polly's other arm.

He took the hall extension and spoke into the receiver: "Yeah, it's me, the superstar. You making a bid on my next story?"

Lamont's voice came through at around ten decibels. "Listen, hotshot, you ever hear of Mat Dougal?"

"Mat Dougal? Can't say that I have . . ."

"Well fifteen years ago he had a scoop on the police involvement in the Brinks caper. I sold fifty thousand papers the first hour it hit the streets. Had to run five editions. Now he's serving soup at St Anthony's Kitchen!"

"Maybe he likes the company there."

"Maybe his tush got too fat to fit in his pants!"

"Naw. You would have just bought him bigger trousers, Lamont."

"Listen, bird brain, you still have that check I gave you?"

"What check?"

"Well, don't try to cash it for a few days."

"Why not?"

"Got some cash-flow problems, Radkin. Temporary shortage of funds."

"How temporary?"

"Until we find out whether we can sell enough papers to offset any libel costs."

"What libel costs, Lamont? What are you getting at?"

"It's a little too late to play the innocent, Radkin. Unless you got something else to sell."

"Hey, Lamont, who goosed you? I thought you said you could stand the heat!"

The voice went two decibels higher. "Stand the heat? Why you mangy turnip, I can stand anything as long as it sells papers! I don't even give a shit if you lie! But if the feds decide to fight it in court, you better have some heavy ammunition!"

"I'll stand by what I wrote, Lamont. Will you?"

"I'll stand by anything that makes John Q Public spend his last dime on my newspaper, Radkin. And I'll defend his right to know—whatever turns him on. What I won't stand by is bankruptcy!"

"The Genesis Files are the real thing, Lamont. Trust me . . ."

"You got people in high places who are ready to substantiate it?"

"How come you didn't ask me that before you ran the story?"

"Because usually the feds don't take what I print seriously enough to sue, you idiot!"

"Well that should tell you something, Lamont. Seems like we've touched a sensitive nerve."

"I don't think you're understanding me, Radkin. I'm not in business to touch sensitive nerves, unless it's the twitching impulse to buy papers. Some people sell popcorn. I sell scandal. I don't particularly care whose scandal it is, as long as it's ripe and juicy. If someone wants to sue, that's fine by me. I usually

232

end up selling even more papers. But the feds are another matter. They got ways of making it kind of hard for me to operate. They also got these high-price lawyers who just sit around waiting for cases like this to pop up. And they don't mind dragging it on and on. So, with that in mind, you got to look at the balance sheet . . ."

"How do you balance truth and justice, Lamont?"

"Radkin, if you weren't so dumb, you'd know that everyone is on the side of truth and justice. It just might mean something different to people like me than to lame-brains like you."

"So what are you going to do, Lamont? Throw in the towel?"

"Throw in the towel, Radkin? No, that never sold papers. I'd sooner see you eaten by the tiger that you're riding. Who knows, maybe you'll be able to come up with someone in authority who might substantiate your wild claims? Maybe a general of the army or the head of the American Medical Association. Maybe not. Maybe you'll at least find a second-rate doctor or a third-rate lieutenant. Who knows?"

"You get a response from the AMA?"

"Seems I did, Radkin. They think your story is ludicrous . . ."

"Yeah. Well, last year they said there was no reason to condemn the nuclear industry just because the rate of childhood leukemia was ten times greater in towns located by atomic power stations."

"Maybe they know which side their bread is radiated on, Radkin."

"I'm sure they do, Lamont. Do you?"

"You bet your sweet virus I do!"

Joseph glanced up. He saw Polly standing at the other end of the hall trying to balance Abe and Tanya in either arm. His voice became softer and more serious. "All bullshit aside, Lamont: are you going to stand by me?"

"All bullshit aside, Radkin: get me some legitimate confirmation or I'll drop you faster than a red-hot turd from an atomic cow!"

*

233

"Sure he's a bastard!" Joseph yelled. "All newspaper publishers are bastards! It's a requirement of the trade just like monkeys are required to have tails to swing from trees!"

"Don't shout!" she said. "You'll wake the babies!"

"How can you call someone a bastard and not shout?" He glared at her. "That's like asking me to take a crap without having to wipe myself!"

"Only you could think up such sweet metaphors, Joseph. Let me remind you, I'm on your side. I worked on the story too!"

He pursed his lips. "I'm sorry, Polly."

"You want a drink? A Scotch?"

"Thanks. Make it a double. On second thoughts, make it a triple."

"I'll make it a single," she said, going into the kitchen. "You'll need your wits about you . . ."

He followed her inside. "Why? Wits haven't helped me much so far. Maybe I'd do better if I acted like most professional journalists and wrote my stories in liquid form."

"You're not most professional journalists, Joseph. If you were, I wouldn't be living with you now." She brought him the drink and sat down next to him at the table. She stared into his eyes. "You're a fighter, Joseph. You don't give up so easily."

"Who said anything about giving up?" He let his gaze drop.

"No one. But what you forgot—what we both forgot—is that you can't just write a story like this and not think that the people, the institutions, the forces you attack are just going to turn over and play dead. You've exposed them. So they're closing ranks. Of course they'll deny everything. Didn't you expect it?"

"Yes, Polly, but . . ."

"You wanted it on a plate. OK. So did I. That's not the way the world works, though, is it?"

"No, but . . ."

"So now you're under attack. Lamont is nipping at your heels. No one in authority says they know anything about the Genesis Files. The medical establishment denies any new virus has been discovered or any increase of female carcinomas. The hospital administration sticks to its guns about its reason for closure. You're in a pickle for sure. So what are you going to do?"

His eyes were opened wide, like a little boy's. "Yeah, good question. What am I going to do?"

"You're going to consolidate your forces. Right?"

"Right! Uh . . . what forces?"

"The forces that you supported and that damn well ought to support you." She ticked the list off on her fingers. "The Nurses' Union; the Department of Public Health; the obstetricians who Gorbachev interviewed; your friends at the vet centers; the immigrant community; progressive scientists; ecologists; humanists; mothers with children . . ." She ran out of fingers and stopped.

"How about the neighborhood dog?"

"If it can stand on its hind legs and holler, yes."

He ran his hand nervously through his hair. "You'd think that some people would start coming forward, Polly. Some scientists maybe or decent bureaucrats . . ."

"They will. But they're frightened, Joseph. They can be discredited too, you know. People like Robin and Nicole and Malcolm all had access to the files. I'm sure they all tried to publicise them. You've gotten further than most because you write for a scandal sheet. If you worked for a liberal editor you probably wouldn't have gotten as far as the man with the Gorbachev strawberry-mark on his head."

"So what do we do?" asked Joseph, turning up his palms and showing them empty.

She pulled back her chair and stood up. "What we do first, Joseph, is start calling our friends."

The study had been returned to him. The bassinets were moved into the bedroom. The desk was freed of diapers, creams and pins. In their place came index cards and files and dirty cups half filled with stale brew and soggy cigarette butts.

Once more *Guernica* had come down. Again, a piece of butcher paper had been tacked into the wall. On it had been penned lists of names and telephone numbers followed by date of contact and response. It was, of course, a Polly-thing to do.

He was wearing the green eyeshade she had once gotten him as a joke after they had seen the old version of *Front Page* at the cinema. With a smoking butt dangling from his lips, stains of java on his shirt, and the receiver tucked into the crevice of his neck, he looked the part of any harried reporter struggling to make a deadline.

"How's it going?" Polly asked, bringing him in a fresh cup of brew and jiggling a baby on her shoulder at the same time.

He looked up at her and gently pulled at a tiny toe that dangled by his face. "Can I use this to stir my coffee?" he asked.

"Good!" she said. "You're starting to joke again. That means you're on to something."

He smiled. "I've got Janet Baker on the line . . ."

"The nurse you met at the Cherry Blossom Restaurant?"

"Yeah, The executive committee is discussing a motion of support. She just went to find out what happened."

"Whoopee! Score one for our side!" She gave the baby a bounce.

Joseph held up a finger and spoke into the phone. "Janet? Yeah, I'm here . . ." Suddenly the smile faded from his lips. "What? Why the hell not?"

Polly watched him with growing concern. His face whitened. His voice grew softer. "Sure, Janet . . . I understand . . . Thanks for your help . . . Bye."

He put down the reciever and looked up into Polly's eyes.

"Why, for heaven's sake?" she asked. Her voice was filled with disbelief.

"They don't want any part of it, Polly. Janet says they don't want to confuse the issues. She said it's hard enough for them to gain any credibility as it is without launching off into science fiction . . ."

"Science fiction?" Polly shouted. The baby began to cry. "Quiet down Abe or Tanya or whoever you are! This is important!" she scolded.

236

Joseph rubbed his watery eyes. "She's got a point, I guess."

"A point? What about solidarity? Jezus, you stuck your neck out for them."

He shrugged tiredly. "Think about it, Polly. It's their hospital we're talking about. University research has been going on for a long, long time. It's never been an issue with them. They had no notion that military work was going on. That part of the hospital was sealed off. It's their neck that would be sticking out. Mine's already on the chopper."

"I think you're being overly generous, Joseph. They knew the salmonella thing was used as a ploy and that they were simply scapegoats. You brought out issues that no one else discusses in the press."

"OK . . . but what proof do we really have that what we say was going on really happened?"

"We have the Genesis Files, Joseph. And we have the photos."

"But no one is coming forward to substantiate our evidence! What we have are documents. How the hell do we know for sure they're not forgeries?"

She narrowed her eyes. "Whose side are you on, Joseph?"

"Ours, damn it!" he shouted. He stood up and pointed to the butcher paper on the wall. "Look at that giant contact sheet you made! Do you see anyone there who's rushing forward in our defense?"

"It takes time for people to come forward, Joseph," she said in a softer voice. "You know that . . ."

Suddenly a shrill cry from the other room cut her off. She turned instinctively. "God!" she cursed. "Talk about Pavlovian responses. One of them yells for milk and my faucets start leaking like mad!" She handed him the baby in her arms and went off to feed the other. "I'll be back to continue this discussion after the commercial break," she said.

The little eyes were opened wide. He peered into them and said, "Which one are you?" He smiled in a stoic sort of way. "I guess it doesn't matter."

And then he lifted the baby higher and put its head against

his cheek. "I feel a surge of energy when I lift you up like this," he whispered. "You're so warm, so vital, so alive . . ." He turned his head and looked into its face. "You were born of this story, you know. Yes. Your life emerged into this mystery. And now you're here and it seems to be fading away . . ." He nuzzled against the softness of the newborn infant. "I want you to be safe," he whispered.

The telephone rang and he picked up the receiver. "Yeah?"

"Mr Radkin?" It was a male voice, husky but cultivated.

"That's me."

"Mr Radkin, please consider what I have to say with great care . . ."

"I always consider what people have to say with great care. Unless it's my mother speaking. And then I sort of shrug it off. Who am I talking to, by the way?"

"My name isn't important, Mr Radkin. What's important is that you listen carefully. I want to warn you that you're walking a very dangerous path. Very dangerous indeed. Nasty things could happen if you insist on continuing . . ."

"Excuse me, but which path are we talking about exactly? You're being a little vague, aren't you? I'm a pretty literal person and I need people to spell things out a bit more precisely."

The voice grew harsher in tone. "If you persist in helping the enemies of liberty with your vile accusations, Mr Radkin, certain events may come to pass which would not be to your liking . . ."

"Wait a minute!" Joseph said, cutting off the voice. "Is this a death threat?"

"It's a warning, Mr Radkin."

Joseph slammed down the receiver and shouted, "Fuck you!"

The baby began to cry.

Chapter 17

The soft, damp light of dawn filtered through the shades, casting its shadow on the waking chidren, crying like ducklings for their food.

His groggy head could hardly direct him to the fridge. The light had yet to penetrate the hall. He stubbed his toe and let out a stream of random curses.

A voice groaned through the cacophony of baby cries and manly screams: "If you're doing the morning run, please do it with a little more finesse. I want to sleep."

He glared back at the bedroom. If looks could kill, he thought to himself, Polly would be a goner now.

Carting the bottles back, he heard her call again. "Remember to test the temperature . . ."

"What?"

"The temperature of the milk. Not too hot, not too cold."

"Milk's supposed to be drunk cold. I added a little chocolate . . ."

"You didn't!"

"All right! All right! Don't get upset! I'll warm the bottles!"

Back in the kitchen he put on a saucepan of water and inserted the bottles. He sat down at the table and buried his head in his hands.

"Remember not to let it boil!" she called out.

"Have a little respect for the dead," he moaned.

Realising it was useless to try and sleep, he fished a stale butt from the ashtray and smoothed it out. He lit it and then took a long and grateful puff. Then, as he heard the water start to boil, he stubbed it out and leapt over to the stove, turning off the flame. He grabbed the bottles, fumbling them once or twice, and then, regaining hold, tested the milk on the back of his hand, nearly scalding himself in the process.

"If it's too hot, put it in some lukewarm water for a minute. But hurry up! The kids are shouting for their breakfast!"

"The voice from ten thousand leagues under the sea!" he muttered.

He got the temperature tolerably drinkable by switching the bottles back and forth from hot to cold. Then he stumbled clumsily to the bedroom. "OK, you guys," he said in a rasping voice. "Who's first?"

"The one with the reddest face."

"I'm color blind this hour in the morning!" Joseph shot back.

"Just take them both into your study and stick the bottles in their traps!" she said, flinging the covers over her head.

"Fine way for a mother to talk!" he chastised, lifting the babies from their cribs.

He tucked the screaming infants under his arms and brought them into the study. After a frustrating few minutes of trial and error, he managed to get them both into position and the bottles, as Polly had so succinctly put it, in their traps.

Then the phone rang.

Glaring at it, he said, "If you think I'm going to answer you after all this, you're crazy!"

"Answer the phone, Joseph!" yelled Polly.

"Your master's voice," he explained to the babies and, making a face directed towards the bedroom, he tried to pick up the receiver while, in his arms, the two children were still sucking furiously at their bottles.

It took him several moments to accomplish this feat of dexterity. When he finally did, he shouted: "I don't accept death threats, eviction notices or subscription pleas until late in the afternoon! So . . ."

"Mr Radkin?" It was a woman's voice.

"Yeah. Who's calling?"

"Mr Radkin, I want to speak with you about the Genesis Files . . ."

"At five a.m? Listen, lady . . ."

"I'm sorry, Mr Radkin. It's impossible to talk over the phone. There's a message waiting for you under your doormat."

"Under my doormat? Who is this?"

240

The call was disconnected. He dropped the receiver and almost one of the babies as well. "Fucking hell!"

"Who was it?" Polly asked.

He went into the bedroom and lowered the two infants till they were resting by her side.

"Does this mean you're going back to work, hotshot?"

"It means I've finally made it to the land where cuckoos sit on clouds and sing," he said, struggling into his pants.

The note had been written in neat, precise handwriting. "Like a proper schoolgirl," he said to himself as he tried to start the Vespa.

It read: "Please meet me at the parking lot overlooking Seal Rock in twenty minutes. You won't see me at first. Wait there. I will contact you. Remember to destroy this note."

"I wonder if she wants me to eat it," he grumbled as he drove down the foggy road. He shivered. "I'm not cut out for early-morning melodramas."

The old Vespa wasn't cut out for early-morning travel either, as it turned out. It kept stalling every time he stopped. Then he had to kick through a barrage of sputters and pops to get it started again.

With a car it wasn't more than twenty minutes from his house to Seal Rock, especially at that hour of the morning. But the Vespa took longer than a bicycle. When he left it was a quarter after five. By the time he got there it was six.

The parking lot, which overlooked the remains of Sutro Baths and the rock where the Pacific seals congregated (for reasons known to no one but themselves), was empty when he arrived. He leaned the Vespa next to a tree and walked over to the edge of the cliff to gaze down at the ocean.

The fog had just begun to dissipate in the morning sun. Below, a group of black birds were swirling around the jagged rocks, caught in currents of air that swept them, like tiny living missiles, perilously close to death before sending them back up again in a strange dance which seemed to have neither a beginning nor an end.

241

He looked far out to sea. Because of the clouds, there seemed to be no distinct horizon. Perhaps, he thought, the ocean went on forever. Perhaps, if you set sail, you too became a black bird caught in a circular stream. Perhaps there was no end at all.

"Mr Radkin?"

He turned around and recognised her at once. She was taller than he expected. She stood quite straight. She had a look of self-assurance, like someone who knew herself well and also knew what she was after. He couldn't see her eyes; she wore dark glasses.

"Hello, Robin," he said. "I've been looking forward to meeting you."

She smiled in response. It was a serious, rather dignified smile. And it faded from her face as quickly as it came.

"We can't speak together for long, Mr Radkin. I must leave soon. But I wanted you to know that I admired your article . . ."

"Then why all the subterfuge?" he asked. "You could have just sent me a fan letter."

"I suspect you're having some problems at the moment," she went on. Her light hair was taken up by the morning breeze; it made her seem to be constantly in motion.

He rubbed his unshaven beard with the side of his hand. "You want to help straighten some things out?"

"I'll help you any way I can."

Joseph narrowed his eyes in a look of suspicion. "Why?"

"Because at this point I think we need each other's help, don't you?" She looked out to sea. "There's very little time . . ." Then turning toward him once more, she continued: "And so much to accomplish."

"Other labs to bomb? Is that it, Robin?"

She lowered her dark glasses for a moment and glanced at him from over the top. He saw her eyes. They were baby blue. Pushing the dark glasses back again she asked, almost in a bemused manner, "Do you think I'm a terrorist, Mr Radkin?"

"Aren't you?" he replied.

"I suppose there are people who would say I am," she

242

admitted. "I suppose there are people who would claim that anyone who stands in the way of established authority or who tries to expose this secret madness that threatens to destroy our world is a terrorist. Maybe there are those who would call you a terrorist, too."

"There's a difference between writing stories and tossing bombs," he said.

The swirling black birds caught her eye. "It's curious how those who are certain to bring us to the brink of Armageddon have redefined the word 'terror'." She stopped for a moment and then turned back to him. "What if you could stop a program for mass destruction with one bomb, Mr Radkin? What would you do?"

"I don't know, Robin. But I think I'd find it especially hard to throw if my brother was in the room . . ."

Her body stiffened. And then she caught herself and smiled, though weakly. "I was warned you could be . . . abrupt."

"I have a reputation for saying what's on my mind, if that's what you mean. But I don't think I'd be any match for you at Russian roulette."

"Do you smoke, Mr Radkin?" she asked.

"Like a house on fire," he said. "But unfortunately I didn't have time to bring my cigarettes or wallet . . ."

"That's a shame," she replied, showing just a trace of nervousness.

"We could take a run up to Sutro Village," he suggested.

She shook her head. "We haven't time." Then, straightening her body again, she said, "Mr Radkin, I'm not a terrorist. At least not in your sense of the word. I didn't blow up the lab that night."

He tried to stare through the dark glasses into her eyes. "You didn't?"

"No."

"Then who did? Was it Malcolm?"

"There may have been a time when Malcolm could have done such a thing. But it wasn't him . . ."

"How do you know?"

She was silent for a moment. Then she said. "Ask yourself this: in whose interest would it be to destroy the lab?"

"I have asked myself that question. Many times."

"And what answer did you come up with?"

"Many different ones. But I don't have enough information to make an educated guess."

"What information are you lacking?"

"Who was your contact, Robin? Who was giving you inside information about the Genesis Files?"

"You don't know?" she asked.

"No. I have my suspicions, of course . . ."

"It was Krohl, Mr Radkin. It was Dr Krohl."

He stared at her in amazement. "You mean the genetic engineer? But it was his project!"

"You find that surprising?"

"Of course I find it surprising! Why would he inform on himself? Why not just stop what he's doing and expose the whole thing in a public way?"

"Think about it," she said. "Dr Krohl was given a lab and a great deal of government funds to find a cure for a terrible disease . . ."

"Caused by a virus that he created . . ." Joseph put in.

"Caused by a virus that mutated. The virus Dr Krohl created was made with the best of intentions . . ."

"Greater love hath no man . . ." Joseph repeated sarcastically.

"The point is Dr Krohl was using the lab for good purposes, not for evil. However the virus was created, it was in everyone's interests that an antibody be found. He didn't want to threaten that work . . ."

"But the Montagnards! I saw the photos!" Joseph shouted.

She nodded. "Yes. The military had made certain demands, one of which was top-level secrecy. They had rounded up as many Montagnards as they could and were trying to convince Dr Krohl to use them as laboratory subjects."

"So what you're saying is that Krohl wanted the whistle

blown on the military but, at the same time, he wanted to keep control of the project to find an antibody."

"He couldn't be seen as the informant, Mr Radkin. We all felt it was better that he keep his position as secure as possible."

"All?"

"There are a number of us."

"But the Genesis Files! Certainly publication of those documents would have pointed to Krohl!"

"So it would."

"But Draper, the journalist, tried to . . ."

"We convinced him the time wasn't right. He allowed me to take the documents from his possession."

Joseph scratched his head. "And Nicole—how much did she know?"

"She was not part of the inner circle."

"And your brother?"

Robin looked down for a moment and then back up. "I didn't want to get him involved. But . . ."

"He found the documents you had hidden?"

"Yes."

"When did you last see him?"

"I met with him the night before . . ."

"After Charlie?"

"Yes. Charlie had been there. Malcolm was still doped up when I arrived. I had to give him some tranquillisers to bring him back down. I told him everything. He wanted to join us . . ."

"Join you?"

"In our attempt to free the Montagnards."

Joseph held out his hand. "Wait a minute. You were planning to free the Montagnards?"

"With Dr Krohl's help, of course."

"The three of you?"

"There were four of us."

"But, Robin, how could you hide a tribe of Montagnards? What were you going to do?"

"We had arranged with a man, a refugee, to take them away on a boat . . ."

245

"Dr Minh! You mean Dr Minh!"

"Yes."

"Where was he taking them?"

"That was to be left up to him."

A great wave suddenly lashed against the rocks. The mighty sound made them turn. They watched as the black birds scattered into the sky.

He looked at her. "Then the bomb . . ."

"They must have found out."

"The military?"

"The military, the CIA, the FBI. They're all the same."

"It was meant to destroy the evidence?" he asked.

She nodded. "Once it was found out that Krohl was our informant and the Montagnards were to be freed, they couldn't take a chance that their secrets would be exposed. They'd sooner blow us up and forget about the antibody. We had planned our meeting for three a.m. Two of us were late."

He took a minute to mull over what she had told him. Then, pressing his lips together, he said, "I'm sorry, Robin."

"For what?" she asked.

"For what I said back then."

Her face seemed thinner now. More tense. "I wanted to meet you," she said, "to thank you for writing what you did."

"I'm sure you haven't told me all this just to thank me," he replied.

She smiled. "Of course not. I want you to join us, Mr Radkin. That's why I met with you."

"Join you?" He laughed. "I'm afraid I'm a family man . . ."

"I understand. But what I meant was that we need people like you who understand the media."

"Whoa there, sister!" he said, taking a small step backward. "The media and me have never understood each other!"

She held out her hand. "We'll be in touch."

"OK," he said, shaking hands with her, "but please, no more calls at five a.m."

Suddenly she turned and waved. In the distance a car started up and then drove to within a few yards of where they were standing.

246

She walked over to the car and opened the door. Before she got in she turned back to him. "Goodbye, Mr Radkin. I hope I've been of help."

"Well, at least you've given me a punch line," he said.

The car started up and then roared away. He recognised the driver. It was the man with the Gorbachev mark on his head.

He stayed by the water for a while. Walking on the beach helped him think about things. The ocean breeze seemed to clear away the cobwebs in his mind.

It wasn't till nearly noon that he drove the Vespa back toward home. When he reached Noe Valley he decided to pay a call.

He drove up Hill Street to the big Victorian and parked the Vespa outside. He was about to walk through the hedge to the cottage in the back when he saw her coming out.

"Hey, Radkin," she said. "What are you doing here?"

"Thought I'd drop by for a visit, Gerry. How were the redwoods?"

"Still there," she said, continuing to walk up the path. "I read your article . . ."

"Yeah?" He kept pace with her even though she walked a mile a minute. "What'd you think?"

She threw him a cock-eyed look. "Pretty far-out stuff, Radkin. Maybe you ought to write fiction."

"I thought of that, too," he said. "Hey, you training for a race or something?"

"I got an appointment," she said, glancing at her watch. "and I'm late as it is . . ."

"Can I give you a lift?"

"Sure. Where's your car?"

He pointed to the Vespa. "You game?"

She shrugged. "Anything's better than the bus!"

Joseph started it up and she climbed on the back. "Where to?" he asked, turning his head around toward her.

"The Department of Public Health. I'm applying for funds to start a new clinic. You know the way?"

"Do I know the way?" he said, letting go of the clutch. "Can a duck lay eggs?"

"Not funny," she shouted through the wind. "Not funny at all!"

If you have enjoyed this book and would like to receive details on other Walker mystery titles, please write to:

Mystery Editor
Walker and Company
720 Fifth Avenue
New York, NY 10019